MURDER IN DETROIT

a novel
by

Al Parker

Pittsburgh, PA

ISBN 1-56315-260-6

Paperback Fiction

First Printing — 2000
Library of Congress #99-65321

Request for information should be addressed to:

SterlingHouse Publisher, Inc.
The Sterling Building
440 Friday Road
Pittsburgh, PA 15209
www.sterlinghousepublisher.com

Cover Design: Michelle S. Vennare — SterlingHouse Publisher, Inc.
Cover Art: Michelle S. Vennare — SterlingHouse Publisher, Inc.
Typesetter: Beth Buckholtz

Printed in Canada

TO MY CHILDREN:

Cheryl, Daniel, Joel, Frank,

AND

Jeffrey, Travis

Detroit, the most historically representative city in America: the one place that everybody can agree on by agreeing they no longer want any part of it.

Jerry Herron, from his book,
Afterculture: Detroit and The Humiliation of History

CHAPTER 1

The man who wrote the first Bible story was an artist. They made him religious, which is a lesser thing. They took what he had made and changed it.

That's what I was thinking, as I stood on the corner of Woodward and Grand, in Detroit. I was lost in the thinking of it. I was not paying attention to where I was or what I was doing. I was in a city foreign to me, doing something that was foreign to me. Yet, here I was thinking of things familiar to me. My refuge, I considered. My home. My safe, sad and lovely place.

A tall man was standing next to me, waiting for the light to change. He did not turn to look at me. He was talking to himself. "It's like stepping into an old-fashioned Christmas card," he said.

I looked where he was looking, trying to see what he was seeing. There were snowflakes coming down in swirls, soft and impermanent, the first snowflakes of the season. Beyond the snowflakes were the tall buildings of New Center, offering a different scene than the squash of squat buildings behind us. I could see nothing old-fashioned. I saw only the snowflakes and a multi-hued maze of cars moving in slow formation around the corner and the sparkling red and green of the flickering traffic lights. I stepped into the busy street.

The man spoke again, not whispering.

"A man hears about the lucky few that win millions of dollars at Lotto. He sees the sports figures he admires being given salaries in the millions. There is a million dollars in real cash being transported in the truck he is in. He kills his partner, the man he has been working with for months. Shoots him dead, without a thought about the man's wife and children, whom he has never met. The million dollars has lured him into a crime he might never have committed, being the fine son of a fine father and mother. Who is responsible? Why, the killer is, of course. How can we see it otherwise?"

I stopped, turned around, stared at him. The tall man did not look crazy, merely thoughtful. He was gazing past me into some vast distance.

"Excuse me," I said.

"What?"

"You were talking," I said. "I thought it might be important."

"You mean, out loud?"

"Yes. Something about a million dollars."

He looked puzzled, then mildly embarrassed. One golden shoe tapped on the curbing, then stopped. Traffic resumed behind me, and I climbed up alongside the man.

"I was? Oh, that!"

"So what's it about?"

"Don't you watch the news?" he said.

"No. I'm new to town. What happened?"

"Just what I said, I guess. I was reflecting upon an armored car robbery. Happened last week. Decent, poor man, hired to watch over a lot of money. Couldn't take it any more. Tempted. Who wouldn't be?"

"And he killed the other guard?"

"Yeah. He and his partner, the outside man."

"Black men, I assume." It seemed a natural conclusion to me, but his looked raised the question. "It's Detroit," I added, explaining everything.

"You got something against Blacks?" he said.

"Not me. I just got here, remember?"

"But just because this is Detroit...?"

"Exactly," I said. "Why not?"

Anger was playing at the corner of the tall man's lips. It rippled up into his eyes and lay there, waiting. There was a sudden rigidness in the air between us.

"You certain you're all right?" I said.

"Sure, I am. Why shouldn't I be?"

"You were talking to yourself. You know what they say about people who talk to themselves?"

"No, what?"

'I dunno. I thought you'd tell me."

He blanched, swallowed, grinned. The tension between us melted like snow.

"Okay," he said. "You got me with that one. Why are we having this conversation? On a street corner? In good-old Detroit?"

"You started it. I thought you were talking to me."

"Funny " he said. "I never used to talk to myself. Now I do it all the time."

"I do it, too. All the time. It does kind of drive other people away."

"You do?"

"Yep. And I walk into Christmas cards."

CHAPTER 2

My wife died in the Spring of 1996. After ten years of fighting cancer, she was tired, she said. You've got to let me go, Marc, she said. I want to go. Let me go.

"What will I do without you?" I said. "I'll always be with you," she said. And I said, "It's not the same."

She took a finger to the back of my hand, like somebody writing a letter. I can still feel the cool pressure of her touch. And then she left me.

On my way to becoming a minister, I discovered philosophy. That was years ago. With philosophy, you learn to play a game, a mental game, a word-picture game. For a man on the way to ministry, discovering philosophy can be an unmitigated disaster. Religion seeks certainty, while philosophy is a realm of uncertainty. Religion brings the comfort of knowing, while philosophy — at the heart of it — admits to knowing nothing.

Philosophy is a kingdom of unanswerable questions. No answer will ever satisfy the questioning mind, for long. A question, it turns out, is merely a stepping stone on the way to a better question. For years, I practiced ministry. But I played, always, at philosophy. Philosophy was my joyous avocation. Now the game was over.

I had won at it. And I had lost.

My wife died in the Spring. My daughter was killed in the Fall. She was killed by a hit-and-run driver in Detroit. Though I flew to Detroit to identify and claim her body, I never did find out what she was doing in Detroit. She had business in Boston. Afterwards, she was supposed to take a direct flight home to California. She did not take it. She went to Detroit, instead. I have raised the questions. An unexpected business stop-over? A momentary curiosity about a strange city? A reaching out for a pleasurable new experience? A rendezvous with a lover? What else? I don't know. I still don't know. All I know is she flew to Detroit and she died.

My sons — both of them — have handled this far better than I have. They have busy lives. One is an architectural engineer, living just outside of Los Angeles. The other is a commercial pilot for one of the major airlines. He travels the world. They have busy lives, but mine has suddenly stopped. I stopped it. I could come up with no reason for it to continue.

A man must have a reason for what he does. That's the way the game is played. But I have given up the game — all games.

Life is not any fun, anymore.

When I got to Detroit the second time, I found it different from any city I had ever been in. I heard it called a failed city, a city humiliated by its own history. Detroit was a good example of what a modern city should not become. There was a huge hole in the middle of Detroit left by the flight of the middle class, both white and Black, after the race riots of 1967. Having lived close to the Watts riots in 1965, 1 had some idea of the ravages of riots on neighbor hoods. Detroit remained exceptional. At one point, not very many years ago, there were 15,000 empty buildings within the city limits of Detroit. A good number of these provided tinder for the likes of Devil's Night, when setting fires seemed like the thing to do for Halloween.

I learned these things on the night before I met Denys Fowler. A black City Cab had transported me from Metro Airport to the St Regis hotel. I had opted to go for a walk in the cool of early December and ended up at a Burger King. I ordered a burger, vanilla shake and fries. I sat at a plastic table on a plastic chair. Three students from nearby Wayne State University were debating the subject of Detroit history. I listened in as they argued. They came close to blows at one point. One student was from out of state. His two companions had been born and raised here and were busy defending the ex-mayor, Coleman Young.

I asked a single question and received an entire semester's education as answer. Detroit's fate was a thing to be avoided, clearly. Worse was to be Black and live here.

"This dude don't know nuthin'," one Black boy said to me, smiling happily. "Less than nuthin'. He ain't got a brain in his fuckin' head."

"Just because he's from somewhere else?"

"New York. That's where he's from. What we gonna expect from somebody from New York?"

"At least, New York still functions as a city," the boy said, defending himself, proudly. "That's more than can be said for this place."

"Listen to him," the third boy said. "Then why is you here, man?"

"Usual reason," the boy said. "My father got himself transferred. That's why. Otherwise..."

"Otherwise, nuthin'," the first boy said. "You be dumb in the head, wherever you from."

As they went out, the boy from New York stopped at my table, leaned over and whispered in my ear. His face was full of small scars, and he smelled of onions. But his dark eyes were deep and kindly.

"Don't plan on living here," he said. "This place will eat you alive. Understand?"

I nodded, as if I did.

The boy looked back one time as he went out the door. He gave me a thumb's up, jabbing it up hard, like a poke in the ribs. Then he smiled a glorious smile.

I nodded again, not understanding anything.

Then it was the next day, and I was in the same Burger King talking to a guy who walked into Christmas cards. Or imagined doing so, as he talked to himself, or to me. Denys Fowler was tall, square of shoulders, regal. His camel-hair coat was flecked with new snow. Denys was white, soldierly, with a trimmed mustache and large hands. His hair was sandy colored, and his eyes were blue, specked with green. He fidgeted with his food, not eating.

"So you're from Oregon?" Denys said.

"That's right. Gresham, just outside Portland."

'And your name is...?"

"McDaniel. Marcus McDaniel. Call me, Marc."

"Sorry. I have to do that. Set it in my head, you know? Otherwise, I'll forget. Repetition helps. My memory's not what it was."

"Was it ever?"

"Huh?"

"Your memory. Was it ever good?"

"Blunt, aren't you?"

"Sometimes. When it seems to matter."

"Well, you might as well know. A few years ago, if I remember right, I had a good memory. Things flowed, you know, like history. Now things are...what'll I call it?...disjointed. Yeah, that's it. Unconnected. As my doctor used to tell me, I live in a permanent *now*. No room for yesterday in the old noggin. It's a strange feeling."

"You familiar with Potok? Chaim Potok, the writer?"

"No. I don't think so. Why?"

"Well, in one of his books, called *The Gift of Asher Lev*, the wife of the main character was writing a story she called, 'The Cave of Now.' It was to be a children's book, but it sounds like you."

"Is that right? Well, what do you know? You read a lot of books?"

"I inhale books, Denys. At least, that's what my wife used to tell me. Like eating."

"She doesn't tell you that any more?"

"My wife is dead, Denys."

"Oh, sorry. I didn't mean..."

"It's all right. She was sick a long time. Her death was a blessing, some say, trying to be kind. As for me, I'm not sure."

"But she's dead?"

"Yes. Eight months and four days ago. Seems a lot longer. It doesn't seem like any time at all."

I expected platitudes from Denys that I didn't get. He sat in the restaurant looking at me, his food untouched. He sat there looking at me with sad, soulful eyes that appeared as if they should brim with tears, but did not.

"So what's good about Portland?" Denys said, as if he had just awakened and was trying to discover where we were in this conversation. "You did say Portland?"

"Close enough. Portland's fine. A nice city. It's just too far from the ocean, that's all. I'd have preferred to live in Lincoln City, right on the water. But you go where you are called."

"Called?"

"Sorry," I said. "I was a minister. Still am, I guess. My ordination's good, and I still have standing."

"Is that right? I never knew a minister up close. So what are you doing here?"

"I don't know for sure, Denys. I've got a mystery on my hands I can't quite understand. I guess I'm here to see if I can figure it out. What about you?"

He leaned back, yawning. "I work at GM, in Corporate Production Scheduling. A strange thing happens to me when I walk into that building, Marc. Nobody can explain it. I go through those doors; I become somebody else. Mr. Efficiency, they call me. But when I'm outside, I'm apt to diddle along like a schoolboy. That's why they like me to bring my lunch. I work right through and never take a break."

"But you broke out, today?" I said. I watched a very old woman at the counter, struggling to make up her mind. A very young waitress was reviewing the menu, loudly.

Denys ignored the noise.

"Yes, I did," he said. "I needed a bit of fresh air. That's what I told them, anyhow. What I really needed was time to think. That robbery was bugging me. How does it get described: extravagance living next door to degradation? That's not right, but you know what I mean. Wealth next to poverty; a surfeit of goods next to those who have nothing. I'm very troubled by it. I'm not sure why. I'm on the right side of the fence. But that kid wasn't, so he stole. Why wouldn't he? Why wouldn't I, if I were him?"

"The dividing line is Eight Mile Road, I hear."

"That's right. I live in Bloomfield Hills."

We sat in silence for a long time. I had started thinking again about 'The Cave of Now.' It was a fascinating, if impossible, concept, good feelings extended into a long-lasting moment — an eternal now! If you removed the "good feelings" idea, you ran straight into theology, which I did not wish to do, not at this particular moment. But my mind raced around, as it often did when it ran across ideas that beat in it like drums, causing reverberations.

"Where did you go?" I heard a voice say.

It repeated itself; an echo.

I blinked and shoved thought aside. Slowly, I came to focus on the tall man sitting across from me.

"Sorry, Denys. I vanish sometimes."

"Everybody's a little weird."

"Ain't that the truth," I said.

"Nice to be with someone who recognizes that fact."

"Yes. The company of the insane."

A strange look came over Denys's face. And I knew, in that moment, that this handsome man had spent a lot of time in institutions, a world I never knew.

CHAPTER 3

I sat in the dark in my room in the Hotel St. Regis and stared out the window into the darkness, outside. Off to my left, slightly, were the lights of downtown Detroit. They glimmered in the cool of evening, the sky having cleared, the snow having stopped. It was too early for snow, even in Michigan. Maybe, by Christmas. Off to my right, slightly, were the four tall towers of the General Motors Building. GM was connected to my hotel by a skywalk over Grand Boulevard, linking it to the shopping area of New Center One, at Crowley's Department Store. A person could walk from the General Motors World Headquarters to New Center One to the Albert Kahn Building, north, or to the Fisher Building, east over Second Avenue, and never go out of doors. For those who hated the natural elements, it was a great arrangement.

It was dark, and the telephone was ringing. But I didn't care. It couldn't be for me. Only my sons knew where I was, and they seldom called to chat. They seldom called, period. One of them calling would amount to a minor miracle. I no longer believed in miracles.

It was neither Jim nor Rick. It was Denys Fowler, asking if I was free for lunch, tomorrow.

"Why?" I said. And he said, "Why do you think, Marc? People eat. People talk. People get together for lunch. It's what people do, Marc." I laughed to cover my embarrassment at being so neatly and gently chastised. "When you put it that way," I said. "I'd love to have lunch, Denys. Where shall I meet you?"

"How about right there in the hotel," he said. "The St. Regis Room is as good a place as any."

"Fine with me. What do I know?"

"Hey, if you don't want to?"

"No. That's fine, Denys. Looking forward to it."

He was silent, but I sensed he wanted to say more. I was not in the mood to wait for him.

"Denys, can I ask you a question?"

"Sure. Yes. Of course, you can."

"Well, I'm sitting here up on the sixth floor, looking down over Detroit, and I'm thinking about the Titanic. You understand?"

"I don't..."

"Representation, Denys. I'm thinking about how the Titanic represents all ships that are sunk in the ocean. Unexpected tragedies, you know?"

"Like with the Edmund Fitzgerald on the Great Lakes. Yeah, I follow. That is what you mean?"

"That's it!" I said. "As with Schliemann's Troy. A single place or a single event that represents so much more than that single event. One thing signifies all."

"Gotcha. So...?"

I was beginning to feel a little foolish, like a college professor who had carried his lecture home to the dinner table. The wife was sitting there, trying to catch up to where the man was in his thinking. But her mind was still on the pot roast. Was it done as he liked it, a bit rare in the middle? Would dessert be what she wanted it to be? Would they make love after? The professor was missing the signals. He should come home. He should pay attention. He should leave his lectures in the classroom.

"Well," I said. "I was with some kids last night, listening to them talk about Detroit. They were telling me how representative a city it is. This city stands for a lot of cities. Maybe, all cities. But, as with the Titanic, it signifies what to avoid. It sounds funny, I know, but Detroit needs to avoid its own past, its own history, if it's going to have a significant future. From what I hear, that's not about to happen, Denys." I stopped, because I didn't know what else to say.

"You're asking did the kids have it right? You're asking can I confirm or deny what you heard? That it?"

"Something like that."

Denys was silent. I held the telephone to my ear hard enough to hurt. I pulled the phone away, changing ears, and rubbed at the soreness.

"Tell you what I'll do, Marc. I'll bring a guy with me to lunch tomorrow. Name's Charlie Eusted. Charlie will be able to answer your questions far better than I can. How would that be?"

"Great! See you then."

"Okay. See you."

I sat at a table in the St. Regis Room, drinking coffee and waiting. I was early, as I usually was for everything, and I was relaxing, inside.

There was a commotion at the entrance. The man who had seated me was arguing quietly but intensely with another man in a wheelchair. The man in the wheelchair was not stopping. He shoved himself into the restaurant, looked around. Here we go, I thought, a bit of local scenery unfolding for my edification. But the man called to me.

"You McDaniel?"

The man was sticking out a huge hand, black as his aged face. The hand was well worn and calloused.

"Well, yes. McDaniel, that's me."

"Charles Edward Eusted. Denys sent me to find you."

"Charles Edward...? Oh, Charlie! Sure. Nice to meet you."

The protesting maitre d' backed off, his hands waving from side to side. Then he rushed forward to remove one of the chairs from the end of my table. Charlie Eusted rolled himself into the empty space.

"Where's Denys?" I said, when Charlie was in place.

"He'll be along in a moment. Long time since I been in this place. They don't cater to the likes of me. Not because I'm Black; that's not the point. You've got to be couth to be in here. Uncouth, that's what I am."

Charlie was toying with the edge of the tablecloth, as he spoke to me. His fingers ran up and down the fine linen. He had a tender smile on his face.

"Couth?" I said, trying hard not to laugh. "Now there's a word I haven't heard for a while."

"You don't understand it?"

"Not that, Charlie...Charles. I used to use it, myself, as a description of the kind of people I liked. A mite pretentious, I suppose, but the best I could find."

"Charlie will do, seeing as your a friend of Denys's. What you're talking about sounds aristocratic. What are you, a poor but acculturated white boy?"

"Yes," I said. "That's exactly what I am."

"Then you won't like me."

"On the contrary, I like you very much, already."

Still, I was thinking: Who the hell is this guy, who acts like a bum, yet talks like a college graduate?

Charlie Eusted began to laugh. His laugh was as bold and uninhibited as the man was. His laugh rang through the restaurant, causing people to pause in their idle conversations and stare our way.

There was Denys, heading toward us, grinning from ear to ear. Over his shoulder, I could see the maitre d' shake his noble head from one side to the other.

"You're not hard to find, Charlie," Denys said. "I see you two have met. What have I missed?"

"Nothing," I said, with Charlie echoing me. "Nothing at all."

"Well, then, let's eat. I'm starved."

We sat around wine after our lunch and chatted about little or nothing. The wine added nicely to my chicken-breast croissant sandwich and Caesar salad. I was feeling mellow. So was Charlie Eusted, apparently. His back was to the luncheon crowd, so he was ignoring them. He was lost in some private world of his own. I was content to be quiet, but I was also waiting for Denys to get us to where we were on the telephone, talking about Detroit. Had he forgotten? I could broach the subject, myself.

As if reading my mind, Denys Fowler said, "Another murder, Charlie. Another fire. Another burglary. Another rape. It makes the news, I guess. Destroys the hoped-for image we all want for Detroit."

Charlie's eyes flicked from Denys to me. The eyes fell down to the glass of burgundy he held in his hand. The hand was way too large for the slender glass stem. He cradled the bowl of the glass, warming the wine. Charlie looked up again and focused his deep, brown eyes on me.

"What does Archer expect?" he said. "A couple of sports stadiums and a few casinos aren't going to change things much. There's a hole in the city that used to be Detroit. That's what's got to change. But he can't see it. Why should he? There is this gaping hole and Whitey's got money enough fill it; that's what he can see. Bring in the money and plug up the hole; why not? But it ain't gonna make no difference to the people already here. What's it they say, 'One man's development is another man's eviction notice.' Got that right! Except that the people are already gone; those that matter. Those to be evicted, now, are just leftovers."

"Who's Archer?"

"Dennis Archer, the mayor," Charlie said. "A good man stuck in the middle. The usual place."

"What's he hope to do?"

"Rejuvenate the city, what else? Detroit has got to be saved! That's the party line. Anybody's party. Everybody's party. Except that nobody wants to live here. Not with the city as it is. So why save it?"

There was no hint of laughter in Charlie's voice. It had dropped at least an octave and was rolling around on the basement floor, like a preacher's voice when a point needed to be made about belief. There was a marvelous roll to the man's voice, and I could easily visualize him as a preacher. Some of our best American preachers were Black.

They had that same deep, rolling voice.

"That's what Marc wants to know," Denys said. "Why should this failed city be saved? Tell us, Charlie."

"What for?" Charlie said.

"Huh?" I said.

"What do you want to know for, Marc? Mere curiosity? Or are you able to do something about it?"

The question stopped me cold. Why did I want to know? Was I simply being my usual curious self? Had I any justifiable reason for knowing? I was certainly in no position to do anything about it.

"His daughter died here," Denys said, as if that were reason enough.

"Oh," Charlie said. "Where? How?"

I told him.

He was quiet, intensely quiet.

"What?" I said.

"I saw that," Charlie said. "I saw it."

"You did? The police said nobody saw it. How did you? Where were you? What did you see?"

Charlie stayed quiet.

"If he saw it," Denys said. "He was at his usual place. The bus stop by the State of Michigan Building, just north of the corner of Grand. Charlie has been writing a book, over a lot of years, about happenings on the corner of Grand and Woodward. Things he sees happening. How he feels about what he sees. I haven't read it. Nobody has read it, right, Charlie? But it's written. If Charlie saw it, he wrote about it. So he knows."

"I don't...? How...? Why...? Why didn't you...?" I was stuttering, trying to get the questions out.

"I saw it," Charlie repeated. "That's all I can tell you."

"But...?"

A hard look from Denys shut me up, but it left me with something I hadn't felt in a while. I had buried my futile rage at Laura's gravesite. Or so I had thought.

We finished the wine, and the friends left me, going out together past the maitre d', who was standing like a soldier at the entrance to the restaurant, his chin jutting into the air. The man glanced over at me, and I watched his thick eyebrows climb up under his hairline. I offered him a shrug of my shoulders as consolation, but he ignored me, granting no forgiveness.

Neither, I thought, will I.

CHAPTER 4

I dreamed. In it, a magician was busy doing his magic tricks on a bright stage. His partner, a much smaller man, ran around doing all the usual assistant things: dragging in the props, encouraging the audience, acting wondrously surprised — yet knowing — as each act unfolded. In the end, the magician explained to the audience one of the simpler of his tricks. As he talked, the assistant performed, surprisingly professional. It is all deceptive motion, the magician informed the crowded house. Every single action is planned for effect. No action is ever what it seemed to be. The common gets changed into the uncommon; ordinary activity becoming mere cover for the extraordinary. "Slight of hand?" he said. "Oh, no! Slight of all body motion. Watch!"

The magician ran his assistant through the routine one more time. Then he turned his assistant, so that the small man faced the other way. We could see what audiences are never shown. The cigarette, dropped to the floor and stomped on, is not dropped to the floor, but palmed. The lit butt gets stuck into the small man's farther ear. A new cigarette is not lit with a flashlight, though it appears to be. The hat brim is not adjusted, but used as motion to cover the plucking of the lit cigarette. The magicians performed again, slowly. With a little practice, everyone in the audience could do that trick. What, then, of all the other tricks we had seen? Could we do them, too?

I woke up certain of it: Every action is not what it seemed to be. Someone had murdered my daughter. What was known about the accident was cover for what really happened. If I could penetrate the cover, I would find the killer. All action is deception, I told myself. If I figured out how the killing was done, I would also find out why it was deemed necessary. Nothing about innocence; lots about guilt. Magicians are merely artists who plan deception carefully. They know how gullible people are. They know how often we long for illusion, not appreciating all that is ordinary in our lives. The world is made up of smoke and ashes, but who lit the fire?

Someone knocked at the door. I answered it, assuming it would be the maid, looking to straighten up. A lovely, young woman stood there, leaning on one foot and then the other. She was tall and slender, not thin enough to be a Twiggy, but not heavy, either. Her soft beauty seemed almost squared off, her body the shape of someone who has been ill and not fully recovered. The face was bony, the eyes bright. She had high cheekbones, high forehead, slender nose and chin. Her lips were compressed too tightly, like a person holding something in or something together. I couldn't tell which.

"Mr. McDaniel?" The lips hardly moved.

"Yes. Something I can do for you?"

"I'm Alicia...Alicia Fowler."

"Oh? I'm sorry, I don't...?"

"Denys Fowler is my husband."

I hadn't heard from Denys that he was married. I waved the young woman into my room and considered the necessity of leaving the door open. It closed of its own accord. I heard the click of the lock.

"I'm sorry to bother you," she said, while taking in the room and the view out the window. The sun was bright outside, and its glow angled in, making a golden trail.

"It's all right," I said. "Won't you sit down?

Of the two chairs in the room, Alicia Fowler chose the one closest to the window. She seated herself gracefully, an unpracticed performance. I had to admire it and her. Alicia Fowler was a very attractive woman, I determined, who looked like she had been through a great deal of pain, yet retained great poise.

Alicia appeared to have forgotten me. Her gaze was fixed out the window. I watched as a hard look glazed her face. She was staring off to the right, toward GM's four tall towers. Then her look softened. She remembered where she was and turned back to me.

I sat down on the opposite side of the small table in the corner of the room and tried a smile.

Alicia Fowler's eyes fell to the purse she held in her lap. Then she looked up and stared at me, stiffening.

"Denys makes so few friends," she said. "I felt I had to meet you.

"Friend? I just met the man, Alicia. I don't think I qualify just yet."

"But you do," she said. "It isn't a matter of time."

"That's...?" I bit back words that were unkind.

"Odd," she said. "But Denys is different, you know. He isn't like any man I've ever met."

"He leaps into things?"

"Yes. I don't know why he's that way. He just is."

"But you love him."

"Yes, exactly. Denys is bright. Brilliant, actually. That's why they keep him over there. In spite of, you know, all the strange things he does or is apt to do. They keep him on a short leash, I guess you'd say."

"That does sound strange. Big companies have a way of getting what they want out of you. But they don't usually condone odd behavior."

"I told you, Denys is brilliant! He saves them scads of money."

"The bottom line," I said, laughing lightly.

"Yes. They have a man or two designated to watch him. They're not obvious about it, but they keep him under control."

I glanced at a picture on the wall. It was a nondescript painting of flowers, done mostly in purple and pink to match the colors of the room.

"So he had gotten away," I said, "if I may put it that way, when he met me."

"Yes," Alicia said. "They do let him loose, once in a while. It's a kind of safety valve thing. It makes me think of monks in Japan being given one day of debauchery a year in order to be under discipline the rest of the time.

"You've been in Japan?"

"Yes. We both have. A long time ago."

At that moment, there was a knock at my door. I was thinking echo and shrugged my shoulders at Alicia Fowler and went to find out who it was.

It wasn't the maid. It was a man, big in the shoulders, dressed as well or better than Denys Fowler dressed. He had thin, blonde hair and a bright scar on his forehead. I admired the man's obvious professionalism, but I was beginning to think that people around here had a specific uniform they were required to wear. Depending of who they worked for, that was probably true enough.

"Mr. McDaniel?"

"Uh, yes?"

"I represent...Oh, Alicia. This is a surprise!"

The man was looking over my shoulder. Suddenly, he seemed disconcerted, and apologetic. He had planned an approach, as to a new client, and things weren't working as they should.

"I'm sorry to interrupt," the man said. "I can come back. I'd better, I guess."

"It's all right, Jack," Alicia Fowler said from behind me. "We were just talking about you."

I turned to stare at her.

"You were?" Jack said, puzzled, too.

"Is there an echo in here?" I said. "You might as well come in, Jack, I guess I should have been expecting you."

"I'll, uh, come back," Jack said, softly.

He backed into the hall, then reached into the room to haul the door closed. The door was chasing him out. He waved a brief goodbye as he faded from view. It was a comedy exit, but it wasn't funny.

Behind me, Alicia Fowler burst out laughing, anyway.

"Should have expected that," Alicia said, struggling to get words out. "They check on Denys's friends. Anybody he talks to gets a contact. Secrets, you know?"

I nodded, but I didn't know.

An hour later, Alicia and I had finished the bottle of Asti Spumante I ordered up to the room. She talked a while about herself and asked about me. As neither of us was willing to push it, we learned very little beyond the fact that we liked each other, immediately. I saw Alicia's lips lose tension and her supple body ease itself. It was due to the conversation, I told myself, and to the fact that we had hit it off. None of it was due to the wine. Maybe poor Jack had acted as catalyst to a new friendship. I had no way of knowing, so I kept my thoughts limited to things I could handle, avoiding feelings.

It was another hour before Alicia left. When she had gone, I felt the vacancy in my chest. It was as big as down town Detroit, all knotted, sad and empty.

CHAPTER 5

When I looked back on my life, I realized that I had spent the last thirty years trying to figure out why a Near Eastern phenomenon of a couple of thousand years ago should be of concern to modern Americans. I was one of those modern Americans, of course. I could not find out how it related to me. How then was I to relate it to others? It wasn't just the God-talk, or even the Jesus-talk. It was the fact of a different world view. Things had changed from Biblical days to now. There appeared to be little connection between the two world views. If there is to be conversation between the ages, there must be a certain amount of connection beyond the simple fact of sin. But what is sin? Is it merely a natural potential, similar to disease? Frankly, I don't know what sin is.

Reflections on religion; my major preoccupation. When I was preoccupied, I hardly heard the call of nature, never mind the ringing of the phone. I picked the instrument up without thinking about it. The conversation was well underway, before I caught up with it. When I did, I wished I hadn't.

"Mr. McDaniel?"

"Yes."

"This is Sergeant Berra of the Detroit Police Department"

"Yes, Sergeant?"

"We heard you were in town, sir, looking into your daughter's death. We wanted to assure you, sir, that we haven't forgotten her. The file on the incident remains open, and the investigation is still active. We wanted to assure you of that fact. Of course, as you are aware, Detroit is a busy place for criminal types. But you haven't been forgotten, sir. The perpetrator, or perpetrators, of your daughter's death will be brought to justice. You can rest assured of that fact."

I reviewed what had been said.

Then I said, "Sergeant, what's my daughter's name?"

"Sir?"

"My daughter's name, Sergeant Berra. Could you tell me what it is, please?"

"Uh, sir. I don't have that information in front of me."

"I assume whoever asked you to place this call does."

"Yes, sir. I'm sure he does. Sorry, sir."

"It's okay, Sergeant. You're just doing your job."

"Yes, sir. That's right, sir."

"May I ask why you were asked to call me. How did you know I was in town? Who told tales out of school?"

"I don't know, sir."

"Maybe, you should start an investigation of your own, Sergeant."

"Yes, sir. You're right, sir. I will, sir."

"And while you're at it..."

"Yes, sir?"

"Find out why anybody would care?"

"Yes, sir. Yes, sir!"

I went walking. It was cold and blustery, but I didn't care. I had to get out of the hotel. I was frustrated and angry, and I couldn't tell myself, for sure, why I was either of those things. It was as if there was something lying just outside my grasp, like the sound of a dog whistle to the human ear. I knew it was there; I just didn't hear it. I felt as if there were people behind a screen, laughing at me. I was some sort of joke. A comedy routine was in progress, and I was the foil-like butt of it, being talked about, played around, hit at, buffeted by adversaries I could not see and would never recognize. So I walked, enjoying the cold. But the wind was another matter; I could have done without the wind.

I walked a circle — sort of — by going west and then north and then east and then south. And then west again and north again and east again, until I was back where I had started. It seemed as if Denys was waiting for me, though he claimed our being in front of the St. Regis at the same time was pure accident. Still, it was good to see him. It was good to see anybody I knew, as I knew no one in Detroit. Denys made me aware of how glad he was to see me, clapping me hard on the back, until I stumbled and almost fell.

"Easy," I said. "I'm fragile."

"You don't look it."

"See these skinny bones? I'm twenty pounds lighter and an inch shorter than I was ten years ago, Denys."

"You're joking," he said, jokingly.

"I wish I were."

"So that's what old age does to you."

"To some of us, Denys, old man. Others sag in all the wrong places. That's one of the things I've noticed; when I dress for swimming, say.

The guys I used to envy, I don't, anymore. They were building up terrific muscles, you know? What they didn't realize was that they'd have to maintain that into old age. So they're sagging, while I'm not, not having anything to sag. So skinny I'll stay, and be grateful for it. Besides, I hear undernourished is the in thing; a better old age for the thin ones like me."

"Damn! And here I went and built up this beautiful body in my sheltered youth. And here it's going to fall apart. At least, down."

"Sorry, buddy. Truth must be told."

Denys laughed on cue and drew me to him for a hug. I'd rather have had him slap my back, but I didn't say that. He was enjoying himself, like a boy at play.

"So, you looking for me?" I said.

Denys told me he wanted to invite me to a party being given tonight at his house, but he wondered if ministers drank. There would be drinking at the party. He knew that Catholic priests drank; what about Protestant ministers? Of course, I could just have wine. This minister drank harder stuff, I told him, moderately. The party was tonight, Denys repeated, was I free? I told him I was, and he said he looked at the party as a celebration of a new friendship. I told him any reason for a party was a good reason. He agreed and said he would pick me up after work, okay?

"You sure you want to do this?"

"You got something else planned?" he said.

I told him I didn't, and he nodded and shook my hand and left me, crossing the street in the middle of the block. I watched him head into the massive GM building to become somebody else.

My son, Richard, called just as I came out of the Jacuzzi. I felt I was spoiling myself, taking a bath in the middle of the day. The call was guilt ringing its bell. I was unaccustomed to the luxury and had been spoiling myself just by being in this hotel. That's what I told myself. It was and was not true.

I lay nude and hot on the bed as I took the call. Timing is everything, somebody said.

"Dad, how are you?"

"Good, Rick."

"You enjoying yourself?"

"At this moment, wonderfully. On the whole, I don't really know."

"How's Detroit?"

"I'm not certain. I guess I don't know what criterion to use." I had been puzzling on that, myself.

"I mean, are you enjoying being in the big city?"

Rick didn't seem to be able to get to the unanswerable question: What the hell was I doing here, anyway? What did I want from Detroit?

I told him that I found Detroit fascinating, unlike any big city I had ever been to, including New York and Los Angeles and Boston. The city had an aura of its own, I said. I didn't explain, though the quiet on the line suggested I should. I told him I was invited to a party this evening, so I should meet some people. Maybe, I would have a better picture for him, after. When he called again, I would fill him in on what I had learned.

"Hey, sounds great," he said.

"Yeah. Yes, it is!"

Then there was silence. Conversation with either of my sons was a strain. Since they had entered into their own lives, we had less and less in common; less experience together, less to talk about. The things we shared were coated with grief. No desire on anybody's part to talk about that. So we strained at ordinary conversations that, for most persons, would simply flow.

"I saw Jim, yesterday."

"You did?" I said.

"Yeah, Dad. He was passing through Los Angeles. We did lunch." I waited for Rick to say more, but nothing came. We had entered a vacuum of words.

"So how is he?" I asked, finally.

"Good. So he says." But Rick's voice was trembling.

"What do you think?"

"The divorce has blown him away, Dad. He realizes that he is responsible, but it's still hard. The life of the romantic flyboy doesn't seem so glamorous to him any more."

"Is that what you think? Or is that what he said?"

"That's what I think. You know, Jim. He doesn't reveal much. You have to know how to read him."

"Which you do?" I said.

"Sure. He's my brother. When you live with a guy, and he's bigger than you are, you learn to read him in order to survive."

"That bad, huh?" I remembered that it was. Brothers are brothers, and there is often little love lost between them. At the very least, they fight. "And how are the kids?" I added, quickly. "Does Jim get to see them?"

"Oh, sure. Almost as often as before."

"He was gone a lot. Can't blame Leslie, entirely, I guess. It takes two, as they say."

"Yeah." Then Rick was quiet again, quieter than before. With Rick, silence often spoke more loudly than words.

"Something wrong?" I said.

"Yeah. I guess you'd have to say that something is wrong. Jane left me, Dad. She said we weren't going anywhere. And she's met this guy."

I took a moment to change the phone from one ear to another and to shift my position on the bed.

"Sorry, Rick. This guy anyone you know?"

"Why do you ask that?"

"It usually is," I said.

Rick didn't respond, and I cursed myself for asking. It was habit, a minister's probing into the core of a problem, needing to know what to be sympathetic about.

"Sorry," I said. "You've got enough to deal with, without listening to me."

"It's okay, Dad. I do know him. I never thought..."

The words trailed off, silence returning like the cat who came back. I could picture Rick ducking his head, in his peculiar way, when troubled. His right hand would then come up and stroke his chin, rubbing it hard. Then he would clear his throat, in order to say something else.

"I've got to go, Dad. I've got a client to see. As if I gave a damn about clients, right now."

"Okay, Rick. Talk to you, later."

CHAPTER 6

The party was a blast. I had never been in a place with so much bawdy humor and raucous laughter going on, not that I could remember. Apparently, I made the most of it. I woke up the next morning in a room I did not recognize. It was stylish and very modern. The furniture was Danish, walnut, and light in scale, with burl accents in the wood. A voice was calling at my door. It came from a lady I thought knew. She was tall and slender and beautiful, and I could have fallen for her, if I were a younger man.

"Breakfast in ten minutes," Alicia Fowler sang. "That is, if you want breakfast."

I started to say something wise, but my head throbbed and my chest ached and my mouth tasted like mush. The lady held a steaming cup of coffee in front of my face.

"Ten minutes," she repeated, leaving me alone.

I drank the coffee. Then I staggered into a bathroom and washed my battered face. After combing my hair, I picked up the empty cup and walked down a long hallway, following the sound of voices and bright laughter. In a well-lit and colorful kitchen, I found Denys and Alicia Fowler holding hands. Denys was licking at one of Alicia's ears. She was laughing at him, unnaturally. When they saw me, they stopped, but only for a moment.

I poured myself a cup of coffee and then noticed the quiet figure sitting on the other side of a large breakfast table. Charlie Eusted was ignoring the goings-on at the far side of the room. He pointed at the pots on the stove, and I helped myself to bacon and eggs, shoved the timer down on a toaster, and sat down to eat. I wondered if I could, but I did very well and felt far better, after.

"Well, what'd you think of the party?" Charlie said.

I thought he was simply making polite conversation, so I said, "Fine."

"C'mon, what'd you think? Forget the lovebirds there."

"Well, it took me a while to figure out what was wrong with it. Then it came to me."

"Wrong with it?" Charlie said. He was scratching at the back of his head with his fingernails and yawning, and I wondered if he felt as badly as I did.

"Yes, wrong with it," I said.

It was too early in the day to know what I was thinking, but I wasn't thinking well. The fog in my head covered my eyes.

"You always look on that side?" Charlie said. "Oh, yeah, a minister."

"Sinners in the hands of an angry God," I said, mockingly. Might as well play the saint.

He laughed at me, a huge, belching laugh which caught the attention of the lovebirds, for a moment.

"C'mon, out with it, " Charlie said. "Man, I've seen your kind. Spit it out."

"Okay, how about this?" I said. "I saw their eyes, and it scared the shit out of me."

"Their eyes?"

"Yes, their eyes. You can learn a lot about people, when you really look into their eyes."

"So what did you see?" Charlie's head was tilting sideways, revealing the doubt in his mind. But he was a man to pursue things, no matter how strange, no matter where they led him. I was altering my judgment of Charlie Eusted but had the feeling I would never know him well.

I also noticed that Denys and Alicia were listening to us. They still touched, but the necking was over. The room seemed suddenly filled with tense expectation.

"They are people who have been yanked out of childish innocence into whatever you call what comes after. Maturity. Adulthood. Reality. Whatever. That's what I saw."

"Yanked?"

"Yes, Charlie," I said, hesitatingly. "Something tore innocence right out of them. They are all people filled with pain."

Charlie was silent. He glanced, now and again, over to where Denys and Alicia silently stood. I saw Denys nod once back at Charlie. There was communication going on, but I was not part of it.

"Tell him," Denys said.

"Can't. You'd better."

"Charlie, you got the words. You tell him."

Charlie's fists tightened on the arms of his wheelchair, and I thought he was about to crush the metal. Instead, he let his fingers relax, and he stretched them until they made a cracking sound.

"We talk about it," he said. "Denys and me, we talk about it." His chin came up, and he stared at Alicia. "Her, too. We talk about it, often."

I waited.

"We all have holes, inside. That's how we describe it, Marc. We're hollow, deep inside. It's the best description we can come up with. When man...a woman, too...gets past a traumatic experience, there's little to be done. You got it right, Marc. Those folks last night, they've been torn out of whatever youth they had. All of us have. We grew up, or *something*, too fast."

"In different ways," Alicia Fowler added. "But a great leap, or something. It left a hole inside. We're empty, in one way or another."

Denys was nodding, rapidly.

"Vietnam," Charlie said. "For Denys and Alicia, both, it was Vietnam. They were there. For some of the guys and gals last night, it was big city things. An accident, maybe. Or a murder. Drugs, you know. For a few, it was rape. Man or woman, rape. For one I know about, it was an illness. A kid and about to die; that's what he thought at the time, that's what they told him. He didn't die, but there's this hole. It sits there, you know?"

"What about you, Charlie?" I said, doing what I do in counseling. Doing what I did.

"The big war, WWII. And this damned city!"

"Detroit? I don't...?"

"Of course, you don't. *You don't live here!*"

Charlie's voice rocked me. I felt as if I had been hit in the chest by one of his big fists. His voice reminded me of the Voice of the Bene Gesserit in Frank Herbert's *Dune*. It struck me so powerfully that I could not move.

Charlie was whispering something, after his outburst, and it dawned on me, finally, that he was saying, *sorry*, *sorry*. I didn't know if he was saying it to me.

"It's okay, Charlie," Denys said, quietly. "You don't have to say any more. We know."

"He doesn't," Charlie said, lifting a chin at me.

I didn't say anything.

"You need to live here, Marc," Charlie said. Then he swallowed, hard. "If you want to understand anything, you need to live here. That's all I'm saying."

"You mean, Detroit?" I said. "I hear its not a white man's city anymore, Charlie. But can a white man live in it enough to know what you're talking about?"

"I don't know," Charlie said.

"What do you think?"

Charlie sagged in his chair. He was thinking about things he would rather not think about right now. That's what I was thinking.

"I don't believe so, to be honest with you, Marc," he said, finally. "But you I'd have to give it a try. You want to try?"

"Me?"

"Isn't that what we're talking about?"

"You mean live here?" Things were happening too fast. I was not a man to jump into things.

"Yeah, live here," Charlie said.

"You're asking a lot, Charlie," Denys said.

"I'm not asking nothin'." Charlie was looking at his own, large, calloused hands.

The silence grew, mocked only by the ticking of the old clock on the wall. A Regulator, if I wasn't mistaken. Had it once graced the wall of an old schoolhouse?

"Marc came here because of his daughter," Alicia said, speaking softly, the words rising and falling like the calm wash of waves on a beach.

I looked carefully at Charlie Eusted. He had not moved in his wheelchair, but something menacing about the man moved across the room and touched me. I would not want this man angry at me. Chair or no chair, he would get to me — or anyone else, I thought — even if he had to crawl to do it. The power in the crippled man oozed out of him; the muscles in his face, his arms, his muscular torso strained to restrain themselves. I witnessed a victory of will over feelings. Soon Charlie looked, once again, like the man I had met, a gentle, highly educated, son-of-a-bitch. He was the kind of man I could admire, not having lived close to one since childhood.

"Make a suggestion," I said.

"Stay in Detroit, awhile. You might learn something."

"Live here?" He had to be joking, but he wasn't.

"I have a place you can stay at," Charlie said. "Of course, there's a fee. You'd have to pay rent."

I glanced at the pair across the room.

"Charlie owns a few places," Denys said. "That's how he makes his living."

"A landlord?" I said.

"You interested?" Charlie said. "You can have it cheap for awhile.

You decide to stay on, the rent becomes what it was before. I doubt you'd stay."

"You'd take a loss? How long are we talking about?"

"Three months, no obligation. You pay by the month for that long. After, I'd want a lease signed."

"You sound like a landlord. Where is this place?"

"Right near the hotel you're staying at. I spend my time nearby, so I'd keep an eye on you."

"Black neighborhood?"

"Pretty much all Black. Except for you and a certain priest we all know. You and he may have a lot in common. More than church, I think. We'd see."

"I'd be the only white man?"

"The guy who lived there before was white. So there's precedence." Charlie was smiling. He was enjoying this. "In case that worries you too much, there is a white woman who lives next door."

"An apartment?" I asked.

"A big old house. Brownstone, you'd call it. I bought it and fixed it up. Made six apartments out of it, four downstairs, two up. It'd do for you."

"It's quite clean," I heard Alicia whisper. "And if anything needs fixing..."

"What happened to the guy who lived there before?" I said, thinking it wasn't a place for me.

"Killed himself," Charlie said. "Or had it done for him. The police aren't sure."

"Holy shit!"

"I never heard of that kind," Charlie said, almost laughing. He was enjoying himself now, for sure.

My mind was running around. What in the world was I thinking about? Why would I want to stay here? Detroit, of all places? The world was full of places to go, places to stay for awhile. I couldn't picture Detroit, Michigan, as one of them. But I also felt I wasn't done here. There was something about my daughter's death; yes, a mystery, with promise of revelation. And there was something else. An echoing, you'd have to call it. Detroit sent shivers down my spine, because of repressed memories of my childhood. I grew up in a mill city. Factory city Detroit made my mind throb. Was yesterday intruding into now? Was I getting old enough to reflect on beginnings? I guess that happened often enough to be a possibility, even for me.

"Well, what'll it be?" Charlie said.

"I'd want to see it," I said.

"Sure," Charlie said.

He squirmed in his chair and dug into his pants pocket. He dangled a set of keys in front of me. He set them on the kitchen table and reached into a shirt pocket and dug out a small pad of paper, the pad on which he placed his jottings as he sat north of the State of Michigan building and commented on goings on near the corner of Woodward and Grand. He wrote for a moment, tore off a piece of paper. He waved it in the air.

"The address," he said. "And a note to be shown to whoever gets in your way, saying you can look."

I waited a moment, then stood up and walked over to him. On his face was a challenge, I thought. I took the bit of paper and scooped up the key.

I did not look behind me, at Denys and Alicia, but there was communication going on, silently, between old friends. They had little need for words.

CHAPTER 7

"He smokes most evenings," Alicia Fowler said.

We were standing at her doorway, saying goodbye. Over in the driveway, Denys was holding open the car door, while Charlie worked himself inside. They were talking. A lot was being said. Their conversation kept me in low gear. I felt they should have all the time they needed. Alicia's remark did not register as significant, at first. Then I thought: So Denys Fowler smokes evenings? So what? I shrugged. Her comment carried no message for me.

"He sees things in the smoke," she said.

I turned away from watching Denys and Charlie and looked her square in the eye.

The eyes were swimming with water. They asked me for understanding.

"What does he see?" I said.

"Things from, you know, back then."

"Vietnam?"

Alicia nodded

"What kind of things, exactly?"

"Killings. Mutilations. Horrible things!" The words were coming out, needing visualization. I could not provide them with essential content.

Alicia was trembling. I didn't know what to say to her, and I didn't think it appropriate for me to hold her. I didn't know what to do.

"Come with me." she said.

We went back into the house, me following her like an obedient child. We went down a corridor, went down some stairs, went through at least three doors. The room we entered was dark, until Alicia threw the switch. The room blared, suddenly. In it was the unbelievable. In it was a man's past made present. In it was hell.

"Good God!" I said.

What was in the room was imprinting itself in me, but I wasn't sure I'd ever accept it.

"We'd better get back," Alicia said.

"Yes, we'd better. But this...?"

She was nodding, but neither of us knew exactly for what reason. It was a thing to do, a closure.

"I had to show you."

"Of course, you did," I said. "I'm glad you did."

"You are?"

She stopped in the hallway by the last door. She stared so intently at me, I thought she could see my soul. Her look made me afraid. I nodded affirmation, and she said, "You're his friend." I thought it was a question for which I didn't have an answer. "I think so," I said."I'd like to be, if he'll let me."

"Good," she said. "That's real good."

And she took me by the hand and led me the rest of the way, to Denys and to Charlie and to my ride back into Detroit.

The door whooshed behind me as I entered the building. In front of me was a dark hallway. The second door on my right accepted the keys I had been given. I glanced back at the stairway going up and wondered for a moment who lived up there. It didn't matter, except that one of them would be above my head if I decided to stay in this brownstone for awhile. Then it would matter.

I did not turn on the light but went over to the window and raised a blind. The window looked out onto the street, which had little traffic and few pedestrians. The view was of an ordinary neighborhood but of a mixture of structures, one- and two-story residences and larger brownstones tied together in a jumble, without obvious order. I had to ask myself what planning went into such a collage of buildings? None, probably. The neighborhood was built before such considerations.

Walking over from the hotel St. Regis, I found myself entering a quite different world than the one I had seen on my circular walk, earlier. I now entered a world in which everyone was Black. No one accosted me; no one blocked my way; no one spoke to me; no one looked at me directly, but I felt my oddity, a sharp sense of not belonging. A world upside down from my usual; is that what Charlie Eusted was confronting me with? If so, he hit hard and fast. To accept his challenge, even given his support of the venture, was to make a journey to a foreign land. Looking out the window, I was still not certain I wanted to go.

The rooms were furnished, right down to the sheets and towels and dishes in the cupboard. That was a good thing, because I had not brought anything with me and had no desire to pay for household stuff. I turned away from the window and wandered around, opening drawers in a bureau and a desk, opening doors to cupboards and closets. The refrigerator was empty and had been recently cleaned. I would need to fill the freezer, fill the shelves in the pantry, put snack stuff where it would be handy. All that was easy enough, assuming there was a grocery store nearby. There had to be, of course. There were people living here who had to shop somewhere. And, assuming not all of them had transportation, that somewhere had to be around a corner, nearby.

I returned to the front window and stared out. It was getting colder out there. A stiff wind was blowing. It was cold enough to snow, though it wasn't snowing. The few folk who did pass by were bundled heavily into themselves. They were hurrying. It was not a day to loaf in, or meander, not a day for the park. It was a day to be home, to drink and smoke, to do whatever you did when you were stuck and alone. Well, alone with family, hopefully. Then you could play games or make crafts, or simply bicker and fight. It was a day for indoor things, and thinking about indoor things made me think of my childhood residence: home.

It was not all that different from here. Take away the idea of Detroit, take away the Black folk on the street, add a few more fences and a lot more noise, and you had my home-town, my street, my place. And here I was looking out a window, as I so often did, then, musing on the confusion that was my childhood world.

Not everything changes, entirely.

I shut the blind and locked the multiple locks on the door and went outside. I had the feeling that I was being watched closely as I walked away. Other people with nothing to do but stare out of windows. I was of momentary interest, nothing more, yet. I spun left at the bottom of the concrete stairs and walked slowly by the house next door. It was purple in color, an assortment of purples, from light to dark on flat and trim. Who would do that to a little house set back far from the street? But then, it wasn't that nice a house. It looked old and dried up, the bright paint fading to dull tones, duller, now, on a dark day. With the wind blowing as it was, the tiny house seemed to rattle. I expected it to simply fall down.

The grass out front was being stroked by gusts of wind that pushed the grass toward the front porch of the house. In the middle of the lawn was a tree, the shape of which said gingko to me. It looked dead. Perhaps, that was just its winter shape, I couldn't know for sure. I only remembered the gingko from cemeteries in California, where the tree leaves turned golden before they fell; the whole tree, golden and then, suddenly, bare. This tree was a lonely sentinel and could be merely a dried-up stick stuck into the ground, the planter hoping to build a tree-house in it one day. Whoever put it there should have chosen a maple or an oak, better trees for better living, not fossil trees, no matter how pretty.

I stood still, remembering. My boys had done that once, digging a hole and putting into it the limb of a sycamore, hoping for life and growth. They watched it for days, weeks. Finally, they gave up and pushed it over. I found them on that day carefully examining the end of the branch which had not grown roots as expected. They fingered it, soft and muddy.

"Why didn't it?" they asked me. The sadness in their eyes was palpable.

"Why do you think?" I said.

They stared at me for a moment.

"We didn't do it right," Rick offered, hesitantly. "We didn't water it enough. We goofed."

Jim plopped down on his eight-year-old duff. Then he sighed, as only a frustrated eight-year-old can sigh.

"Tree limbs don't grow," he said, the insight frustrating, if clarifying. "Why did you let us?"

"Would you have believed me?"

They looked at each other.

"No," Jim said, finally, speaking for both of them.

"That's why," I said.

"Man, whatcha staring' at?" a voice said from beside me. The voice dragged me back into the cold of now, in the city of Detroit, not California.

"Huh?"

"Just dat ol' house," the voice said. "What yo' lookin' at that for?"

It was a boy of maybe eleven or twelve years of age; maybe younger, I couldn't tell. His fingers were locked into the small chain-linked fence, and he was looking over at the house, not looking at me.

"I don't know," I said. "Because it's an odd house, I guess. An odd color, anyway."

"Yo' plannin' to buy it?"

"No." I chuckled. "I'm thinking about living next door, over there, for awhile." I was lifting my chin toward the brownstone, not wanting to take my hands out of my pockets. It was too cold to hold the fence.

"What yo' wanna do that for?"

"I'm not sure, to tell you the truth. The apartment has been offered to me."

The boy was shaking his head, somberly. His hair was cut short on his head, tight curls showing in what remained. The boy's face was handsome, but a small scar cut into one eyebrow, spoiling the symmetry. It glowed light against the boy's dark skin.

"Don' know why any white man'd wanna live der. The boy's head was shaking, harder than before.

"No white folk around?"

"Yeah, they is. Ol' woman live in there. Her's it. A white man, once, but he kill his fool self. White guy with a gun live in here, sometimes. He mean mutha."

"A gun?"

"Sure! Lots of guns 'round here."

"Is that right?"

The boy suddenly stared up at me. He seemed to be trying to puzzle me out, find out who I was and what I wanted. Everybody wanted something, right? That's the way the game got played.

"Should I get me a gun?" I said. "If I decide to live here?"

The boy nodded at me once, quickly.

"Damn right! Befo' some mutha put a gun in yo' face! Gotta take care of yo'self 'round here."

I said that maybe I'd do that, and the boy nodded his head with satisfaction. His gaze returned to the purple house deep in the lot in front of us. He was staring at it through the fence, as if entranced.

"Whitey lived there once. Big man, huge! Tore a hole in da place, jus' to get him out."

"That right?"

"Tol' ya'"

"So you did. Sorry."

I was beginning to feel very cold and was wondering why I was standing on a street in Detroit, talking to a small boy about an old, purple house.

I looked down and found the boy looking up at me.

"Yo' got lots to learn, yo' live here," he said.

"You teach me?" I said.

The smile, huge and wondrous, was devastating in its effect upon me. This was going to be one handsome kid. His smile transformed him.

The boy was making small circular motions with a thumb against its neighboring finger.

"I don't know if I can afford you," I said.

The smile fell away.

"Look, man," he said. "Yo' can't not afford me. I save yo' life. That's what I do. If yo' gonna live here, yo' gonna need me. Yo' hear?"

I told him I'd think about it, and his attention returned to the purple house. He stared at it, intently, muttering something. I heard words stuck in a throat.

"What's the problem?" I said.

After a quick glance at me, his gaze went back to the house. His voice was fierce, dangerous.

"Gonna own dat place some day," he said.

"Why?" I dared to ask.

"Grandmama liv' there, long time ago. She liv' there again. I make it happin'. That why, okay?"

We stood together, quietly, for a few minutes. Then the boy walked away from me, heading down the street.

After a moment, I called after him.

"What's your name? You didn't say."

The boy turned back and smiled his glorious smile, the one that turned him into a movie star.

"Henri Aloysius Budd, dat my name." The smile grew larger, mocking me. "Say 'Hey, Hank!' That be 'nough."

"Okay, Hey Hank. I'll do that. See you!" I waved at him before turning away.

The boy nodded, smiled.

It was as if the sun had come out.

CHAPTER 8

At the hotel, I was stopped by a man in a uniform. It was blue. The man was short and heavy-set. He was muscular. He had one muscular arm out in front of him, blocking my way. I looked into a crabby, tough, clean-shaven face. I guessed that the man was not used to smiling, given the lines and cracks I saw in that face. He was not a man to fool around with, or lie to, or try to deceive. In the Mafia, he would be an enforcer. He was not with the Mafia. He was one of Detroit's finest.

I stopped in front of his raised hand.

"Mr. McDaniel?"

"Yes ?"

"I'm Sergeant Berra. We talked on the phone."

"Oh, yes. Sergeant. I remember."

"I want to apologize for being stupid on the phone. I want you to know I should never have been conned like that. I want you to know, also, that I don't have any answers for you, yet, but I want you to know that I'm looking into it. You ask hard questions, but I'll get answers for you. I'm looking into it. I want you to know that; that's what I want you to know. You understand?"

I took what he was telling me in, slowly, trying to adjust to what I was being told that he did not say.

"Okay," I said, after a moment. "I appreciate that, Sergeant Berra. I do, more than I can say."

He nodded.

"I don't have any answers, yet. But I will. You can bank on it, Mr. McDaniel. Place a bet, if you want."

"Good, Sergeant. I'll do that."

"Intriguing case. Lots of questions."

"That right? I hadn't heard," I said. "I thought it was just me."

"Well, don't you worry. I'm on it now. I'll get some answers for you. Bet on it."

As he finished speaking, he shoved by me, going fast. I did not know how to stop him. He pushed through the door, and I watched the hotel help get out of his way. They knew the man. They had sense enough to get out of his way.

I felt intimidated, glad he wasn't after me.

I turned away from the hotel entry and started walking toward the elevators. It was quiet in the large empty space. The help at the hotel counter were watching me.

I stood in the elevator, looking back, as the doors closed. There was silence out in front of me. A stillness. It was eerie as a morgue out there. Nothing, no one, was moving. I watched as the size of my viewing screen squashed, thinned out, became a vertical line, then nothing.

I rode up to my room.

I was packing and, therefore, had made a decision. Or had I? Had the decision made me? I folded things neatly into my bag, thinking there would soon be need for a laundromat. I hadn't brought much clothing with me. It would be either wash often or buy more. Maybe, a lot more. Assuming I had really decided to stay.

I sat at the small table when I was finished packing, gazing out the window. The sky had turned a solid blue, not a cloud in the sky, anywhere. Detroit's outline sat in the distance, a city skyline like any other. Closer at hand were GM's four towers. They had been around for a while; since the roaring twenties according to a brochure now on my table. The Fisher Building next door, I had been surprised to read, was supposed to have been three buildings, filling the block, with a middle one taller than the others. Due to unforeseen fortunes of commerce, only one building got built. Still, lit up at night, the place was impressive. At least, in a picture at the center of the brochure.

I placed calls to my sons and left messages on their respective machines, giving no explanation, but providing them with my new address. They would have to write me or I would have to call them. The latter was the more likely. I couldn't remember a single letter from either of my sons.

I took my lonely bag in hand and headed down toward the desk to check out.

"Leaving already?"

"Yes, ma'am."

"Well, just a moment."

She worked the computer in front of her with deft hands, then offered me the results. I signed the bill, authorizing the amount on my MasterCard account.

The girl was young and pretty. Even the stark uniform suited her. She could have been a stewardess on an airplane; the image was the same. Still, she smiled and seemed happy at her work. Not every word she said came out of her training. At least, I didn't think so.

"I hope you had a nice stay." I took the receipt she handed me and stuck it in my pocket. I caught a whiff of her sweet fragrance on my fingers.

"Yes, ma'am. It's a nice hotel."

"Yes, it is nice. Heading home, huh?"

"No, ma'am. Not quite yet."

The girl had a question, but she was not supposed to ask it. Her eyes asked it. I did not answer them. I strolled toward the exit, feeling the heat of the young girl's dark eyes on my back.

"Cab, sir?"

"No, son. Thanks."

The boy reached automatically for my bag, and I held it away from him as I passed by. There are many people taught what to do if they are to serve the public. It becomes habit and ruins personality.

There were cabs at the curb that had drivers that were looking at me, not quite expectantly, but looking anyway, just in case. In cold weather like this, people looking to ride will head quickly their way, seeking refuge, seeking warmth. All the others are oddities, intent on something near at hand; the bank or, perhaps, a restaurant. It was the bag that was drawing the hungry drivers to my scent. They soon looked away, watching for movement, watching for the good fare.

I walked quickly up Grand Boulevard to Woodward Avenue. I turned left. It wasn't far to the street I wanted, but, now that I had a suitcase in my hand, people were apt to watch me. A suitcase meant something, a traveler lost on the road. I walked quickly, acting like I knew where I was going. It was the only way. I was not simply another white guy who strayed away from the New Center area. I belonged here. Or thought I did, or would. Use the direct approach, I told myself. Be bold. Things bad only happen to those who hesitate, who don't know their head from a hole in the ground. I was putting my ass on the line, wasn't I? Why should anybody bother me?

I shifted my bag to my other hand and walked up the steps to my new apartment. I listened to the whoosh of the door behind me. I walked a few steps down the nearly dark hallway and proceeded to unlock a door. It took a few moments of fiddling and fitting keys into locks. I entered a room and locked a few locks. I felt scared, yet safe, in the room. I wondered, again, what I was doing, but it appeared to be too late to turn back. I raised the suitcase in my hand and looked at it.

Easy enough to retrace my steps and get the hell out of here. Instead, I dropped the suitcase onto the bed and opened it. I put my things away. I paused for a minute, when I was done. Then I unlocked my door again. I went out through the whoosh of the main door. I walked a few blocks for a paper bag full of food. I returned the way I came. Now they all know.

I'm staying.

I had been confined for hours and had walked circles around the room. I was wearing a hole in what carpet there was in the place. This will never do, I told myself. I have got to have something going. I can't sit still. I was not a cop to plunge into an investigation, not knowing how. So I will bug a certain policeman by the name of Sergeant Berra. What can the man do, anyway? What else? I can't just sit here and stew all winter. Think of it as a sabbatical, I told myself. Study. Of course, I can do that. Got to find out where the local library was and get a card. But what to study? Not religion, not theology. Something in the liberal arts, the humanities.

Wait a minute, there was a guy living here before me. What was he like? What did he do? Why did he kill himself, if he did, in fact, kill himself? Why? The greatest of the human questions. The one that permeates both philosophy and religion. There is a reason for everything; that is what we tell ourselves. Even God has a purpose, though we often cannot tell what that purpose is. Jesus killed himself or let himself be killed. There had to be a purpose for that act. The Church was built on the answer, in some sense it was the answer, to the question, Why did Jesus die? Well, here was another man who died. I'd try to find out why.

Reasons and purposes. We cover our mental landscape with such things. To hear evolutionary theory talk, there is no reason or purpose in anything that happens. It's all accident, the result of chance. So divvy up your ways of knowing, depending on what you want to know. If it's facts you're after, go with science, and with evolutionary theory. But if it's meaning you need, go with divine motivations — no matter how difficult to figure out — or go with common sense, the lowest and most natural form of human reasoning. A simple division, what's the harm in that? But neither side seems content with simple things.

So, Jesus dead, or some other man dead, and there is or is not a reason for the dying. Who can tell for sure? You pay your penny, and you take your choice. Stuck inside, I was beginning to feel dead, myself.

I grabbed for my jacket and headed out the door. I slammed it shut. I locked up, strode down the hall, pushed open the whooshing door. I plunged right into the arms of the biggest man I had ever seen. I was stopped cold. There was no way to knock him over. He held me in two outstretched arms, as if I were a GI Joe doll in the hands of a large boy. There was no recognizable expression on the man's face. He held me, that was all. I waited for what came next. I had no choice in the matter. The man appeared to be waiting, as well. The collision of our bodies had not fazed him in the least. He acted as if this had happened to him before. He was trying to remember what he had done the last time. I waited, looking him over. I realized that nothing physical could touch him. He was of a race superior in strength and toughness to mine. He was Neitzche's *Ubermensch*, a kind of superman. I was looking at physical perfection, but wondering about what was inside. Was he in control of himself, as he appeared to be? Or would he rage in a moment, as my offence of his person became certain? I considered all that might happen to me. It was something to do.

"Meet Bubba," I heard a voice say.

I followed the sound to its source. There was Charlie Eusted, in his wheelchair, grinning up at me.

"Bubba, meet Marc McDaniel, my new tenant. See that he gets treated right, okay?"

Bubba nodded once, very slowly.

"I don't want this man hurt, ever. You hear me?" I was trying to deal with the laughter at the back of Charlie's deep voice.

Bubba nodded, again, as slowly as before.

"Now, put Mr. McDaniel down, Bubba."

I smiled up at Bubba as his face floated away from mine. There was no way to shake his hand until he let me go. By then, it was too late. Bubba left me to prop open the door behind me. He walked back down the steps and picked Charlie up, wheelchair and all, and carried him into the building. I made it a point to stay out of the way. At the apartment, Bubba waited patiently for me.

He was like an elephant in the hallway, filling it. I was the one in a hurry. I wondered if Bubba could move fast, if he had to. I did not wish to find out. If he did, he could be an entire football team, all by himself.

By the time I got into the room, Charlie Eusted had rolled himself over to the desk by the window. He was staring outside, as if something was going on out there.

"Gonna snow," he said. "Feel it coming."

"Old bones?" I said, to say something in response. I was fidgeting, looking for somewhere to seat myself. I settled for a corner of the bed. A small kitchen, off to one side, had a pair of chairs and a small table in it. But it was too far away from Charlie. I needed to stay close enough to the man to talk. I leaned back on my elbows, as backrest. Bubba remained standing.

Then Charlie gave Bubba a sign, and the big man left my room. I assumed he would wait for Charlie out in the hall. Or in his car parked outside.

"Well...?" Charlie said.

I raised my hands, questioning.

"You have any questions, Marc?" Charlie asked me. I quickly made reference to the man who had lived here before me. Charlie's attention was immediate.

"Good place to start," he said. "The man lived here, therefore, he must have some experience with living here. I see what you're thinking."

"What can you tell me about him?" I said. "You were his landlord, you must know something about him."

"Very little, Marc. His name was Gregory Barton and he kept pretty much to himself. He had an occasional lover in here. Pretty women. But they didn't stay long. He was a writer with a couple of published books to his name. He was friends with the poet who lived next door, a few years back. That house has been empty for awhile. He was also friends with a local priest, name of Father Rene, you'll meet him. That's about it. It's all I know."

"But why did he live here? Why choose this place?"

"Don't know, Marc. He was living here when I bought the place. He payed his rent on time, so I let him stay. Same with the old, white lady next door. The people around here accepted him, but not as a friend. You understand? I think they worry about white guys who are writers. They fear exploitation, you know. If they care at all. He seemed to be a self-contained sort of guy, the kind who need only a few friends. He took things that came his way, as some men do. Could be that's how it was."

"His books have titles?"

"Sure. Try a bookstore. I don't know them."

"You're a big help," I said.

Charlie made an indescribable sound.

"I keep my nose out of other people's business, Marc. That's a lesson you need to learn, if you're going to live around here."

"You've got your nose in mine," I said, feeling sudden anger. "What about my daughter?"

He was quiet before he spoke.

"I can't tell you about that, yet."

"Why not? When can you tell me? What can you tell me? I need to know what you know, Charlie. That's what I'm here for. That's why I came to Detroit."

My chest was thumping. I didn't remember standing up, but I was standing over the man in the wheelchair, feeling like hitting him.

"You can leave anytime you want," Charlie said, calmly. "But if I were you, I'd stay."

"Why?"

"You'll find out why soon enough. Bubba?"

The big man listened for his name. He entered the room, and Charlie beckoned to him. Bubba lifted Charlie as gently as a baby. He carried Charlie out the door, carefully, so as not to knock his head.

I bruised my knuckles rapping them on the doorpost.

CHAPTER 9

The first night passed. It wasn't so bad. I did cringe at a couple of sharp sounds I thought were gunshots. But, outside of that, I slept well. Morning came with sunlight full on my face. I squinted into it and fell back onto my bed. It was cold and clear, just like the forecast had said. The clear I liked; the cold was not for me. I decided that I needed heavier clothing. The thought came unbidden: If I was cold, how did the homeless survive? Detroit had its share of homeless people More than its share. What about them? Nothing I could do about that, except not become one, myself. That thought surprised me. Had I shed ministerial robes? Had I become somebody else? Why didn't I care more? I cared, and I didn't care; how could that be?

There was a rapping going on, on my door. It was the sound a woodpecker makes in a tree in the distance. It was a gentle noise, not loud, but persistent. After a while, you were apt to notice.

The man standing in the hall, like a supplicant, was quite short. In the dimness of the hall, his priest's outfit did not stand out, but his white collar glowed. It defined him. Know one priest, know them all, they say. I had known a few priests. They were as unlike each other as the rest of us. To know one is to know one. Dismiss the uniform, then. It is a disguise, a commonality donned in order to confuse.

"Yes?" I said.

I was speaking to a crop of shiny, black hair, combed close to the man's head. His eyes came up, dark as his hair. His eyelids blinked, once, twice, three times. I was counting, a kind of curiosity. It was like memorizing license plate numbers, a habit developed while acting as a police chaplain in Huntington Park, California. I served a church there that closed its doors after I left. I did do a few unusual things in the company of police officer friends. I developed some unexpected habits, as well. Like counting. I wished to avoid Sherlock Holmes's judgment of Watson, "You see, Watson, but you do not observe." In each other's company, we all become a bit weird.

"My name is Father Rene DuBois," the man said. "I am a priest from St. Edwards. I used to visit the man who lived here before you. This is my parish, and he was my friend."

"So I've heard."

"You have?"

"Yes, I know little else than that; you and he were friends. He had few friends, I've been told. You were one of them. Won't you come in?"

Father Dubois hesitated. He shifted from one foot to the other, as if he were being pulled in two directions at once. Should he come in? Should he not? I was not about to help him. I didn't know what he knew about me.

He came in slowly, slipping to the side of the doorway, once he was in the room. He looked around, like someone who expected great change. Then his look softened. The room must have been exactly as it was before. He sighed and turned to look at me, directly.

"I expect to see him here. I am sorry."

"His name was Gregory Barton, I hear," I said, trying to help the priest be at ease. But he was a wound-up man, it appeared to me, who lived mostly on nerves alone. "And he was something of a writer."

"Yes, Greg. That was his name."

The priest almost stuttered, making him hard to listen to, but he did not actually stutter. It was more an accent. It hinted at a deliberate attempt to always find the right word. Otherwise, he might be misunderstood. It was always so easy to be misunderstood.

"What do you wish of me, Rene?" I said.

His head cocked like a spaniel's. I saw his mouth fly open and a startled look leap into his eyes. He seemed suddenly flustered, like a man who had just come across a familiar, friendly ghost in a children's movie.

"You do not call me *Father*?" he said.

I said nothing.

"Greg would not call me *Fathe*r, either." Rene said. "It had something to do with his experience as a child. He lived in a Catholic neighborhood, Greg told me once. I am still uncertain of the connection."

"I like Gregory Barton, already," I said. "I lived in a Catholic neighborhood, too. Condemned forever to Hell, in the view of some of my friends. Such a judgment's a rather unnerving experience, when you're just a boy."

"Unfortunate," Rene replied, carefully. "But things have changed, have they not? You are a minister, I have been told. Surely, things have changed."

"You want to discuss Pope John?" I said. "As over against the present Pope? Things haven't changed, Rene. it's only the appearances that have changed."

Rene said nothing, but his face spoke eloquently.

"Let's not talk about popes," I said. "Tell me about Gregory Barton. Tell me about him and you."

"I don't know if I can do that," Rene said. Then he proceeded to recount a good deal of his life and ongoing conversation with Gregory Barton. The more Rene told me, the more I had trouble believing what he told me. Catholic priests and ordinary mortals do not wrestle with such things as Biblical criticism and religious doubt. Not together. I had known a number of priests, from college lecturers to diocesan functionaries. Of all of them, I only got close to one, who was a monk of the Order of St. Francis. He and a disgruntled Missouri Synod Lutheran and I used to breakfast together in the city of Vista, California. Father Alban was unique. Was this man like him?

Father Rene talked for a long time, as if he had stored up a welter of memories since Gregory Barton's death and could face them no longer without imploding. When he was finished, Rene began apologizing for all that he had just told me. The apology ran on and on, until I stopped it.

We sat looking at each other across the room, he in my desk chair and me on the edge of the bed. The silence lingered. You could almost visualize it. It wrapped itself around us, drawing us together in ways that mere words could not. There was grief in the man and intense, unconquerable pain. I listened to sad echoes, for myself and others. It was eerie sitting there, knowing that another person knew what you knew and felt what you felt. Without saying anything, we knew we were brothers, looking out on the world, trying to understand the endless suffering. If there was purpose, God kept it well hidden. This priest knew that, as I did. It was a secret we shared with Job. Our lives were "hedged in" by very human ignorance.

I felt restless after the priest left, so I went out. I had a sweater and a jacket on; it didn't seem to be enough. Oregon had cold winters but not as cold as this. I'd better find warmer things to wear.

Right now, I wanted a hot meal, the good taste of somebody else's cooking. I didn't know where to go, except for the Burger King on Woodward. I should have asked the priest. Father Rene would have known where to send me.

I walked awhile. There were few people on the street I walked Woodward Avenue, heading south. I reached Grand Boulevard and turned east. I walked until I found myself by a freeway. There was traffic below me and a railroad track above. I felt squashed by the noise of train above and cars and trucks below. I spun around and headed back the way I had come. I decided to walk to New Center One, where there were restaurants that catered to professional people. Why not me? I felt my mouth watering as I thought about a steak and potatoes. A real meal, done right.

As I walked past a Mom-and-Pop store, a half-dozen youth came out of it. I heard yelling behind them, an angry voice cursing loudly. One of the young men was calling back, "We didn't take nothin'! We'uns is good kids! Momma done brought us up right!" All the while, he was laughing and waving a bag of cookies in the air above his head. His friends were reaching for it, but the boy was taller than they were. They had little chance of success. Then the bag broke open and the cookies were grabbed at as they fell. A number of cookies fell to the ground. These were ignored or stomped on.

The group ran into me.

"Hey, man! Watch where yo'all goin'."

"Sorry," I said, trying to slip around them.

The tall boy dropped the cookies. He stepped quickly in front of me. I was suddenly surrounded by faces that were rocking to a music I could not hear.

The boy said, "Where yo'all goin', man?"

Everything stopped. I stood still, waiting. Groups of youth did not usually faze me, and these young men were joking, still. I was a momentary amusement, I figured, like the taking of cookies from the store. A harmless caper. It was a way to kill a little time and have a little fun. I assumed I would survive, but still —.

"Whatcha doin' here? Yo' think yo' own the street?"

"Sidewa'k," a shorter boy ventured. "He think he own dis sidewa'k."

"Da't right? "Yo' own the sidewa'k?"

The boy was taller than I was, and wider across the shoulders. He moved his shoulders, raising one, dropping the other, as if he were walking or playing in a basketball game. His hips swung back and forth, too. I pictured a dance going on in his head. He was swaying with a lovely partner, as athletic as he was. They were graceful together, a matched pair. Handsome, too.

"Not today," I said, trying to keep it light. I'd get through this, if I didn't take it serious.

There was quick laughter. I watch two of the boys playing tag, reaching around another boy's butt to hit each other with slapping fingers.

"Fo' sure," the tall boy said. He still wore a smile, but there was something else in his eyes. "Here, we own da sidewa'k. Alla time, yo' hear?"

He had a long finger jabbing up under my chin. I started to feel things, emotions that grew from down low, but I had also noticed a gliding motion of white in the street. A car passed us, but was now easing toward the curb.

"Actually," I said. "I think he owns the street."

I tilted my chin away from the boy's long finger. I jerked it twice toward the idling car. The boy laughed.

"Yeah, man. Yeah! But when he not 'round..."

"I think I'll go now," I said.

The boy's grin got broader as I walked away. The music in his head was really rocking. In spite of myself, I felt a sense of great relief. I didn't believe I'd enjoy being hassled, robbed or beaten up by a gang of city kids. Not by any kids, anywhere.

I went by the idling patrol car. The uniformed woman sitting in the driver's seat did not glance at me. She was watching in the rear-view mirror. Unlike mine, her chin was set. She knew what to expect, and she knew how to deal with it, when it happened. She knew the story.

I wandered around the shopping area known as New Center One, feeling safe. I watched two modern, glass-sided elevators run from top to bottom. I watched people shop. I took myself out of the way of business people hastening here or there. The pace was extraordinarily brisk. I decided that I did not wish to work here or live here or shop here. They might be planning an "Urban Village" around this place, but they could count me out. Let those who had fled Detroit return to this spot, bringing their money with them. What I saw in and around this place was intended to spread like a beneficial disease; a healing spot in the city. A place to point to and say: "This is Detroit." At least, its hoped-for future. Call it a dream. The section north and east of here, where I was presently living, was scheduled for light industrial use in the sketches I saw. What else would you expect city developers to do with it? Of course, that means removing people from those battered streets to somewhere else. Nobody seemed to care where.

I spent time walking an indoor route designed for workers in need of exercise. There were a few building-to-building loops pictured on displays. There was a Two-Tenths-of-a-Mile Loop on the GM Building main floor. There was a Quarter-Mile Loop on the Fisher Building main floor. There was a Third-of-a-Mile Loop on the second level of New Center. One that included the three skywalks. In summer, there were walking loops outside, around a couple of city blocks, and a loop that ran for a mile up and down Grand Boulevard from the Henry Ford Hospital to Woodward Avenue. Obviously, the people who live, work and shop here want to stay healthy. It's part of their creative life-style.

I got weary of the glitz and headed outside. While I walked back to my new quarters, I realized how secure I had felt in the New Center One complex. That's the idea, of course: security and safety. No gang of kids to threaten you while in there. There were guards to make certain such things did not happen. Order and harmony was the pattern of each day. What a contrast I entered by walking across one single street. My new world belonged to somebody else, not to any wealthy, upper-middle class.

I didn't know who that somebody was.

CHAPTER 10

T*hings belong to those who want them mos*t. Where did that thought come from. Everything must come from somewhere. Is nothing truly original, then? Did Plato have it right: Learning is remembering clearly. You already know all you need to know, you've just forgotten it. Would that concept apply to everything anybody could ever know? I couldn't accept that idea. Perhaps it applied only to the essentials, to the things that made us human and kept us human. I had to realize, again, that we think with words, and words are fickle. They won't sit still, even when you believe you have them locked in their places. Words are like drops of water in a river; they tend to run away with you, taking you with the current.

Denys Fowler knocked on my door, canceling thought. I hastily let him in, glad to see him. He spent a moment looking around.

"Not much of a place," he said.

"I don't require much," I said.

"There was a white guy living here before you. I guess you heard that. He was experimenting with a certain kind of writing style. I guess it didn't work out. I think he was experimenting with a way of living, too. I think it killed him. That's what I think."

"Thanks, Denys," I said. "You make me feel better."

"Bad habit of mine, saying what I think." Denys looked contrite enough that I believed him.

"I didn't know the guy," Denys added. "Charlie talks about him."

I was looking at Denys Fowler and thinking of Detroit. The two images did not go together. Of course, there were endless numbers of whites who came daily into Detroit to work. Their jobs were still down here, even further into central Detroit than the New Center Area. Otherwise, white people showed up in Detroit only for the special things, riding down Woodward or Livernois or I-75 in order to go to the Opera House or Symphony Hall or Renaissance Center. Or they might come to Greektown to eat, especially if they were tourists wanting the sights and taste of Detroit. But Denys looked comfortable here.

"You settling in?"

"Yes, Denys. I think so. I'll tell you if I'm not."

But Denys had vanished from me. He walked slowly to the window and looked out. He wiped at the edge of the window with his fingers, as if checking for dust. He leaned a hand against the window's upper sill and then leaned his weight against his hand. I was tempted to get up and go over to the window to see what he might be looking at. I decided that he wasn't looking at anything out there, so there was no sense in my trying to see what he was seeing. I waited on the edge of my bed for him to come back to me.

"I wish I could feel settled somewhere," Denys said. He was speaking into the window glass, and it took me a moment to figure out what he had said.

"You have a nice house," I said.

Denys turned to me. There was a ton of sadness in his bright eyes. I thought there were unspilled tears there. I felt a pull inside me, like a guitar string had broken and was ruining the folksong I was playing.

"It's her house," he said. "Alicia's. We bought it together, but I thought it should be hers. So we bought it that way. Just in case, you know?"

"I understand."

"Do you?"

"Probably not."

"Honest man, are you?"

"Probably not."

Then Denys borrowed a page from Charlie Eusted and began to laugh, uproariously. I thought he was going to split a gizzard, as my old mom used to say when somebody laughed much harder than expected.

"Me, neither," Denys said, when he found his voice again. He dug out a handkerchief, embroidered on the edges, and wiped tears away. "It's better to lie, Marc. That's what I think. If you tell the truth, people get hurt. Truth is, people don't want to hear the truth, because it does hurt. Society runs on lies."

"So I've noticed."

"But you tell me the truth, don't you?"

"I haven't told you much, so far."

"But it's all truth?"

"So far, Denys."

We were quiet together. I didn't know quite what Denys was driving at or why his questions seemed necessary. But I let it go. Denys had begun to fidget in his heavy camel-hair coat. He had not taken it off, and it was warm in my room. Denys had too much on. The heat comes on and goes off, noisily. I had begun to ignore it.

Suddenly, Denys went out my door. I focused on the tail of his coat. It slipped out last, just as the door closed. I thought for a moment that I had offended him, somehow. But I couldn't think of anything I had said that should have driven him away. He had simply gone, vanished. Then I had the odd feeling that Denys had not really been here, that I had imagined him. There was no Denys Fowler, never had been. And that was crazy. Then I noticed that my hands were shaking. I thought: Denys is a presence that has no pattern, none that I can discover. We humans depend upon patterns, including patterns of behavior. How else civilization? We all do what we do, conditioned pretty much to the doing. It is the way things work, especially in cities, where people are jammed together. Denys did not appear to fit that mold. It seemed that even he did not know for sure what it was he was going to do next.

I took a set of deep breaths and waited until my hands had quit their shaking. I struggled with breathing, because the room seemed empty of air. It was as if I was suddenly trapped in a vacuum jar, with the oxygen drawn out of it with nothing left to breathe.

Then I was all right, again.

I stumbled over Father Rene on my way out the front door. The tiny priest was coming up the stairs as I went down them. Rene had his hands in front of him, protecting his body from the bulk of me, while slipping off to one side.

I apologized, admiring his nimbleness, especially on the cold, icy steps. All priests should be as nimble as Father Rene, with words as well as deeds.

"You are in a hurry, my son."

I looked at him, nonplused. I hadn't been anybody's son since my father died.

"Uh, yes. And no."

"Both?"

"Umm, yes. Both."

"When in a hurry, slow down," Rene said, as if he knew what I was talking about. "It is a saying an old priest told me; one his father told him. We are all in too much of a hurry, so we should always choose to slow down."

"Oh."

"Most things we are in a hurry about are not worth being in a hurry about," Rene added, assuming I had given him permission to lecture.

"Your old priest told you that?"

"No. That I determined by thinking about the possible reasons for never being in a hurry."

I told him that, from what I had seen so far, Rene had not taken the lesson to heart. He asked me how I could know such a thing. I told him I sensed it from his nervousness, a statement which clearly upset him. Rene wished to be seen as something other than what he was. Like most of us.

He stood, quietly. We were both shivering in the cold. A gust of wind lifted his black fedora. He grabbed at the hat before it flew away. I got a glimpse of his thick, black hair, combed straight back, glistening with oil in the slim light of the sun.

"I think we need to talk," he said in a voice that made me think of my mother. She used to use those words, too. Especially after I had done something simply foolish. We talked often, my mother and I. Long discussions about people and their habits, the need to cultivate very decent qualities of social relationships, exploring, particularly, the ways of men and women in our tumultuous world.

"I don't think so," I said.

"Then, at least, walk with me, Marc."

My mother never pleaded. This man was pleading, and I wondered why. A person should never beg for anything; that one of my mother's adages. I set it over against Rene's request. But I surrendered, anyway. Whoever wants to talk to you, hear him out, my mother had also told me. Only then can you make an informed decision. I made it a point to obey my mother on certain occasions.

We walked in silence up one block and down another. I was just out for the walk, so direction didn't matter. The room had closed in on me and driven me from it. I just needed the walk, the air, a view of the sky.

We walked in silence, and I got to wondering what Catholic priests spent their time thinking about. Surely, it wasn't always the spreading of the faith. There were immediate concerns, of priest and of parish, to consider. I thought, then, of that which I spent a lot of time working at: how to get this or that program off the ground. Like many people, I went into the ministry to preach, teach and counsel. But I ended up dealing mostly with administrative and managerial affairs. It's the way things are in ministry, as in other organizations. A person cannot avoid the essential day-by-day necessities of the job. Whether you like it or not. It goes with the territory, as they say. I never liked it. I still don't.

Rene had stopped, and I stopped walking to stare back at him. He was looking toward an alley across the street.

"A girl has been raped," he said.

I stared at him, not comprehending. Then I looked over at the alley. It seemed an ordinary alley, between a set of red brick buildings. It was like all other alleys.

"In there?" I said, dumbly.

He nodded, very slowly.

"The assailant is dead," he said, oddly.

"They caught him?" I said, meaning the police. I assumed a shootout, but I should have assumed nothing. Things were not as they ought to be in this place.

"No," Rene said. "Someone else, Marc. You will notice, after awhile. No crime goes unpunished on these streets."

"Unpunished? But the police are..."

"The police have nothing to do with it." Rene's voice was fierce, as if he were angered and upset and pleased, all at the same time. He could not sort out how he felt about whatever it was that was happening in his parish. As priest, Rene felt responsible for everything here. That's the way good priests and ministers are. Not all, but the good ones. Helpful and responsible, regardless of that which they could or could not control.

"I don't understand," I said, keeping my voice level, even non-committal. "Who, then?"

"We don't know, Marc. Nobody knows."

Rene left me hanging on that thought. Nobody knew? Nobody knew what? Somebody did something bad on these streets, and he or she faced immediate punishment? Was that a possibility? Was any community like that? In the old West, maybe, with its take-the-law-in-your-own-hands kind of justice. But not in our modern society. No way.

"How come?" I blurted out, finally. "How long has this been happening? How large an area? Are there any suspects? Is there a police investigation going on? You can't solve a crime by committing a crime, Rene. The citizenry can't permit that to happen. What the hell is going on here?"

Rene spoke softly, almost to the point of not caring whether I heard him or not. He stood on the curbing, shivering in the face of a cold wind, staring at an alley across the street, his mouth working, his mind working, but his heart in turmoil, filled with obvious grief. As he spoke, I could agree with all the feelings he felt. I quickly came to have them, myself.

"To take your questions. one at a time, Marc," he said. "It has been going on for nearly ten years now. The area covers a few blocks; the blocks we are walking, the blocks you live in. These few city streets, Marc. They are safe streets, more or less. Much more than other city streets, certainly. They are protected by someone, but no one knows who."

Rene paused, and I waited, questions flooding my mind. He sighed, after a moment, scuffing his shoes on the side-walk's broken curbing. A few cars went by him, a parade of fancy colors, red and blue and green and yellow and orange. A mixed bag of colors. We had come a long way from Old Man Ford's day, when you could have any color car you wanted, as long as it was black.

"There was an investigation, once upon a time," Rene continued. "It has since stopped. At least, I have no awareness of one going on at present. I think the police are content with the way things are, though they will never say so. Why should they say so? They have enough to do elsewhere. If this section of the city is being cared for, even if it is tinged with violence, why shouldn't they leave it alone? Of course, once in a while, a complaint arises, and things are stirred up, even here. But when the dust settles, nothing has been done. Yet justice has been served, in a way."

"You say that so casually," I said, feeling suddenly angry. "Surely, the citizens would not allow this to settle down. There are killings going on, Rene. That's what you're saying."

"Yes, that is what I'm saying," Rene said. "But look who is being slain."

"Don't give me that," I said. "You're a priest, dammit! You can't abide this in your parish." Then, as if it had come to me as an after-thought, "Can you?"

"I can't seem to do anything about it," he said. "And I'm not sure I want to try."

"But...?"

"No, Marc. I no longer wish to try."

He bowed his head to me and walked away, leaving me standing in the cold, actually and figuratively. I tried to force my feet to take me across the street, as if there was a clue to all of this to be found in the alley over there, where the girl had been raped. Then I wondered who the girl was. A neighbor, probably. Already avenged.

Already avenged; I had to repeat it to myself. How was that possible? We were people obedient to law, no vigilante justice allowed. Yet, as I was discovering, the inner-city of Detroit — or any big city — was a different country. Did different rules apply, then? Was it right for someone to speak and act for those who, otherwise, felt helpless, even if the arm of the law was available to them? What if the law was, unavoidably, ineffective? The inner-city was a place of danger and drugs and sudden, inexplicable violence. Did it take a different kind of justice to hold things in check here?

I would have to find out.

CHAPTER 11

I was walking, not paying attention to where I was going, lost in my anger at a priest, lost in anguish over a sorry situation that was not mine, lost in thought. The rain was sudden, and I was caught in it. The rain turned to hail at the front of the storm. The hail streaked cross my face, cutting at me on cheek and chin. The front passed by, and the hail dissolved slowly into snow. The snow was being carried by gusts of cold wind that whipped at me. The wind settled down, and the snow became a steady falling of huge, white flakes. I was cold and wet and still blocks from my home. I was closed into myself, plunging ahead, oblivious to anything except my discomfort and the plaguing question as to what I was doing in Detroit in winter.

Then I was on my knees.

A voice was in my ear. My head was ringing, though the blow had been muffled by my new hat, a thick muff of a hat bought at an old, discount store. A knee was in the middle of my back, holding me still. I was shaking my head to clear it. The voice in my ear was saying, "We just be takin' your wallet, man. Jus' lie still." I slumped to the sidewalk on command, my face in the slush. It was cold and wet, but I did not feel it. The knee in my back slipped away, and I felt fingers, fumbling in my pants pocket. I heard a shout of glee and the words, "Be still, man! Be very still!" I listened to the crush of feet, walking away.

I stayed where I was for a long time. Finally, I pushed up with my hands and lifted around to sit. I could see nothing but falling snow.

Then a voice was in my ear, a whisper.

"Here," it said.

I glanced at the face. Hey Hank was sitting on his haunches staring at me. His wide eyes were blank. I could read nothing in them. I took the wallet he offered me and opened it. All the money was gone. Everything else seemed to be there.

"I tol' yo'. Yo' need me. Dumb, man!"

"But how did you...?"

"Don' ask. I get them to take jus' the money. Yo' a fool. But yo' a friend."

"Now look, Hey Hank, I've just been robbed..."

"I tol' ya', don' ask. Yo' ask down here, yo' ass sit in a hole. Or yo' dead meat. Dig?"

I stared into his face and saw nothing. The boy had developed the adult ability to hide his feelings, already. It gave him a certain dignity, a certain strength. A small boy in the city needed all the power he could command. I would get nowhere questioning this kid. Besides, as I had heard, this kind of thing was known as a caper, not a crime. It was a way to get a few bucks for drugs, or whatever. It was no worse that stealing piping out of abandoned, or not abandoned, houses to sell. If you could get away with it, it was the thing to do. Nothing serious.

"No, I don't dig," I told Hey Hank. But I slapped the empty wallet against my knee. "But thanks, I owe you."

"Don' owe me nuthin'."

I nodded, but thought otherwise.

"Help me up," I said.

To help me, Hey Hank would have to touch me. I saw him hesitate, then reach for me with both hands. Using Hey Hank for leverage, I heaved myself to my feet. I felt woozy, but okay. I felt pretty much as I did as a kid, playing skinny end on our school's losing football team. I was hit often, catching a pass, or trying to. The feeling was the same as now, when I worked to get back up. I get hit, I get up; a life story. For a guy whose bones were too close to the surface, offering no cushion, woozy was the normal scene.

"Yo' make it?"

"Yeah," I said, taking my hat off to feel my head. A bump was growing there, a small one, not worth mentioning. Hey Hank had probably known worse.

"Good. I gotta go."

He went, glancing back only once.

The snow was lighter, and I looked up into it. The sky way up high was gray and pocketed by the tiny flakes that were now falling onto my face, refreshing it. I stuck my tongue out, like a kid. "The rain falls on the just..." I was glad it was snowing.

By the time I got home, the snow had stopped. I felt badly about that, for snow was a gift to the big and dirty city of Detroit. It was a gift to any city. It hid ugliness and the cramped distortion that humans call loneliness. It hid both pain and sorrow. The snow covered things over; its main attribute. It was the only attribute that mattered to cities. For the rest, the snow meant it was cold, and the homeless shivered and struggled. The poor became grateful for the tiniest bit of housing, the least amount of warmth. Others found it merely annoying. There was no place for skiing and snowboarding in Detroit.

I turned my back to my lonely room and faced my window. I pulled up a chair and sat on it. I stared out. I stared for a long time. I forgot time. I was lost in looking at a city street that was like a million other city streets. Not a thing was happening on it; the people were all indoors, staying warm. Once in a while, somebody braved the weather, heading for the market to buy the necessities: food, hard liquor, beer, videos. Gotta get a Lotto ticket? Why not? I thought of what I might find in my cupboard, pantry, fridge. Did I need anything? Not a thing. I have enough to live on, if I'm willing to open a package or a can. I'm willing, but I opened nothing.

The hours went by, and I saturated myself with a street. I ate it for lunch, for dinner, for breakfast. I sat and stared at my street. The next day was cold and the day after colder. I roused myself only for aspirin and for coffee; my necessities. I watched the street. It was an enigma, a use less thing. I watched the occasional venturing forth of a neighbor. Didn't anybody go to work from this street? Didn't anybody go out to play? I was turning into a surveillance camera. I was marking it all down. Life in the big city, in winter. My findings would be my legacy. It's a nothing life, Dullsville. What was it Charlie Eusted expected me to learn about Detroit? Whatever it was, I had not discovered it. I had learned nothing.

Then a man came to install my phone. I welcomed him in, grateful for the interruption. It took him a very short time to see to the installation. I tried to delay him, by offering coffee, tea, wine, beer. Nothing delayed him. He was in and then gone, on his merry way. Not merry. He was a sour man, unemotional and insensitive. His face was a prune. I was glad he was gone.

I placed a call to my son, Jim. As I expected, he was not home. I left a message on his answering machine, that included my new phone number. I called Rick, and he was not home, either. I left a similar message for him. My sons are both capable and decent people, but they are very different from each other. The one is a tough, get-on-with-it, sort of fellow. The other is a fragile, resilient, take-it-easy guy. They are brothers, after all; they should be different. But differences such as theirs astonishes me. How could they both be mine? From where, in me and their mother, did they glean such distinctive personalities? How did such unique clusterings come about?

Jim was the normal first-born son. He fit the picture attributed to first-borns. It was Rick who surprised. He was never the second-born rebel.

Quite the contrary. He was a sweet child, and he remains a sweet man. That, of course, is part of his problem. I should have taught him how to be mean, occasionally. It's an essential ingredient in the business world. All sweet people get mangled in the modern corporate battles; competition is the essential thing. It's a matter of *survival.* I repeat the word: *survival*. Talk about foundational? What a hell of a life we moderns lead. With all the well-armed competitors out front, guess who survives.

I saw the woman walking down the middle of the empty street. She had on a warm coat, tan in color, a scarf of a darker brown wrapped around her head. Tan boots covered her feet, and tan mittens protected her hands. She looked as warm as toast, in spite of the cold outside. I looked closely at her, trying to make out the color of her lipstick and rouge. *Cafe' au lait* was the color of her face — coffee laced with cream. Her lipstick appeared to be a tint of darker brown. I could not make out rouge, for certain. I was too busy absorbing the loveliness of her face.

She walked by, firm of stride. I watched as she ambled slowly past me. I was an obvious voyeur, if she happened to glance my way. She did. She stopped walking, nodded once, turned and marched toward the door of my apartment building. I felt a knotting in my chest. Then I caught a glimpse of a small figure, trailing the woman. Hey Hank was smiling, grimly, while dancing to a tune in his head. He spun softly around, now and then, his small body bending and swaying. I saw him bend down once and scoop up a handful of slush. He formed it into a snowball and hurled it in a wide arc, over the line of cars parked by the curb. He laughed, and I felt I heard him laugh. Then he stood still and watched his mother heading my way.

There was a knock at my door. I was afraid to open it but I did, anyway. Did the woman have friends as big as Charlie's Bubba? They didn't have to be that big to put a scare in me. Just about anybody would be big enough.

"Mr. McDaniel, I believe," the woman said.

The woman's voice was throaty, and her perfume smelled wonderful. I found myself reeling as her perfectly shaped lips curled into a perfect smile. I was trying to place the accent in her voice, but could not. It was her own, belonging to this woman and nobody else. I surrendered to her without a fight. Nations should give in when they are out-gunned, or out-styled, or outclassed. I was way out of my class. She was smiling, waiting.

"Yes, I'm McDaniel," I said. "Marc's the name."

What's the game? I'm thinking, inanely. Poetry that rhymes is sometimes the realm of idiots.

Her hand was out, minus its tan glove.

"Rebecca Coltrane," she said. "Nee Budd. Does that ring a bell?"

"Coltrane? The music. Budd? The sailor. No, the boy."

I had caught on quickly, and she rewarded me with a smile as wonderful as my memory of her son's. But her smile contained other dimensions, as well, dimensions her son would never understand. I couldn't be attracted to her. It was not a possibility for me. Not in Detroit. Not anywhere. I was a one woman man and my woman was dead. There could be no other. Yet, I had these feelings racing through me, as Rebecca Coltrane moved into my room. She did not look it over. She sat herself on my one chair as if she belonged there. In my view in that moment, she could stay there as long as she liked. My room was hers. But I would have to defend my heart.

"That rapscallion son of mine told me of your unfortunate experience. I apologize to you for it."

"You do? I never..."

"We are a decent neighborhood here, Mr. McDaniel. At least, we try to be. There are other elements, of course. You need to understand our situation. Often, there are no jobs, you see. Often, there is hunger. Often, people use drugs, as escape. Often, a lot of things. But we try, Mr. McDaniel. I want you to know we try."

I was not really listening to her. I was captivated by her and trying to make sense of my feelings. I raced now to catch up to her words, before they fled away and were gone. I didn't want them to go. Her, either.

"Make it Marc, please. May I call you...?"

"Rebecca. Becky, if you wish, though that tag makes me feel little-girlish. I keep wondering whether I like it or not. I'm not sure, even after all these years. Something from Tom Sawyer, you know?"

"Rebecca sounds fine to me," I said. "Quite lovely, actually. I don't believe I've ever known a Rebecca."

She smiled, and her tinted lips were full and beckoning. I watched the crinkle in her cheeks and the way her eyes got smaller as her skin intruded upon them, with lines reaching out below her eyebrows, marking her as older than I probably thought at first. I began to wonder about Hey Hank, outside. This obviously very cultured woman and that boy? Could he truly be her son? It was as if Rebecca could read my mind.

Most likely, I had glanced toward the window and that had told her something. Woman were more apt to notice subtle things.

"Henri," she said. "You must forgive him his idiom. It helps him blend in, he says. So I let him do it, though I do not like it. Hey Hank, for example, as his name. But he is my son and must live here. I cannot protect him, always. The streets can be hard on a young boy. Harder than you can imagine, I think. Harder than it is for me."

"He doesn't appear to need protection," I said. "Like I do."

My last words hung between us, momentarily. Rebecca Coltrane appeared to be replaying them behind her eyes. I gazed steadily, now, into her eyes and found them to be dark, sparkling and very beautiful. I waited for the snide remark that, thankfully, did not come.

"I think," she said, "that on the whole, you can take good care of yourself...Marc."

There was a pause before the saying of my name, and I filled that gap with all kinds of things that, most likely, were not there.

"Yes," I said. "I have for quite a while now. Though never in Detroit. I should add, however, that Detroit is a lot like home. By that, I mean a place made desolate by the desertion of industry. There are echoes for me here. The loss of jobs meant anger and pain. You had to try to find a way out of a mess you were part of, but did not make. Then you discovered there was no way, short of leaving the place. Yesterday was gone; you had to try something else, by going some place else. Or you suffered through, if that were possible, at all."

Rebecca was listening, intently. With her, listening was a way of drawing you in. If you were a man, I thought, you could drown in her rapt attention. You would enjoy the drowning.

"Yes, that's it," Rebecca said. "You're a very perceptive man, Marc McDaniel. I like the way your name rolls off my tongue."

"I like it, too."

We were silent awhile, simply gazing at each other like old friends who had been apart for a time and were back together, trying to determine what had changed. A lot had changed, but was it good or bad? There was no way to be certain. There was never a way.

I cleared my throat. I needed to return us to whatever it was we had been talking about. I was feeling pleasantly dizzy, and I had this odd desire to remain that way. It was the way you often felt having just drunk two glasses of wine. It was a perfect feeling, but it would not stay. Nothing ever stays. Nothing.

"Am I correct in assuming that Hey Hank can speak, ah, differently? More like you? That the way he talked to me is part of an act. His 'fitting in,' as you say?"

Rebecca's knuckle came up and rubbed at the skin on her face. She reached higher still and wiped the beginning of a tear away. It was a happy tear.

"Oh, yes," she said. "Henri Aloysius Budd is one bright boy. He is two grades ahead of his class. He would be farther ahead, if he wished to be. Henri has a sharp mind and wit to match. But here, in this neighborhood and this city, he is smart to hide it."

"I understand," I said. "I've spent a lifetime trying to fit in, myself. Not into a neighborhood, but into a higher class, I guess you'd say. Higher than the one I came out of. Unfortunately, you are always where you come from. That's partly true, at least. You can't shake the source, so you never fit in anywhere else, exactly. We all do the best we can. May I say, excepting you. You don't look like you belong here. But you know that, already."

"I'll assume that's not just a line you're using, Marc," Rebecca said. "No, you're right. But every community has room for one oddball. I am it around here, you see. There are plenty of the other kind, of course. Misfits. Hey Hank actually makes it easier for me by acting the part he does. Another reason to let him do as he wishes, you see. I can also visit you, Marc. That would be risky for any other Black around here, unless he were working a scam. But as I am odd, already..."

I nodded, trying to catch all the ramifications of her words. Charlie said I would learn. Had he steered Hey Hank and his mother my way?

Rebecca Coltrane stood up and went toward my door. I did not want her to leave, but I didn't know how to ask her to stay. She shouldn't stay, I told myself. There were gossipy tongues that would wag. They were probably at it, already. Why provide gossips with more stuff?

Rebecca turned and offered me her hand, knuckles up. I kissed it and bowed. She laughed, lightly. We were playing a game of charades.

"Goodbye, Mr. McDaniel. Marc."

"Goodbye, Ms. Coltrane. Rebecca."

I went back to my window and watched her march, head-high, down the front steps. She paraded out into the middle of the street, heading back the way she had come.

A few yards further down the street, Hey Hank scooted out from between parked cars to join her. He stopped her by dragging on her hand. Together, they bowed deeply to me. Rather, he bowed and she curtsied. They overdid it, holding the deep position. They came up laughing, together, as good friends do. Or mothers and sons who happen to like each other very much. Very much, indeed.

Rebecca's fragrance lingered in my room.

CHAPTER 12

The dreams came in frightening fragments, and I bolted awake a dozen times during the night. I woke up, exhausted. It would have been better not to have slept at all.

I licked my tattered lips and longed for a drink of cool water. I had to get up and get it for myself. I rolled off the edge of the bed and almost fell to the floor. My ankle was rocking, a cramp had pulled on tendons. I pushed the foot flat to relieve it and listened to the crack that came after. The foot went flat to the floor and let me lean weight on it. I walked slowly into the kitchen and found a glass. I poured water into my throat. The back of my hand, in front of my face, was shaking. There was the feeling of someone writing words on my skin.

Memories of Margie rose up and reprised:

My wife's face floats in the air. I see us at beach, running hand-in-hand. The surf crashes on us, softly. It tickles our ankles and washes up our legs. We stop in the surf and kiss. It is a long kiss, one that is not given up until a surprisingly large wave sends cold fingers up above our knees. I see my fingers in her hair and feel, again, the soft stiffness of each strand. I let the fingers wander as my eyes probe hers. She is smiling at me, and the love we make is gentle and warm. We roll off quilts on a living room floor, and I let my hand slide from her face to her breasts. She places one hand over mine, forcing me to stop where I want to stop. We lie there, content together, content to be together before the children come home from school, before children come into our lives and change us altogether. We lie there and look at each other, and the moments blur, one with another, over a good many, wonderful years.

I let the memories run and think of them as study, as of Scripture, where any passage can be used to understand and enrich any other passage. Time has no meaning, then. Time coalesces, as meaning does. Who is to say what is the simplest truth? The mind does its own thing, and the mind is a wonder in its own right. Ah, what God has wrought! But God took away what God had given. Who in his right mind wants a God like that? God is gone. Memories, in all their confusion, crawled down from my mind to my heart and mingled with the feelings surfacing there. Finally, I took the glass in my hand and rubbed it on my face.

My daughter, Laura, who was unlike her mother and very much like me, was dead. I leaned up against the sink and saw the pair of them walking through the mall, chattering up a storm, like good friends do. There are packages in their hands, as they stroll toward me. They have forgotten I am standing there waiting for them. They are busy with each other, and I am amazed that they belong to me. No one truly belongs to anyone else, of course. Laura's dark hair, cut short, belongs to Laura. And Margie's hair, lying like a breeze on her shoulders, is Margie's hair. But the hair is all mine. They have the same eyes and the same indomitable spirit and the same way of wrapping me around a finger. I watch them come, and I thank God for my blessings. I do not call God a him. But, now, God, who is invisible and beyond human understanding, has taken reality away and left me with only haunting images of those I love.

Nobody walks toward me anymore.

There was a mouse living under my sink. I stooped down to locate it, only to discover the scratching sound was an echo. I toweled my face and opened the door.

A woman stood there. She was as short as Father Rene, but heavier. There were folds to her skin. She was wearing an apron, but there was no flour on her hands. Her dress was old-fashioned, with ranks of flowers cascading from shoulder to hem. Her shoes were slippers, with flowers like the dress. The flowers did not go together; the dress was fall, the slippers were spring. Her face was a welter of movement, as if her cheeks were used to her mouth being in action, nibbling on something, talking about something. The woman's eyes were blinking and one bent, thin-fingered hand worried the fall of gray hair running onto her forehead. A net was in her hair, holding the rest in place. She looked at me intently.

"You live here?" she said.

I nodded, wondering. She couldn't have come in off the street dressed like that. She would have frozen in the cold outside. Where had she come from?

"I thought so," she said. "You're quiet. Another man lived here. I had to make sure somebody was here. Keep it quiet! I don't like noise. Hmmm. I do not like you. I did not like him. I do not like you any more than I liked him. But maybe you're quiet. You'd best be quiet, or I'll have the manager get after you. You hear?"

Her words were clipped, as if cut by scissors. I shook my head, trying to understand.

"I do not like noise," she suddenly screamed. "Can't you appreciate that?" She shouted again, and I backed away. Would she follow me into my room?

"Men! What do they know? Bastards! That's what men are. My husband was a bastard. You are, too."

I put my hands out in front of me, just in case, and held onto the door. I wondered if I should be screaming also, calling for help. I didn't know that anyone would answer. The woman tugged at her curls with the fingers of both hands. She let the hands slip to the front of her fancy apron. The fingers wrapped themselves in flowered cloth. "Shhh!" she whispered, as if quieting a child. She sighed, deeply. She shook her head and walked off down the hall. I heard the door of the next apartment slam. I heard her yell, "Quiet! Shut up, you old fool!"

I had been told that Mrs. Hedley lived alone. Who was she yelling at, then? Herself? A cat, maybe? Some image of a dead husband still lodged in her memory, seemingly alive in her empty room?

I closed my door, quietly. I returned to the kitchen to put on coffee. I knew I would end up drinking drinks that were stronger if I continued to live here.

I dropped my towel on the sideboard. I looked from the towel to the door. It was almost as if I knew there would soon be another knock.

Denys and I walked to a nearby doughnut shop to enjoy things we did not need. The two waitresses were old. They served us fast, but they paid us no other attention. There was loud conversation going on. The women were part of it, an integral part. The epithets streaming about my head were startlingly descriptive. I was stunned, but Denys ignored it as routine stuff down here. Except for the few years that I worked in the mills, I had not spent time with this type of language. As soon as I could get myself out of the mills, I did. And I never went back.

"So, you liking it?" Denys said.

I shrugged my weary shoulders.

"You need to loosen up, Marc. You look tight as a drum. You should become more like me. One day. One day, only. One day at a time. That sort of thing. It relieves you of your overburdened sense of responsibility, Marc. It lets you be free. Listen to me."

Denys was smiling his gentle smile, but I was hearing other words than his. I wasn't listening to him. He kept on talking, totally ignoring the profanity spilling over from the other end of the doughnut shop.

And then, I heard him. I heard him clearly.

"I had a dream last night," he said. "You were in it."

"Me?'

"Yeah. I was back in Vietnam...I dream a lot about Vietnam...and you were with me. As a matter of fact, you were the lieutenant in charge. We were in the middle of a firefight, and we blew you away. I don't know why I should dream that."

I was suddenly reeling, thinking of a room I had been shown. And now I listened to words about a dream in which I was killed. By my own men, yet.

"Shall I get out of town?" I said.

Denys was quiet a long time. Too long. I got to thinking that maybe he was considering killing me. If he fought in Vietnam, he would surely know how.

"It was just a dream," he said, finally. "I probably shouldn't talk about my dreams."

"No, Denys. Tell me. You just startled me, that's all. I don't think I've been killed in anybody's dream before. At least, they didn't tell me about it."

"We did that," Denys said.

I stayed silent. My mind could not accept what I was hearing. Why should it? What I was hearing was impossible. Even though I understood such things happened, I had no personal knowledge about it. Nobody I knew ever admitted to what I remembered was called fragging.

"More than once," Denys said.

I remained silent and, suddenly, very uneasy.

"Three times, I think. To be more exact."

"Why?" I blurted out.

"Best of reasons. To stay alive." Denys leaped to his feet, towering over me. "You're a threat to us, Marc McDaniel. And you frighten me."

I pushed back in my chair, trying to put distance between us. The legs of the chair squealed in protest.

"What?" I said. "I don't...."

"You reek of authority, you know that? Alicia says you don't, but I know it's there. You see things. And you know things you don't talk about. We never do see ourselves for what we are in the eyes of others; they told me that, too. I remember things, Marc. A doctor shouldn't tell me what I am not supposed to know. I remember things. You'd be wise not to forget that."

"You lost me," I said. "How am I a threat? To whom am I a threat? What the hell are you talking about?"

Denys cocked his head, then ducked it.

"They confuse me, Marc. I get rattled. I think you're a threat, because you're an educated man. You may not see things as we do."

"See things? What are you talking about, Denys? I'm new here. I don't see much of anything."

"I think you do."

"Should I leave?"

"No, dammit! I need you. I don't know why, but I do. That's what Alicia says, too. Charlie agrees. Maybe we all need you. We just don't know why."

"Sorry, Denys. I've got troubles of my own."

He said nothing.

I broke into song, "Nobody knows de trouble I seen." I leaned back and rocked, "Nobody knows, but..." I was going great, I thought, but I stopped suddenly. There was an odd silence in the place. When I looked around, hostile faces were focused my way. One man was slowly rising out of his chair. He could hardly make it, but he was rising up and reaching for his cane, a weapon.

"Sorry," I called, raising one hand. "I was...."

What was I?

Denys pushed at me. Then he lifted me to my feet and hauled me outside. He brushed me off, extravagantly. I leaned on him, rubbing my arms and trying to get my eyes to focus once more, so I could see.

"What're you trying to do, get yourself killed?"

"Just trying to determine what's real and what's not, Denys," I said. "I think I just found out."

"Way to go, buddy," he said, shaking his head.

CHAPTER 13

I sat on a bench next to Charlie Eusted, who sat in his wheelchair. This was Charlie's spot, the bus stop just north of Grand Boulevard on Woodward Avenue. He sat here, I knew, every day, scribbling descriptions of whatever happened on and around this corner. Charlie was wrapped up in a orange parka with a fur-lined hood. He peered out from its shadow, like a hawk from the depths of a tall tree. The misshape of blue mittens covered the shiny metal of the chair's arms, and the black of his fur-lined boots covered the chair's fold-up feet. Charlie had not said a word since I arrived. He did not even look at me. His eyes were on the corner and on the traffic in the street and on the bundled-up people rushing toward the tall buildings all around us. Charlie didn't seem to be missing anything.

Then I saw a young man in a tattered jacket and fisherman's hat run quickly across the intersection. When the man reached the other side, he turned around and ran back. He ran the corner a dozen times, not waiting for the signal. Charlie made a note in his notebook.

"How'd you get started?" I asked.

"You want to know?"

"Sure. Why not?"

Charlie breathed out, and the stream of it was clear as morning fog. He watched his breath, until it vanished.

"An accident," he said. "No, I don't mean it that way. I already had these useless legs. I lost their use right over there."

He lifted his chin toward the busy intersection. Cars were turning, obeying the lights. There was a steady stream of cars around the corner.

"A guy ran a light. Right there. I was crossing the street. I ended up asking the usual question in hospital: Why me? I had lived through a war, didn't have a scratch. I came home and wham! It made no sense; never does, I guess. Whatever happens, happens. It's the way it is."

I said nothing, having nothing to say.

"Anyway," Charlie said, shifting to a more comfortable position on his cold chair.

I waited, though shivering hard.

"Then I asked the better question," Charlie said. "I asked: Why here? It seemed the more useful question, don't ask me why. It gave me something to do, I guess. I had money coming in; my lawyer saw to that. What I needed was something to do. So this is it, keeping track of what happens on the corner. Beyond that, I don't know."

"So you sit here, doing research for a book?" I said, trying to understand. What would happen on this corner that someone would want to read a book about? I could only think of one thing, and Charlie refused to talk about it.

"It's what I tell people," Charlie said, chuckling. "I have to tell them something, don't I? Something that might make sense of this? Truth is, I would write a book, if I knew how. I don't. I could learn. Who knows, maybe."

A bus had pulled up in front of us, and Charlie turned his attention to the passengers as they disembarked and ran rapidly toward warmer places. The driver of the bus left the door open a few moments longer than needed. She shook her head at Charlie and smiled. "You still crazy, man," she called. "You a little wacko in the head, you know that?" It was said with affection.

"I know it," Charlie said, perking up.

The woman nodded and pulled shut the door, causing the remaining passengers to return to whatever it was they were doing. I saw a thin boy with his mother, sitting on the bus. The boy waved tentatively at Charlie as the bus pulled away from the curb. Charlie waved back, and the boy grinned. His mother said something to him and rapped him lightly on the head.

"That's Sheila," Charlie said. "She says that to me every time."

"This book you're writing...," I said.

Charlie's face hardened.

"I don't talk about it," he said. "I know what you want, but I can't help you. I don't talk about it."

Charlie breathed in gulps of air, and I could see each puff as it fled from his mouth to vanish into the cold sky, trailing off like smoke.

"You've got to, Charlie. It would help me."

"No, I don't. And I can't help you. Not that way."

"I could force it. The police would be interested."

"I'd destroy it. There'd be nothing for them to be interested in. Believe me, I'd destroy it."

Looking at him, I knew he would. Then I realized that he was not seeing me, but gazing above my head. His features inside the fur hood were swinging slowly from side to side. Behind me stood Bubba, I discovered. Bubba was holding an enormously large thermos. But Bubba's mind was not on the coffee he had brought. Bubba was working himself up, but the shaking of Charlie's head held him in place.

By then, I was half up off the bench.

"It's just coffee," Charlie said. "Isn't that right, Bubba? You've just brought us some coffee to drink. That's very thoughtful of you, Bubba. Why don't you pour my friend Marc a cup of coffee, Bubba? It's cold out here, isn't it, Bubba? I guess it's going to get colder. Coffee's just the thing for us to drink on such a cold day. Good of Bubba to have brought us coffee to drink on such a cold day. He is very considerate, Bubba is. He thinks a lot, Bubba does. He makes the coffee, himself. Don't you, Bubba? You make the best coffee in this world. I could sure use a cup. Why don't you pour me one, son? My hands are cold. I need to wrap my hands around a good cup of hot coffee. Good of you to bring it, Bubba. Awful good of you."

Bubba was obviously wrestling with himself, but he unscrewed the thermos and dragged paper cups out of a coat pocket. He poured a cup and walked by me to hand it to Charlie. I was standing as tall as I could get, and I was staring at Bubba's broad chest. I could not see above it to his neck. Charlie's fingers were waving at me, and I followed instructions and sat myself, again.

Bubba poured me a cup. There was something resembling a smile on his face as he handed it to me.

"Thanks," I said, struggling to get words out. "Thank you very much, Bubba. Smells great!"

And I was thankful.

Three hours later and I was in the Burger King, still trying to stop the shivering. Hamburger and fries had vanished, and I was nursing still more coffee. It was not as good as Bubba's coffee, but it would do. I was going to need a restroom soon. I would probably be in there a week.

I knew nobody in the place, even if it was busy. I should not stay too long. The line at the counter was looking at me. I was taking up room for two customers, at least. I swallowed the last of the coffee and headed home, dropping my tray and its refuse in the proper place on my way out the door. As I went out, still more people were coming in. They wanted the heat of the restaurant, first of all, so they pushed by me as if I were not there.

Home seemed drab to me. And empty. I reminded myself that I had to find something to do.

Finally, I dug in my suitcase, remembering that I had brought a book or two with me from Oregon, though I couldn't remember what the titles were.

They came out, one in each hand. I stared at them. One was *The Lost Gospel*, by Burton Mack, subtitled: *The Book of Q and Christian Origins*. The other was *Jesus: A Revolutionary Biography*, by John Dominic Crosson. The letter *Q* in the subtitle of Mack's book stood for the German word *quelle*, meaning source. *Q* was not a book at all, though a number of scholars think it was once. *Q* represented the verses in Matthew and Luke that were common to both, but were not in Mark's gospel. It was a logical assumption to think of *Q* as a book. But at this moment, *Q* did not interest me. I dropped Mack's book on the bed. Maybe, later.

The other book was listed as a "national bestseller." Isn't that a kick! A book about the Bible, a bestseller! "A startling account about the life of Jesus;" that's what the cover blurb said. Isn't that a kick! On the cover was also a quote from the *New York Times Book Review*. It said of the author: "Crosson paints his Jesus with great warmth and power." Now there was the truth. Crosson's Jesus, not mine! An enigmatic sage from Galilee or a Jewish cynic; those were the choices, apparently. Forget it, friends! Scholars are never satisfied with yesterday's conclusions. Reputations are made now. Who was Jesus, anyway? Nobody knows; that's what I still think. Isn't that a kick!

Got to find me a store and buy a book.

I shoved myself into my jacket, slipped on my gloves, and donned my newly battered hat. Boots, I had to get yet. My old walking Red Wings would have to do for now.

The sun was a thin wafer of warmth in the sky. It did nothing to remove the chill from the air. I walked fast to New Center and hit the stores. Lots of books to choose from. I settled on a rereading of the pair of novels by Chaim Potok I had mentioned to Denys Fowler. Chain Potok is a Jewish Rabbi, whose books are all fascinating studies of Jewish intellectual life. They are about non-gentile men and women trying to figure out what to do with themselves in a gentile world. A couple of the books have been made into movies. But here was *My Name Is Asher Lev* and *The Gift of Asher Lev*, books I had already read and enjoyed. I thought of them as old friends. I broke a fifty to buy copies and stuck the books into my jacket pockets.

Outside, I was stopped by a familiar figure. The man had this distinctive face. It struck me that I had seen it only once before.

"It was not an accident," Sergeant Berra said.

"What?" I said.

"Believe it," he added, walking by me, acting as if we were two spies who had made a pact not to be seen together. We were simply strangers passing on the street.

Then he stopped me with a hand on my arm, swinging me around in a small circle.

"He knows," he said. "But I know he knows, now. You needn't worry any more. I'll get proof."

Sergeant Berra fidgeted. His lips moved, but he wasn't saying anything. His eyes wandered around, examining faces of people on the street. I wanted to scream at him: What is it that you know? Come on, Sergeant Berra, you can't do this to me!

But Sergeant Berra was gone, and the only screaming was inside my aching head. I found myself standing on the sidewalk across from the GM Building in the middle of winter. I was cold, but I was not cold. I was warmed by the heat of a cold rage. That kind of cold lingers. It does not seep gently away come Spring. It hangs around, paying no attention as the seasons come and go. It laughs at the seasons, but it causes human beings to cry a lot.

CHAPTER 14

The tapping on my door was familiar. I got up from my chair to open the door but, apparently, I had forgotten to lock it the night before. The door swung on its hinges, and Father Rene Du Bois walked in. He padded quickly by me. I stood out of his way. "Well?" he said, glancing over one shoulder. Then he leaned over and picked up a book from the floor, where it had fallen. He placed the book carefully on my desk, lining it up well away from the edge.

"What?" I said.

"Close the door, why don't you?" he said.

"Oh, sure."

Trivialities, I thought. Who was there out in the hall to listen in? Why would they want to? Then again, perhaps the priest had something important to say.

"You fell asleep reading," Rene said.

"I did? How could you know that?"

I looked where he pointed and saw that my bed had a crease in it about the size of my body. The pillow was pulled out, but the blankets had not been pulled down. Only the coverlet had been pushed aside as I had arisen this morning. I could be a detective myself, I considered, if I paid attention to little things. Why didn't I pay attention?

"You do that sort of thing, do you?" I said. "Make believe you're Sherlock Holmes?

"It amuses me to figure things out," Rene said.

About then, I wished he were gone.

Rene sat down at my desk, where I had been sitting, and began telling me a convoluted story about trying to explain the Bible to certain immigrants that were flooding into the area. It wasn't simply a problem of language, Rene said. It was a problem of culture and customs, as well. People from the Near East were not much interested in Rene's attempt to convert them. They were much more concerned with practical matters pertaining to survival. What could they work at? What neighborhood could they live in? Rene had scant knowledge of such matters, in spite of the length of time he had lived here. Rene's talk went on and on, as if I should be interested in his dilemma. I was a minister, wasn't I? We were brothers under the skin?

"Rene," I said, after a time.

He rattled on, as if he had not heard me.

"Rene," I fairly screamed.

He glanced up, stunned by my voice. I was waving my hands in the air, like flapping wings on a chicken that had just lost its head.

"Sorry," I said, slightly repentant. "What you are telling me is probably important to you, but I cannot listen, right now. Maybe later, okay? A bit later in the day? I was wrestling with other things that are important to me. I do that most mornings, Rene. It's habit, I guess. I find that mornings are the best time of day for creative thought. For me, that is. I don't know about other people."

"I interrupted you. I..."

He was up off the chair and out my door before I could stop him. I grabbed at his sleeve and missed. I reached for a closing door. I called his name just as he pushed out the whooshing outer door. He was fast; too fast for me. I should be interested in him and his work but, inside, I did not want to let go of my own patterns. I was trying to understand — not get involved with — this place. Ministers got involved; it was unavoidable. I could not do that, yet. That was as good a reason as any for me not to listen to Rene's stories. It was a personal thing and a professional thing. I needed to separate those two, not join them.

"Why are relationships so hard, Dad?" my daughter, Laura, once asked me.

We were snuggled up in front of the fire in our small home in Oregon. It was a chilly day, just before Thanksgiving. Laura was home from college and had been recounting some of her difficulties in the new situation. In her classes, things were going well. In the dorm, however, all was not good.

"I don't know," I had replied, honestly. In spite of all I had come to know over all the years, I still found I used those words, often.

"Any ideas, Dad?"

"You need some?" I said. as she snuggled closer into my shoulder, eyes on the blazing blue, green, yellow and red hues, all mixed together, as the wood burned up, before falling black as the night outside below the grate.

"Yes, Dad. I could use a few. I've thought about it a lot, and I'm stumped."

"Well," I said. "If I were to wrestle with that issue for any length of time, I'd probably come to the conclusion that it had to do with the fact that we all change to suit different situations. Some changes, we discover, are harder to make than others. And we react to different people in different ways, as well."

"Ugh," Laura said. "I'm sorry I asked."

"Old philosophical question," I said. "Identity and difference, the static and the dynamic; how are such things related? Say we fall in love with someone and, a few years later, that person seems to be someone else. We haven't changed, of course. We don't notice our own changes most of the time. We're too close to them. We're not paying attention. But that other person? We can see those changes more clearly. So it's that person's fault, see?"

"The relationship has to change, too."

"Right. It cannot stay the same, ever. Only God can stay the same. Or so the argument goes."

"So if you have a changed situation, you have to become someone else to fit it?"

Laura was thinking deeply, and I had to admire that. My little girl had grown up into a very sophisticated young woman. I was proud to be her father.

"Yes. You've just gone off to college, where you are forced to live where things are very different from home. There have to be some changes."

"Does God change? You said..."

"I know what I said, Laura. You can argue that God changes, or you can argue that our understanding of God changes. In my view, that's saying the same thing. The simpler of the two poles is that God changes. Otherwise, we have a God to whom all kinds of attributes accrue as we learn things about God we didn't know before. I don't see the point of that. Besides, we often say the same thing differently. Especially, where a situation is ambiguous. Our best poetry conveys that idea, if it is an idea. Very likely, it is not."

"Dad, don't."

"Okay," I said. "Let's not get into it."

"It's no wonder you are always in trouble, Dad. You think too much. Clever people and grocers weighing everything, you know?"

"Zorba, the Greek" I said. "Am I in trouble?"

"Only when you try to teach, Dad. As a preacher, you're great. Ask me, I'll tell you."

"Oh, good," I said. "I won't teach often, then."

"Did you and Mom have to change?"

"Are you asking, have we had times of trouble in our relationship?"

"Yes. May I ask that?"

"You're a big girl, Love. You can ask me anything you want. I may not always answer, but you can ask."

"Oh, Dad." Laura lifted her head and nuzzled her hair into my neck. The fire chose that moment to settle, sending out a kaleidoscope of colors, along with a cracking sound, like that of a gun. We laughed at the timing. Laura sank down my arm, waiting patiently. The fire sank, too, remaining logs snapping at center. Neither of us thought to reach over and shake them up.

"We separated once," I said. All of the anguish of those days came back with the words. "We had a 'period of separation,' as they call it."

"I seem to remember that."

"You were small. You might."

I was remembering. Thinking of our separation made it live again. I was driving away in my pickup, laden with my few belongings. Margie was standing out on the lawn by the driveway, slowly waving. The look on her face was indescribable. It was a mix of relief and determination and pain. Her look probably echoed my own. I was hoping she'd relent and call me back. That didn't happen. I drove out of the driveway, staring into the rear-view mirror. My known world vanished into its own reflection.

"Were you considering a divorce?" That was Laura's voice, edging into my memories, piercing them. I blinked and shook my head to clear it.

"Yes, Laura. Rather, your mother was. She was trying to find herself. She thought that, without me, it might be more of a possibility."

"It didn't work?"

"If we hadn't had the three of you, it might have been possible. It might have even been the right thing to do."

"But she couldn't hack it alone?"

"If we had lived closer to family, closer to relatives back home, say, it might have been. Help with all the essential routine of a household. Your mother wanted...needed...to go back to school, Laura. Hard to do that and raise three kids. Expensive, too."

Laura had removed her head from my chest and was sitting up, her brown eyes probing mine, trying to comprehend things she would rather not even talk about.

"So you came back?"

"Yes. Your mother called me, and I came home."

"How did you feel?"

"Hmm. I don't really know, Laura. I didn't want a divorce, but I didn't know what I wanted."

"But you came back. And you stayed."

"Yes, There was you and Jim and Rick to consider. I felt responsible for you all. Your mother and I both felt that way. We were always responsible parents, Laura. Overly responsible, some people might say."

"I don't think so," Laura said.

I smiled at her and drew her to me. I stared over the top of her head at the smoke now trailing up the chimney. The fire needed a fresh log. I could smell the smoke of the fire. I could also smell the lovely fragrance that was my daughter. The mix was satisfying.

"So God changes," Laura said, drawing away from me, her features suddenly intense. She was trying to understand some concept that sat just beyond her view.

"I think so, Laura. I don't often say so, but I think so. It sounds right to me."

"That's the problem, then."

"What is?"

"God keeps changing, and the world doesn't know what God is like, right now. That's why it's so hard to relate."

"Now there's a thought to blow the minds of today's theologians," I said. "If we mortals have changed and the eternal God has changed, it's no wonder there's this sense of separation between God and human beings. Think we ought to divorce? Maybe, we already have."

"I hope not," Laura said, looking troubled.

"Why is that, Laura? Lots of people don't care today. It doesn't seem to matter to them if there's a God or not. Why should you care?"

"I don't know, Dad. I just do. That's all."

"And what about school?" I said.

"I guess I'll change. Don't worry. I'll be okay. I'm glad we talk. It helps me see things differently. See from somebody else's viewpoint, you know?"

"Sure," I said, though I wasn't sure. I've never been sure it really helps to see things from another person's perspective. Laura seemed better at it than me.

The next morning, Laura went off to San Jose State. I watched her drive away in her small, yellow, Volkswagon Bug. I was happy for her, entering into her own life.

Ten years later and she was dead.

CHAPTER 15

I stood on the corner, shivering. This was where she died, my daughter. This was the place. It was not much of a place. There was a building to the inside and a, pole to the outside. In between, death came in one of its many forms. This time, the form bumped and pushed and mangled, dragging the victim out into the middle of the street before dropping her and rushing on, not stopping, not ever stopping; even now, not stopping, not inside my head. I looked where death came from, south Woodward. I looked where death went, east Grand. Death's machine went right through this small space, missing the pole on one side, scraping the building on the other. A bit of blue paint remains. A blurred mark of tires out into the street.

I turned one way, I turned the other; it made no difference which way I turned. Either way, she was dead. Laura was dead. I gazed at the cars coming toward me up Woodward. There was nothing frightening about them. They had grills and headlights and bumpers, some massive, some flimsy. All of them had drivers. A few of the drivers glanced my way as I spun solitary circles on the pavement. Particularly, those turning the corner looked at me. I walked alone in the cold; another Detroit crazy doing his thing. I watched cars run away from me down Grand, reflecting sunlight, what there was of it. I caught some drivers watching me through rear windows. Did one of them do it? Was one of them laden with guilt? Which one? Probably, none.

Fingers wrapped themselves in mine.

I was locked away within myself. It took time for me to come out of myself enough to find Alicia Fowler showering me with her brand of sympathy. She clung firmly to my hand, saying nothing. She wasn't smiling.

I felt the pull of her body, leading me away from the corner. Across the street to the north, I saw Charlie Eusted and Bubba. They were not moving, but they seemed to be. Snow was sweeping down on an angle in front of them. Across the street in front of me, I saw Denys Fowler. He was hunched into his camel-hair coat, waiting. Then they all turned and left the corner. As I watched, they left.

Soon Alicia and I were sitting in a coffee shop on the second level of New Center One. The smell of freshly brewed coffee permeated the place. I felt lulled by it, at peace. My fingers, wrapped around a huge mug of the house blend, let warmth ooze through my skin and into my tense body. I was being comforted from extremities to trunk, as by a gentle rain in Spring. Caffeine acted the purgative — removing anger, frustration and pain. I sipped the coffee slowly, so as not to burn my lips.

Alicia waited.

She has done this before, I thought. This gentle woman specializes in waiting. She's an expert at it. Then she began to talk, as if she could see my brain begin to work.

"Charlie saw you," Alicia said. "I was in having lunch with Denys. Charlie had Bubba call. I came right over. We thought you could use a friend."

I nodded. It was a single lift of my head. It became the swinging of a heavy axe. That's what friends are for, I remembered thinking, though I felt I really didn't know what friends were for. For me?

Alicia's head had tilted in a way that was becoming familiar. Her eyes contained their own questions.

"You're used to death," I said.

"What makes you say that?"

"A feeling," I said.

"I'm used to seeing death. I'm not used to death. I don't think anyone gets used to the idea of men dying."

"Over there?"

"Yes. Over there. Vietnam. The turning point of modern American lives. Vietnam. Our national crucifixion."

"You were...what?"

"I was a nurse."

"Men died."

"Yes."

"A lot of men."

"Yes."

"Young men."

"Yes. Very young. Too young."

Alicia was playing with the edge of her saucer, the edge of the coffee table, the edge of the sleeve on her dress. Her fingers went back and forth, back and forth in an endlessly repetitive cycle of movement. The movement went nowhere, like the war. Nowhere to get to, nowhere to retreat from, nowhere to go. It just went on, like the constant flutter of Alicia's fingers.

"But some men lived because of you."

"Some, I guess."

"You don't seem happy about that."

"I'm not sure we did them a favor, sometimes."

She didn't say anything more. I found myself crawling into a hole I was digging in my head. The hole became a tunnel, a long bitter tunnel, and there was no end to it. We die, and that's the end of things. To live forever would destroy the story that tells us life is precious. When we are gone, we are gone. To be gone was to go to the place where nothing is precious, where all is one. No individuality; no distinctiveness; no specific character. My daughter Laura was gone, and her individuality, her distinctiveness, her individual character was gone. Never to return. There would never be another Laura like mine. Except as memory.

"Where are you, Marc?" I thought I heard Alicia say.

"I don't know," I heard myself answering, whether she had actually spoken or not.

"Welcome to the club," she said. "I mean that sincerely, Marc. On behalf of a host of lovely, lost people, I welcome you to the club. Like us, you wear the mark where we can see it. You wear the mark of pain."

I thought, immediately, of Albert Schweitzer, that old humanitarian, that doctor, that musician, that theologian. Those were his words. A fellowship, he called it, of those who bear the mark of pain. It seemed, I had finally joined a very large company, a select community. It was not my desire to join, but it happened.

I was soon back in my room, savoring a burning sensation, the lingering feel of Alicia Fowler's parting kiss. It was a peck on the cheek like my wife used to give me on the mornings I was rushing away, out to save the world. Margie called it her "birdie kiss," a tiny peck like a sparrow's. All her other kisses were more fun. She saved them for the moments in which I slowed down almost to a stop. Those were the kisses worth savoring.

My cheek tingled, and the back of my hand that rubbed my cheek tingled, too. Woman was touching me. I was lost within that touching. It was a great place to be lost in.

My answering machine had a message on it, when I came back from a quick trip to the store. My son, Jim, asked if I could meet him at Metro Airport at two o'clock, today. He left me a flight number. Jim would be flying the plane. He had layover time. Meet me. Please, Dad. He knew I could not ignore such a request.

A black City Cab got me out to Metro. The driver was the same color as the cab. He had not once looked at me, not when picking me up or dropping me off. While paying him, I made it a point to touch his hand, and he looked up. He did not really see me. I smiled at him, anyway.

Then I entered the terminal, amidst the busy turmoil of too many people rushing through too few doors.

As a small boy, I was a lonely child who learned to love his loneliness. In airports, loneliness is palpable. It throbs. All the activity around you, as you stand in an airport, is empty of meaning. The airport has no purpose beyond getting a person from one place to another, as if that were an important thing to do. For a businessman, it may be important. For other people, most often it is not. Most matters are trivial in airports, except for the loneliness you feel. In your loneliness sits the real you.

My father liked to drive to the airport in Providence, Rhode Island, once in a while. He was never going anywhere, but he liked to watch the planes take off and land. He and I would sometimes stand at the edge of the runway, enjoying the roar of the silver machines as the engines gunned, as they idled before gunning. Watching airplanes was different from watching railroad trains rush by, a thing we could see anytime. Planes leaped like birds into an empty sky. Trains make as much noise, but they are captive to tracks. There is no freedom to trains.

Freedom was what my father wished for, I thought. He was like a railroad engine, pushed down, by the weight of his own living, onto tracks no one could see. Deep down, Dad saw the steel rails that held him; he knew them, intimately. He hated them, on occasion. But he could not free himself, as any responsible person cannot. But the look on his face as he watched the he watched the planes haunted me for years after he died. Every time I saw an airplane take off or land, I have seen that look. I avoid airports.

My son stood in front of me, and I hardly recognized him. James Edward McDaniel is taller that I am, and heavier by far, big of chest and shoulders. He carries himself with a lean grace. He is handsome, in a craggy sort of way. There is something in him that I have never understood. It isn't that Jim is deliberately cruel; it is just that he is careless of feelings. A pet of his might die, and Jim would miss it, momentarily. That was about it. Losses never changed him. Not in any way that I could ever see. But now his marriage was failing; had failed. His casual assignations all ended the same way, I imagined. And Jim could never figure out why. I guessed he couldn't this time.

I made it a point to embrace him. He held me close, then playfully shoved me away.

"It hasn't been that long, Dad," he said.

He was trying to laugh, but there didn't appear to be any humor in him.

In a few minutes, we were munching sandwiches in the Fly-Bye Restaurant. Sandwiches were all that the place was good for, except for the imported beer. Jim was quiet, quieter than usual for him. He didn't even respond to the pass our waitress made at him. Waitresses were always making passes at him. What was it they saw? I often asked myself that but never found an answer. Whatever it was that attracted them soon drove them away. The man was a mystery to me, and he was my own son.

"Rick told you," Jim muttered, finally, his sandwich gone, his coffee waiting for its refill.

"Yes. I tried calling you."

"Gone. I'm always gone, Dad. Once in a while, I remember to call for my messages. Most of the time, I skip it. The messages I get aren't worth the trouble."

I looked at him, quietly, for a while. There were lines etched into his cheek, where none had been before. His eyes had creased edges, and I caught the glimpse of one gray hair deep in the curl above his forehead.

"Has she filed?" I asked.

"Yes. I guess Leslie has had it, Dad. I'm gone a lot. And when I'm there, I might as well be gone."

"Oh?"

"That's the way she puts it, Dad. She's right. I'm not there when I'm there. I just..."

I waited, looking at his face.

"Anyway," Jim said. "It's happening. It's going to happen."

"And the kids?"

"They side with their mother. Why shouldn't they? It is true. They're like their mother, anyhow. Carol has her face. Christie has her eyes and her hair. They're lucky. They got nothing from me."

"That's not true, son."

"Sure, it's true. You wouldn't want to have anything from me, would you? If you were them?"

"They're going to be tall girls. They have your height, which will be a very good thing, especially these days. And they have your directness. Christie, especially. She's not shy. Not shy, at all."

I didn't tell him that most modern girls did not seem very shy to me. "They'll get by, then."

"Is that a question?"

"No, Dad. I used to get angry at how stubborn they became around me, when I was there. Christie, especially. But, now, I think it's a good thing. They'll survive. Being stubborn helps you to survive."

"You wouldn't know anything about that," I said.

This time, Jim did laugh. He leaned back in his chair, with his long legs out front, and laughed at me. It was good to hear him laugh. Then he told me it was good to see me. We should do this more often, he said. Father and son talk, he said. I agreed with him that it would be a goodthing, but I knew it would never happen. Jim was simply unburdening himself. The desire of a father is not often the desire of a son.

When he was done, Jim left me. His flight was heading for Paris, and he had been called for it. I stayed where I was, nibbling on an oddly-flavored piece of apple pie. I couldn't figure out what the flavor was, but the ice-cream on top was delicious. I twisted my fork in that, making each piece of the pie more palatable. Then it was gone, and I sipped my coffee until it was gone, too.

With no other reason to stay, I left.

CHAPTER 16

A couple of weeks later and I felt as if I belonged to the neighborhood. The first blizzard of the season blanketed Detroit, making it beautiful. The white of the snow contrasted surprisingly well with the darker buildings. It coated the streets like a sheet. Then the traffic began to move, following the horrific noise of snow-plows at their appointed task. The roads turned to muck. I went outside to look at my new world more closely and found it brown-stained and ugly, snow piled against sidewalks and onto cars. It was going to be a task to dig them out. A few men on the block were doing just that, hurling show back onto the street from which it had come.

Hey Hank was suddenly by my side. He was looking where I was looking. All of the men out there were waving at him, laughing and pointing.

"Don't min' them none," Hey Hank said to me.

"I missed you," I said. "I thought you were going to teach me about living here."

"I teach you, beginnin' now. You got bread?"

I opened my wallet and dug out a five. I handed it over, and Hey Hank glanced at it and then at me.

"Yo' don't want to learn much."

"Give me a sample," I said. "I need to know something about the product, before giving money away."

"Never give in to nobody," Hey Hank said. "Never give in to nobody. Yo' got d'at?"

"Yeah. I got that."

Hey Hank slipped the five-spot into his pocket, while shaking his head. He was glaring at the men in the street. I wondered what was actually going on.

"That it?" I said.

"D'at it," he said. "Worth what you gimme."

"You can cut it with the street talk," I said. "I heard from your Mom. She probably told you she told me."

Hey Hank said nothing for a moment. His gaze was riding over his shoulder at my building, then again at the men on the street.

"In there, I talk like yo'. Out here, yo' better learn to talk like me. Save yo' ass."

"Is that right?" I said."

Hey Hank nodded, vehemently.

"You're right," I said, having survived both the mills and the military. "I'll try to be tough."

"Yo' better be. Yo' live here, see?"

"Gotcha," I said. "From this moment, I'm a bad-ass, mean motherfucker, and yo' better stay out of my way, man!"

Hey Hank about rolled in the muck-packed gutter, he laughed so hard. But he affirmed the role.

I studied the faces in my new neighborhood. I was beginning to tell one from another, who belonged where and to whom. I also noted that the more I was seen, the less I was noticed. I had become simply another person who lived here. My oddity had all but disappeared over time. But there was one man who didn't fit the picture of another neighbor on the street. I would go out only to find him leaning against a lamppost not far away. He would be smoking one cigarette or rolled joint after another. He did not belong here, I told myself, but he was here. I looked for him, whenever I went out. He seemed, also, to be looking for me.

What could the man be doing?

I made it a habit, when I walked past the man, to stare at him, not taking my gaze away until the last moment. But it was as if the man expected it. He did not look away. He almost smiled, lifting his cigarette with two long fingers. He blew smoke at me through his white teeth. It got to be routine. The corners of the man's dark eyes crinkled up as I approached him and a scar on his cheek ripped up the darkness of his face. The scar had a life of its own. It accented the fact that the man and I were having an ongoing conversation. I had to wonder what it was we were talking about.

Then one day, I found Bubba standing on a corner watching the man who was watching me. I stood on my stoop awhile, taking in this slight change of scene. Then I walked by the man, and he responded as always. He stared at me, then dragged smoke through his teeth. The smoke clouded his face for a moment. I thought I saw his eyes flicker, but I could not be certain. I held his stare, until I passed him by. I did not feel his eyes on my back. But then, I never had.

I went up to Bubba on the corner, but Bubba did not look at me. He gazed over my shoulder, staring at the man. I stood in front of Bubba for a moment, then turned around to look at the man. He wasn't there.

I saw his long frame strolling off further down the street. He didn't look back. I left Bubba and headed for the grocery story around the corner. I did not look back at Bubba, and I did not feel his eyes on my back watching me.

A game is being played, I thought, an inner-city game of chicken, maybe. But were all the cards on the table? I couldn't know that. Chicken was one game; cards another. I wouldn't know if I were seeing all the cards, anyway. I didn't know what the game was. How do you play a game when you do not know what the rules were? Every card game had rules. I had to assume there were rules. Even the game of chicken had rules. A guy could get killed playing chicken.

When I got back to my apartment, I plunked myself onto the bed, jamming my shoulder-blade into the bed's wooden headboard. The gap between the mattress and the headboard had swallowed my pillows. They weren't much, as pillows went, anyway. It took two pillows to make one decent one. The pillows were crushed, and the life had gone out of them long ago.

I reached down into the gap and tugged the pillows out. I heard an odd noise as I did so and flipped myself off the side of the bed and reached under. I discovered a small raft of papers slithering out onto the floor, mingling with the dustballs. They turned out to be loose papers and they had writing on them; poems in the making. I hadn't been told that the former resident, Gregory Barton, wrote poetry. He wrote novels, but these were not the pages of a novel. I examined them, carefully. Each page held a complete poem, scribbled over and worked on. No name was attached to the sheets. The poems were about Detroit, as viewed from some place around here. I took a few of the poems and read them aloud to myself.

I was no poet, but I liked what I read. The poems rang in me like bells, offering pleasant-sad reverberations. I found them hauntingly beautiful. The person who wrote them had a deft touch and a sharp eye. I read:

PRIVATE TRANSPORT

Beautiful maiden, waiting for a bus Botticelli's Venus has nothing on you You are taller, darker, more willowy You hold yourself with fierce pride You are the last member of a noble race that for a time lived far, far away; they dragged your parents here Your birth was celebrated with crack and gin, the sour smell of cheap wine The shell comes and you board. I watch you ride away, your sea a wide street. Your chariot will not reach a finer, better shore Oh, lady, do not fall below your looks! The fish are hungry for your beauty. The waves are restless to devour dusky flesh. I am feeling pain for you, a feeling you do not want or need. You want a better ride a private transport that does not smell of shit. You want sea breezes instead of this dark room. You want a chance to step ashore, boldly and live on some other world

The man or woman who wrote these poems had knowledge and sensibility. The poems weren't just touching tributes, they were signifiers of a great love, both of art and of people in this troubled city. I read:

CEZANNE IN DETROIT

I picture him walking streets North and East of New Center looking at the ragged people forcing them to be beautiful

Change does not touch them they go their separate ways But in his mind, on canvas on the page, they glow

Whatever objects he sees are suddenly transformed yet no brush touches them He lives elsewhere

Raging at the world dragging its dark color into brightness rising in his own ugly face

Yet the writer's final view was despairing. He or she was clearly a worrier, a person concerned with the spread of ugliness, of emptiness, of loss. He or she considered the possibility that Detroit's fate might be universal. All it took was a different way of seeing. I read:

AND SUDDENLY THE RIGHT EYES

You pass down Grand Boulevard your mind filled with your own doings

Behind you, a cathedral created by cars sits in sunset, burying itself

In dark shadows. In front of you, the moon and buildings; always

Buildings, railroads factories, houses, small struggling businesses

Darkness is oppressive Suddenly you're alone and suddenly the right eyes

Grow in your face transforming people into everyone, forever

The author, it seemed to me, caught the gist of the dilemma of Detroit. And of every other large city in this country: What can be salvaged when so much of nature, and of culture, is gone?

I read the bundle of poems once more, going slower. I felt I could not judge them as poetry; that was not my job, certainly not my forte. I was no connoisseur of the fine arts, including poetry. I was just an educated man, appreciative of what others could do. It seemed to me that what this person could do was capture images and moments. He or she caught emotions and turned them into words. He or she transformed pain into beauty. Poignant is the word. What is good poetry? I don't know. But as one scholar said, if you must read the words again, already knowing what a poem says, then it's great poetry! The poems moved me.

I sat at my desk with the sheaf of poems in my hand. I looked out the window and tried to see my new world through other eyes. Cezanne, you tormented soul! Where did your idea of color come from? Where the detail? Could you walk these streets today, and what would you do with them if you did? Would the cruel children pelt you with stones? I guessed they would. They might throw other things.

I looked out the window. The street was quiet. It was late in the day. The sun cast a dull halo of diminished light. The street seemed unreal. I watched a single car plow its lonely way down the windblown street. The car was brown and rusted and banged up. There were deep dents on the doors and fenders. There was rust along the bottom of the doors and in the wheelwells. The hood of the car was of a different color, a replacement picked up at a used car lot. The hood was an icky gray, the color of primers: near blue, near black. There were spots of red lead on the roof and on the trunk lid. The car had been around. Then it dawned on me. The sound of the car's engine was throaty and powerful. This was no slouch of a car. It was a car for get-up-and-go, for racing away from trouble, perhaps, at speeds you would not expect. The car moved off down the street, going slow all the way. It faded out of view, but I could hear the engine long after the car was gone.

The soft halo of sunlight faded. It seeped into the dark crevices between the buildings; it ran onto the roofs of tall houses; it blurred stiff windows, then blackened them. One moment, every window was a mirror, reflecting the light. The next each was dark as coal, reflecting nothing. The change was rapid. I thought I might have imagined seeing the transition, like the green glow a person might see at sunset. Was it there? Was it not? I strained now to see anything at all. My eyes soon adjusted. A few people were on the street, struggling up the street or down it. A car or two or three went by, not quite in an orderly row. Then the people vanished into the houses, and the cars parked and grew silent. Streetlights came on, echoing the earlier effect of the fading sun, with haloes around them. For miles around, I guessed, there were these tiny moons.

I could only see with my own eyes. I knew no artistic revelation, no conversion experience in seeing, no translation of viewpoint. My mind saw what my mind permitted and my sense of sight allowed. What did Charlie Eusted expect me to see? I saw as my species saw, as my diurnal facility saw, as my race saw. I was merely a common man, not an exception. I can add to what I see, even add to what others see, perhaps, but I cannot change it. I do not have the power. Seeing is quite often a euphemism for the heart. "It is not a pretty world, Papa," says a young Asher Lev I've been reading. Papa could not disagree. Why would Papa disagree? It is not a pretty world, but it is often as mysterious as it is dangerous and ugly.

CHAPTER 17

I paced the floor until the light knocking came on my door. It was morning, and I had drunk my coffee. I had two pots of coffee, actually, and I was about to start on my third. I felt like a teenager waiting for a call from his girlfriend. I was circling the door when the knock came. I threw the door open and dragged Father Rene inside. "You're late," I told him, and he shrugged his thin shoulders at me. Rene swirled around and settled on the edge of my bed. "I am late for what?" he said, amusement roiling his face. "For this," I told him and dropped the sheaf of papers onto his lap. The papers slid on his shiny, black, pants and he caught at them, as they slipped off his knees. He fondled pages while still looking at me.

"Whose are they?" I asked.

Rene continued to gaze at me, as if I were the mystery and not the poems on the pages. He finally condescended to lower his eyes, but only for a brief moment.

"They are Frederick's," he said.

"Who's Frederick?"

"Frederick Ragg, the poet. Frederick, the Great...according to Frederick, himself. The Frederick of this neighborhood, Marc. Our Frederick, if you please. Frederick Ragg lived next door, in the purple house. The man who used to live here was his friend. They talked poetry, the two of them. They talked writing. They talked of many things, I believe, but this is poetry. It is Frederick Ragg's poetry. These poems are in print, now. There is a book; I own a copy. These are clearly working copies of some of the poems. Greg Barton must have had them."

"I never heard of the man," I said. "A famous poet?"

Rene laughed. "*Frederique*, as he liked to be called, would be disappointed. He assumes everyone knows him."

"He's alive?"

"Of course, he's alive. He lives in Grand Rapids. A few years ago, he lived next door."

"In the purple house," I said. I was remembering Hey Hank, when I met him, staring at that house over its short chain-link fence, longing in his young eyes. Once that old house had belonged to his grandmother. How galling it had to be to know someone else was living in a that belonged to you by ancestral right. And now, if I had it right, the house was empty. Why couldn't it be Hey Hank's and Rebecca's house?

Lovely Rebecca; thinking of her made me want to see her again. Was my longing like Hank's for the house?

Rene sat waiting. When my attention returned to him, he lifted one of the pages by its edge and turned it my way. I saw it was one of the poems I liked.

"You know poetry," Rene said. "But you don't know this? Frederick would be upset."

"I'll run right out to the bookstore and rectify my failing," I said.

"You don't have to be sarcastic."

"Sorry."

I let myself down into the chair at the desk in the corner of my room by the window.

"Let me explain a few things, Rene," I said. "I came out of a working class family, and I didn't get to college until late. Very late. Actually, after my time in the Navy. I was on my way to ministry when I discovered philosophy. So, it was after seminary that I began my real education. I read history; ancient civilizations, you know? Philosophy, sociology, psychology; those things. Literature, I left until poetry, last of all. I am a novice at poetry, my friend, but I like it very much. It should have been first. I thought I should survey what are called the humanities, Rene. I didn't know poetry."

Rene waited. He seemed to know I wasn't finished. He was good at waiting. Perhaps, because of all his time in the confessional. Perhaps, it was natural to him.

"I was afraid of poetry, Rene. Poetry comes out of the aural world...the world of myths, remember? Biblical poetry still forms some of the world's best poetry, outside of Shakespeare, I guess you'd have to say. But Shakespeare was influenced by Biblical language and by Biblical images. I couldn't get into poetry, I think, because it had to rhyme. Of course, I discovered finally that Biblical poetry didn't rhyme. It depended on a music-like rhythm. The repetition of phrases and such. Modern poetry doesn't need to rhyme, I've learned. So I'm getting into it, slowly. I'm sorry I don't know your Frederick Ragg."

"Poetry as the peak of literature," Rene said. "Yes, I see."

I couldn't help but laugh at him.

"It's either the peak of language or it's a superfluous activity," I said. "Call it a game academics play. To get to poetry, we are apt to get back, also, to nature and see words as metaphors. Scientists don't like that. I think of poetry as a top of the mountain kind of thing. It touches our lost emotions. It expresses both beauty and depth."

"Poetry is not superfluous," Rene argued. "The words Frederick speaks echo Detroit, and they move me with pain and sadness. As for Biblical poetry, there is nothing like the Psalms, my friend."

"And Proverbs and Job," I added. "The end of Job, in particular, where God's power is described. In it lies the wonder of creation."

We sat thinking of passages of Scripture familiar to us both. Our demeanor was like prayer. It was prayer. I found it terribly hard to pray.

"What will you do with this?" Rene said, his thin hand lying on the paper by his side. "Frederick should have these poems. I could see the pages are sent to him, if that is your wish."

"It's all right, Rene," I said. "I've never met a poet in person. A few readings, nothing up close and personal. I'll get them to him, myself."

"You mean, you'll go to Grand Rapids?"

"It's not far, is it?" I asked.

"Far enough. I'll give you his address."

Rene reached into a pocket and drew out a pen and a small pad. He wrote for a moment, then put what he had written on top of the pages of Frederick's poems.

"There is a phone number," he said. "You should let my friend know you are coming."

"I will, Rene."

I spent the rest of the morning puttering around. I thought I should straighten up the place, maybe dust the furniture, sweep out under the bed. I used to do that at home, because Margie wasn't much of a housekeeper, either. The house used to get dirty, and it was a contest of sorts to see who could stand the messiness longer. In most cases, she won. Once in a while, I would go crazy with cleaning house. But then, she would laugh and help and, between us both, the place would become spotless. Until the next time.

When Laura got older, things were better, even though, with the boys, the mess was bigger and came about quicker. Laura just did things. She put our pile of dirty clothes in the washing machine. She washed the dishes left after breakfast and lunch. And her own room was neat as a pin. In contrast, Jim and Rick did little around the house. Inside, at least. Unless I sat on them, which I came to do often. Particularly on those days when I went crazy cleaning. It was kind of a join-in-or-die affair. If you were smart, you saw the day coming. The boys never did.

Finally, I gave it up and went grocery shopping. There was a blue-uniformed guard at the market door. It was his daily post, the market's attempt to keep order.

I packed the things I wanted into a basket and took them to the counter where a smiling cashier took my money and transferred the items to two brown paper sacks, one large and the other smaller. I heaved them up into my arms and headed out the door. I passed by the uniformed guard. He ignored me. I was leaving his area of responsibility and was no longer of significance.

The day was still blustery. I shrugged my chin down into my jacket. I had forgotten to zip it all the way up. I could not reach the zipper to correct it, unless I lay my grocery burden down. I decided to forget it and rushed on toward the street.

A human cry stopped me.

A figure lay on the ground on the far side of the parking lot. It squirmed around, crying. I glanced around and noticed that I was alone. There was one old woman way off down the sidewalk, tugging at a two-wheeled cart. A child walked by her side, hanging on to the woman's arm. If they heard the cry, they were ignoring it. Perhaps, that was the best thing to do.

I tried to walk away.

With a glance toward the store, hoping the guard was looking out the window, which he was not, I walked toward the crying figure. The boy was not very big, a teenager, a drug-stoned teenager, perhaps. I bent down for a closer look. For my effort, I got a fist in my face. The blow stunned me. Behind it was a call of triumph, the cry of the beast who has taken prey.

I was surrounded by a pack of kids. They were laughing, as they kicked at me. My groceries lay scattered in a wide circle around me while the youth were playing a tattoo on my body with their heavy shoes. I noted the heavy shoes and wondered where the soft Nikes were? It was an odd thought for that moment, and I almost laughed. My arms, up around my face, were taking a beating. I didn't dare remove them, for fear of being kicked in the face. It didn't matter. I was kicked right through my arms. There were too many kicks, and I only had two arms.

I was lost in the kicking. I had no idea how long it went on. It was a permanent kind of moment. When the kicking stopped, I found I missed it. Another kick was supposed to come, wasn't it? It didn't, and that worried me. I peeked out through the crack between my two arms and saw a face. It was a dark face with lips moving, expressing concern. I was listening to words of comfort meant for me. The ministration of efficient hands were their extension. Soon I was riding away somewhere. We did not go far. When the riding stopped, so did my brain. The pain I felt was subtle but consistent, not like the sharp stabs of a few moments ago.

I saw green, an ugly, familiar green. I saw white, a common, too-bright white. I was under the care of yet another set of hands and heard the soothing sounds of a commanding voice. Then I was dropped into silence, except for the soft monotone of a single voice that seemed to roll down the length of one long, muscular arm.

"How ya' feelin'"

I groaned. "Where...?"

"Where would ya' expect to be?"

"Hospital?"

"Ah, a genius."

The man was working on my arm, adjusting something. I was feeling disembodied from that arm, except for a numbness that reached all the way up it into my skull.

"This is gonna sound kinda funny, I know," the doctor said from between his thick lips. "But you can go home if you want. You wanna go home?"

I blinked my lack of understanding.

"Bruises, ya' got. Painful bruises. But nothing broken, I can find. Even your nose is only battered a bit. Give it a few days, it'll feel good as new."

Was he laughing at me? Was there a joke being told I could not comprehend?

"Take a minute to decide," the doctor said. "Take the afternoon. We're not rushed."

"But...?" I licked my lips and tasted blood and something else. I didn't know what the odd taste was.

I heard the doctor mutter, "Geez!" under his breath. Was he having fun with this?

"What?" I felt like I did at the dentist, knowing numbness, understanding that pain would come later. The question was, how much later? And how much pain?

"I'd take the warning seriously," the doctor said. "If I was you, that's what I'd do."

"Funny," I muttered.

"Not funny," the doctor said, standing up and walking to the bottom of the bed and drawing the curtain aside. He stood there, looking back at me, making up his mind.

"I'd go home," he said, finally. "I mean, really home. Kids around here don't play games, except with their own kind. You don't have a single serious injury. So the guys held back, you see? It's a warning to you."

"You're joking. Warning about what?"

"I don't know about what. You do."

"But I don't..."

"Well, I'd give it some thought. There must be something. Get outta town, mister. That's the best advice I can give ya' "

He went through the curtain, before sticking his head back through. He was smiling, broadly.

"When you're ready, just call. We'll get you a cab, take you wherever you wanna go. And, by the way, your groceries are out here. Folk gathered them up for you, sent them along. Some good folk out there."

I stared at him, not knowing what to think.

"Yeah," he said, smiling.

CHAPTER 18

I dreamed, and the face I was seeing in the dream kept vanishing. It was off to one corner. It was in the exact center of my lens. It was above my range of focus. It lay beneath the curve of my eyelids. It was one face; it was many. It was huge; it was tiny. It appeared and reappeared. It was calm; it was laughing; it was sad. I could not make the face stay, it came and went of its own volition. The face was a puppet's, a mannequin's, a man's. The face was a friend's face, a stranger's face. I felt drawn toward the face. It drove me away with a look I could not comprehend. I was locked into that face.

One wrecked cheekbone glowed in that face.

There were two voices coming down the hall, waking me. Two men burst through my door without seeking permission. One man was bigger than the other, dressed in a different kind of uniform. The smaller man moved quicker, his thin shoulders jerking up and down as he gesticulated, making a point of argument. The bigger man ignored him, except to snort, a sound that was quickly swallowed by the man's big, battered face.

"Come in," I said, facetiously

Father Rene paused at the foot of the bed. Sergeant Berra strutted around to the side of the bed and stared down at me.

"You look like hell," he said.

Father Rene sighed, his head swinging from side to side, disapproval written into the curl of his lips and the bland deepness of his frown.

"I know who they are," Sergeant Berra said. "You want to press charges?"

"No," I said.

"No?" A jerk of his heavy head.

"I'm not sure I could identify them," I said. "I'm not certain I want to."

"Why not?"

I shook my head. It hurt to shake my head. I felt a grimace tighten up the muscles in my cheek.

"You've got to do better than that."

"No, I don't."

Father Rene's head was a pendulum, swinging. There was humor in his dark eyes. He lifted his pointed chin toward Sergeant Berra. It was a mother's chastisement of a loved, but troublesome, child.

"He knows what everybody should do," Rene said. "You must forgive him for that."

"You two know each other," I said. "Why bother me?"

"You figure it out," Sergeant Berra said

"I was told."

"Good to have a wise teacher. When are you leaving?"

"I'm not, Sergeant."

Rene laughed, a squeak of a laugh.

Sergeant Berra stared at him and said, "Another idiot, Father. Just like you and me. We ought to all get the hell out of here. The city's not worth saving. Not any more."

Father Rene smiled, agreeing.

"Why don't you go, then?" I said.

"I dunno. What else would I do?"

"Like me," Rene said. "He belongs here."

"Hardly," Berra said, angrily. "About these kids, Mr. McDaniel. I'll harass them. It's the least I can do."

"Why do that?".

"They'll expect me to. I shouldn't disappoint them."

"A game?" I said, a glimpse of comprehension dawning.

"Sometimes, the most we can do is keep the lid on," Sergeant Berra said. "It's what I' ll do here. Let them know they've reached the limit of my patience with them. It doesn't hurt them to be sat on."

I got no chance to reply as the sergeant rushed out the door. Father Rene watched him go, sadness revealed in his profile. Then he turned to me.

"He is an abrupt man," Rene said. "You must forgive him."

"Nothing to forgive," I said.

Rene asked about my injuries, and I told him I had known worse. He did not ask how or where or when. He simply nodded at a common truth, one he knew himself. Then a silence fell upon us like a sheet. Rene lifted himself from my bed and went over and sat at my desk. He picked up a pen and began to doodle on a piece of blank paper.

I concentrated on the pain I was feeling and realized that it really wasn't bad. I would be up and about before long; no doubt about that. My pride had been damaged much more than my body. I had assumed I would not ever be beaten up again, after the sometimes frequent beatings of a young childhood. Mine was a tough neighborhood, and I knew early on I did not belong in it. It would kill me if I stayed. So I left. In coming to Detroit, I had returned to pain.

"And you must forgive them," Rene said.

He had quit making marks on paper. He had turned around to face in my direction. He had begun to wear his priestly face. It was set in a cast of firm determination. His mind made up, the course established, he could take the consequences, whatever they were, of saying what he had to say. Sometimes, you must risk friendship.

"Nothing to forgive," I said.

Rene stared at me.

"A difference in philosophy, Rene," I said. "I believe that, if you understand someone, you often find that there is nothing to forgive.

Rene said nothing, but his hard look softened.

"Where I come from, this kind of thing happens, too. It's part of...uh...neighborhood life."

"You understand them?"

"I think I do."

"I have been here for years, Marc," Rene said. "And I will never understand them. That's what I have come to believe."

"You're not from here?"

"No. Boston. Near there." Rene looked embarrassed to have made the admission.

"New England," I said, to help him. "My country, too."

"Detroit is a mystery, is it not?

"In some ways, yes," I said. "We didn't have an overwhelmingly Black influence. That's what I'm trying to learn about, Rene. But this beating? No. I've been there before, a long time ago"

"Violence still surprises me," Rene admitted. "I have not figured out why it is necessary."

"It's not necessary," I said. "But what it is, I'm not sure. I have never liked fighting."

Silence returned like a cloak laid upon us. We were gazing at each other, but not seeing anything beyond the cover of our eyelids. I looked again, and Rene was up and heading for the door. He gave me a blessing on the way. I was touched by the beauty of it, the words and the gentle motion of his hands.

"Rest," he added. "Rest is what you need."

I closed my eyes and listened to the whoosh of the outer door.

My door stood open, and a woman stood just inside it. She was shedding her heavy coat. She shed her dress and the silk slip beneath it.

She shed her bra and panties. She slipped beneath my covers and snuggled her warm body against mine. I was shivering, and then I was warm. My body burned where her body touched it. I felt her long arms go around me. I felt her lips on my neck. I smelled the wonderful scent of female closeness. I smelled a faint perfume. And more. I did not move to get closer. I felt her climb onto me, the movement slow and stimulating, surprisingly vibrant and warm. The woman was smiling at me, familiarly, while whispering something I could not hear. Then I heard it: "Kill them. Kill them. They deserve to die. Kill them all!" And then she made love to me.

I woke up, sweating. My bandages were soaked and sticking to me. I had to do something about them. I had to get them off of me. They were clinging like glue. My poor body had to shed them. It had to. I had to.

I staggered out of bed and into the bathroom. I ran water into the tub. I let myself into the water while the faucet was running. I reached where I could and tugged off the strips of tape that had been placed on me. The pain was excruciating, but I paid it little attention. I was something out of a darkened tomb, trying to become alive again. Trying to live; what's a little pain, when you're trying to live? Pain is life. Sometimes, pain is life's signature. If you are alive, there is pain. When you're not, pain vanishes into the mists of memory.

I relished the pain. In a tub of hot water, I folded into my hurt and let it go. The pain slowly faded away from me. The water slowly turned cool, then cold. I lay in the cold water a long, long time.

When I crawled out, I could hardly stand. I didn't bother toweling off but leaned against the wall, holding myself up, learning to walk. I had no strength to hold a towel. I forced myself to cross the chasm from the wall to the bed. I fell onto the bed and into sleep. I did not try to dream. I did not dream. I did not wake from dreaming. I woke up sometime during the day, and I was cold. It was a good cold, a very good cold, a cold that wrapped me up in a comforter, making me feel warm.

I woke up and dressed.

It was late afternoon when I went outside. I walked up and down the long street on which I now lived. I walked around my block, once. I walked around the block across the street from my apartment. I walked both blocks a second and then a third time. I relished the act of walking. I felt I was making a claim upon a few streets. I was a dog making a mark, but I was not a little dog any more. I had bled here; I was part of this place. I was no longer a stranger; I was family. I made my claim to territory, along with all the others living here. Don't mess with me, my mark said. I am here to stay.

Exhausted, I walked up steps and opened doors and went into my room. Mrs. Hedley's door cracked open as I went by. I paid her no attention. I closed my door behind me and locked it, tightly.

When I woke again, it was morning.

Frederick Ragg's poems intrigued me. I spent the day examining them, trying to explain to myself the magic of a man's words. Frederick Ragg had lived in this neighborhood for a number of years, mostly as a recluse in the purple house next door. But before that, what had he experienced? Whatever it was, he remembered, and in his remembering lay a mystery of merger, facts and human imagination at play. Yes, play. I had learned long ago that poetry was work. But it was also play for those who practiced the art. Maybe the man himself could provide revelation.

I placed a call to Grand Rapids, using the number that Father Rene had given me. The phone rang for a long time. I was about to hang up, when the phone was picked up, and a sibilant voice said, "Yes?" The word rolled up from somewhere deep and brought to the surface resonant tones that echoed like voices in an empty cavern.

"Mr. Ragg? Mr. Frederick Ragg, please?"

"Speaking. Who wants to know?"

My voice had a quaver in it, and I was trying to figure out why I was so nervous. Certainly, I was beyond being affected by fame. Was this man truly famous? Perhaps, in Michigan. There was no quaver in Mr. Ragg's voice. I could not picture this man's voice sounding nervous.

"You don't know me, but..."

"Goodbye."

"Wait!"

I expected him to hang up, but he did not.

"My name is Marc McDaniel. I am living, right now, next door to where you used to live. In Detroit, you know?"

"So?" The aggravation was obvious. I had never heard so much annoyance encased in a single word.

"I have some of your poems."

"My books are popular. I'm glad you enjoy them."

"No. I mean, I have some of your poems in manuscript form. Working copies, I guess. They were stuck behind the bed."

"Well. You must be in Gregory Barton's old apartment. Why in the world would you be living there?"

"Why shouldn't I live here?"

"You are white, right? Your voice says white."

I didn't like the way this conversation was going. I was rewriting what I wanted from this man, as I continued to talk to him. Perhaps, I wanted nothing.

"Well..." I said.

"Certainly, you are. The fact that you hesitate gives you away. Are you ashamed to be white?"

Frederick Ragg's mind was too fast for me. I couldn't let him know that. I was growing angry, myself.

"It's no great honor," I said. "An accident of fate."

The laughter was immediate and loud. It was raucous. I had been told that Mr. Ragg was an exceptionally fat man. I guess I had pictured someone rolly-polly pleasant, certainly not the voice I was hearing. The laughter died after a short while. I could almost see the tears running from the man's eyes. I should have hung up on him.

"You're a good one, Mr...?"

"McDaniel," I said. "Marc McDaniel."

"Mr. McDaniel. What is it you want from me?"

He was in control of himself again, and I reminded myself to be careful. The man was dangerous when he was in control of himself.

I told him I thought he might want his poems back. He said to keep them if I wished. They might be worth something, someday. After he was dead and buried, of course. I told him I didn't want to keep them, but I thought I might get to see him and could return the poems at the same time. He said, why do you wish to see me? And I said, I'm not certain. It seemed to be an acceptable reason. He gave me easy directions. Come anytime, he'd be home.

I told him it would probably be a day or two. I needed to arrange transportation. He repeated that anytime would be fine. He wasn't going anywhere.

CHAPTER 19

I called Denys Fowler to ask for his recommendation as to rent-a-car companies. No need for that, Marc, he told me. You can borrow one of ours. I could hear a conversation in the background, then Denys came back on the line. No problem for us, Marc, if you need the car for a couple of days. I told him that one day should be plenty, surprised, still, by people who did things for each other, no questions asked. I felt inclusion, an almost religious sense of belonging. It was a good feeling. I told him I'd probably be back late, however. He said, no problem. They'd just pick the car up the next day, when Denys came in for work. He was a man used to figuring out usable formats for activity. I should have remembered what his job was.

I raced across Michigan in a dream car. It was a red MGB, one of those tiny, British cars that, when you drive it, offers you nothing but engine noise. Your butt drags on the ground. Still, it's a wonderful machine, and I could picture Alicia Fowler in it, smile on her lips, hair blowing in the wind. I was surprised she'd be willing to lend it out. I'm not sure I ever would. I certainly wouldn't lend it to either of my sons. Jim would have run it out as fast as the little, red car would go. Rick would have run it back and forth through town, picking up girls at every corner. They would have loved this machine, as I was loving it now.

There were no words to describe the lovely scenery I enjoyed once I had gotten past Lansing, Michigan's capital city. I paused at an intersection at Portland, to pick up a McDonald's Egg McMuffin and coffee for my late breakfast. It was late enough that my muffin was the last one offered that day. Next came lunch, with nothing I wanted. The growling in my stomach satisfied, I concentrated on the scenery. It was beautiful, even if that over-used word doesn't really describe anything. It was the best word I had. Where the freeway crossed the Thornapple River, I was tempted to stop. But I did not stop. I needed to see the man.

Frederick Ragg lived where it was beautiful, too, on the east bank of the Grand River, looking slightly south. I sat in the car a long time just looking at the water. There was a soothing gentleness to the flow of it. It was living water, blue and gray in spots, murky and brown in spots, but living. There was life in it, on it, around it. I watched a few birds circling above the rippling, crackling swell of the river. I saw broken rays of light on the cool water. I felt pinpricks to my skin, echoing the ripples, and I saw the deepening, rich-colors on the near and far shoreline. I made out tall trees, mostly oaks and maple. I looked with a mind's eye and saw the river as a painter does, with lines and planes oozing out of reality onto canvas, through the wonderful medium of colored paint. What would Asher Lev do with this? What would Cezanne do? And what of the Spaniard named Picasso? What would he do? I did not understand what any of them would do, really, so I drew the water into me. I sketched the clouds, the sky. I pushed them back out of me onto a canvas of words on paper. The words did not need to be written.

The artist and the medium and the phenomenon we see are one. It is all we have. It is enough.

I crawled from the car a long time later and, only then, realized that I had been watched. A mound of a man was sitting in one of the sun-blotched windows of what appeared to be a sunroom, attached to an expensive, almost lavish home. The man filled the window. I did not assume this large.

The poet caught my eye and waved me toward a door at the far end of his room, nearest the river. I headed that way and slid the glass aside when I got there. A burst of warm air struck me, letting me know how cold it had become outside. I had not felt it.

"You took your time," Frederick Ragg said, not offering to shake hands. His fingers were moving, however. They made a dance of their own on his huge stomach.

"The view...." I waved a hand, helplessly. There was no way to describe what I was feeling. Out the window, the big river still looked beautiful, though not as glorious as it had a moment ago.

"Yes," he said. "I like it, too."

We were both silent, gazing out the large window.

"You see that bend in the river over there?" Frederick Ragg said. "The water curls into the shoreline right there, as if it were a cat licking up milk. If I could keep myself concentrated on that little bit of water, I could write enough poems to fill a barrel. Fortunately, or unfortunately, I cannot do that. Such concentration wears a person out. It wears me out."

"I see what you mean," I said.

"Do you?"

I stared at him, aware that I hadn't looked at his fat face. I was overawed by what he was wearing, the color. I was not used to seeing anyone dressed with a single color. It drove a person down to his knees to be exposed to such uniformity. Green, I could take, maybe. An actress once did that to her home, I remembered. Everything in shades of the color green. All the different hues. But purple? Not a chance. The hues of purple did not seem to blend for me. Each had its own character. Each could — and did — stand alone. Even when directly alongside its neighbor, it stood alone. When I finally found the man's face, it looked to be a pale, whitish dot in the middle of a fantasy of tone.

"Probably, not," I said. "I write a little, myself. Not that much. I do not have your gift for words."

"Gift? Ha! Ha! Curse would be more like it." Mr. Ragg spoke like an actor on a stage. As he did, his hands danced on the man's chest. I watched them until they seemed to notice I was watching them. Then, they stopped dancing. The hands folded together, quietly.

"This is a gift," I said, lifting the pages containing his poems in the air. "It has been to me."

"I told you to keep them," he said.

"I'd like to, but I needed to be certain you meant what you said."

"I always mean what I say. Keep them."

Frederick Ragg let one hand do the waving, granting permission. The other continued to lie still, a flat, white flag on a mound of purple cloth. I suddenly distrusted the hands. The movement of hands, I felt, should accent the words we use. These hands had minds of their own, agreeing with the man's thoughts only where necessary. This was a man who spoke too much, I considered, like an actor or a preacher or a politician. The hands did the talking; follow the hands. Follow the bouncing ball, and be mesmerized. Sing the silly song. I told myself to ignore the hands. I looked for, and found, the man's round face. In its fold, I found his eyes. I focused on the eyes.

"So, you wish to talk about my friend, Gregory Barton," Frederick Ragg said. "Poor man. I do wonder...? Ah, well. It's impossible to know what's actually going on in another person's mind. Often, I do not know what is going on in my own. Ha. Ha."

"Yes," I said. "I would like to talk about him. And about you. I'm interested to discover why the two of you lived where I'm living now. Why did you go there? What did you expect to learn?"

"Learn?" laughed Frederick Ragg. "I expected to teach." The discourse that followed was composed of a flood of allusions I did not always recognize. I listened to names and snatches of poetry and bits and pieces of novels. Interspersed with these came the philosophical underpinnings — I'll call them that — a welter of statements about the mix of races, about boundary lines, about borders that should not be crossed. He suggested images of foreign countries and fusion with lesser stocks. He had crossed boundaries, himself, and should never have left Detroit, he said. It was beautiful in Grand Rapids, but it was deadly, too. He had lost his sense of endangerment and diminishing culture. He had lost his motivation for poetry.

I listened for hours, unconsciously selecting a phrase here, a thought here, an entire universe of human understanding wrapped up in flowing words. To stop the flow was to damage the words; they were a community in transit, and I had no right to dam them. Underneath lay the horrible, a mix of fear and hope, of ugliness and magical beauty. At the bottom rolled the creative mud, generating its own joining of word and meaning. Dragons and Detroit; how were they to be related? I could not figure it. I have heard Christians link Revelation and Gospel, but never with more imaginative verve that Frederick Ragg's linkage of fantasy and fact. The man was a mad genius; he didn't belong to this world. Not anymore. Perhaps, not ever. The Muse had become deranged; that's what I thought as he finished talking.

The hands, which had been still, now drummed on his chest. The drumming was like rollicking laughter.

I was fed lunch mid-afternoon by a mouse of a woman named Hope, Frederick's brother Lawrence's wife. Lawrence himself showed up just as I was leaving at dark. He urged me to stay to dinner. I would not. I did not have the feeling he really wished me to; he merely wanted to talk to me. His eyes said he needed to talk to someone. I went out the door, never happier to getaway from any place in my life. I didn't get far.

Before I could get my car backed up and turned around, Lawrence Ragg was on his knees by my window, talking to me through the glass. He had to lean way over in order to be at my head-level. It wasn't quite enough. I rolled down the side window, holding the little car on the slope with shift and gas. In a moment, I added the brake. Lawrence was talking a mile a minute, and I couldn't hear a word he was saying. I shut off the engine.

"He drinks," Lawrence said, taking a big breath. He was a big-sized man. My car settled into the driveway as he leaned on it.

"So?"

"I mean, Frederick drinks a lot these days. All the time, now. It has done something to him. His mind, you know? He isn't what he was even a short time ago."

"Writers drink," I said. "Nothing new about that. It often goes with the territory."

Lawrence rocked away from my car, but kept a hand on the window. He seemed to be falling into himself, as if his thoughts were deeply buried and had to be dredged up in order to be spoken.

"I know," he said. "Frederick tells me. Crane, Hemingway, Faulkner...drinkers all. The poets, Lowell, Sexton, Dickey; take your pick. The best of them drink; that's what he tells me. That's what he always says. I don't care. I don't know about them. All I know is Frederick can't write. He has no inspiration, no desire. Maybe it's too calm here...I don't know. Hope and I talk about it. He hasn't written a word since leaving Detroit. My brother has always been a pain to me, Mr. McDaniel. But he is my brother. Now Frederick is paying for the gift he once had. That's how I see it."

I picked up the sheaf of papers from the seat of my car. I held them up, riffled them, slid them toward Lawrence outside my window.

Lawrence looked at them, absently. I saw one tear fall, staining the paper. The man at my window let go of the car and sank back onto the ground. He turned his back to me as he skimmed a few pages. Then he stood up and walked toward the house. There were stains on his knees and on his bottom. They will be hard stains to get out. The pants looked new, and it seemed a shame to ruin them.

Through the glass of the house, I watched a big man rage. I heard the cry of muffled voices. The voices, I thought, all came from one man. I rolled up the window, started the car, drove up the slope of the hill. I dared not look back, or I would not leave. I needed to leave.

The trip back to Detroit was a blur of indistinct, unimportant events. The sun had set, it was dark. The road was merely a road, any road. I was simply another traveler on it. I did stop at a Bob Evans' Restaurant at Lansing for dinner. I had sausage gravy and biscuits, a specialty of the house. I like breakfast for dinner while traveling. Then, I was home. Great place to go, when you don't know where else to go. I was tempted to head for the airport, go to my real home. Go west until you can't go any further. Travelers in frontier days, I've been told, headed west until they hit the ocean. Then they cried. There was nowhere else to go. An echo of the present day. Was there any place to go, today, where no one had ever been before? Probably, not.

I got home and found a note taped to my door. It said: *Get out, Whitey!* in a scrawl, like a child's. I balled the note up and tossed it into the trash. Then I dug it out and examined it. It was not a child's note. I couldn't picture any immediate neighbor doing this. I had been here for weeks, and any upset neighbor would have done something long before this. I wasn't the first Whitey here, and there were a few others still around. So this was a ploy in a game somebody was playing. A ploy for what? Getting me gone appeared to be suddenly high up on somebody's agenda. The question was why? And why, all of a sudden, now?

I dug out Charlie Eusted's phone number and dialed it. He answered, immediately. I told him what I had found on my door and what I felt about it.

He was quiet, then he said, "I'll be right over."

"Don't come," I said. "I'm going to bed."

"This doesn't bother you?"

"It bothers me. I had to tell someone. Now I've told you."

Silence on the other end of the phone.

"Sorry about the beating," he said, finally. "I talked to Bubba. He'll keep a closer watch from now on."

"Not your fault," I said. "Kids getting their kicks. Not Bubba's fault, either. He can't shadow me. I'm a big boy, Charlie. I've been banged on before."

"You sure?"

I was picturing Big Bad Bubba camped out on my doorstep. Not a thing to do, too much fear in it. Not a thing to do, so don't do it. These people don't owe me, anyway. You get hurt, you get hurt. The way it is.

"I'm sure," I said. "And I am going to bed."

"I could come over."

"No need."

"Okay. Have it your way."

I usually do, I wanted to say. It's a stupid statement, because nobody does. Frank Sinatra may sing it, but it is seldom a part of real life.

"Goodnight, then. And thanks."

"Good night, Marc. Hang tough."

"Yeah. You, too."

CHAPTER 20

I went to bed after talking with Charlie Eusted, but sleep would not come. It had been too troublesome a day. I picked up Chaim Potok's book, *The Gift of Asher Lev*, trying to figure out where I was in it. Oh, yes, at the place where Asher is trying to explain to his daughter's class what an artist does. It was an English class with a goyim teacher — the school has only believing Jews or non-Jews as teachers; non-believing Jews not allowed — and Asher Lev is the focus of the class' attention because of Rocheleh's essay on the subject of "What My Father Does." What Asher does is not acceptable to orthodox Judaism.

He describes artists as interpreters, each of whom sees the world through his own eyes. Therefore, what they paint is different, not out of the thing being painted, but out of the way it is the way it is seen and the way that seeing is expressed on canvas. Artists are like the great interpreters of Torah. What they offer is interesting, for that reason, is it not? Interpretation is the beginning of great art.

To illustrate his point, Asher draws the teacher, Miss Sullivan, in colored chalk on the blackboard in the various styles of three famous artists: Matisse, Mogdigliani and Picasso. Three views of one person — the power of art Miss Sullivan! The differences presented make life richer, do they not? So it is with the Gospel stories in the Bible. So there are four Gospels — or five, if Paul's is added — and each adds dimension to the rest. Every word of the Gospel writers is the stroke of a painter's brush.

With that thought, I fell asleep.

I woke up with Potok's book on my chest and the light on by my bed. I was dizzy, I discovered, as I placed my feet on the cold floor. The room spun very slowly around me.

I took a step and the feeling vanished. I took another and found I could make it all the way to the coffee pot. The pot was a Betty Crocker electric; just plug it in, and it perks. With my pattern, the pot should be ready to go, water in the bottom, grounds on the top. But the pot felt light. I shook it. Nothing inside: no grounds, no water. I remembered, then, I wasn't here last evening until very late. I was out of town during the time I usually fixed the pot. I turned on the tap and dug out the Yuban coffee. I felt lucky to find it in Michigan, having enjoyed the brand so much in Oregon. The pot was soon doing its thing.

I opened the refrigerator and found doughnuts. They were Hostess doughnuts. I did not care for them, but it was all the grocery store had. You should not go shopping when you're hungry; that's an old adage from my mother's generation. It still applies. I took a bite of a Hostess doughnut and a sip of freshly brewed coffee. That's when the door was knocked on. I went over and opened it.

Hey Hank stood there with his hands behind his back. He reminded me of the littlest boy in the only Black family in my childhood neighborhood. Or maybe his slightly older brother; I could not decide which, and it didn't matter. Hey Hank's heavy, blue jacket added weight to his thin form. He did not look at me.

"Da man say we should take yo' in," he said, even as he gazed up at me.

"Does he?"

"Yeah, he do."

"Quit it, Hank," I said.

The boy glanced up and down the hall. There was nobody in sight, either way. That was not to say nobody was listening from the landing, but it was a start.

"Yes, he does," Hey Hank said. "Charlie sent me to take you home." He was still looking up and down the hall, as if there was a God about to get him for sinning.

"You know Charlie?" I said.

"Everybody knows Charlie Eusted. He's from around here. He's been around here forever."

"So he knows the streets."

Charlie knows *everything*." Hey Hank let a tiny smile crease the edges of his cheeks. The smile remained as Hey Hank's head began to nod up and down, affirming what he had just told me.

"So Charlie bosses this street. Is that the way you say it?"

I was picturing gangsters and gang wars and territory divided up among groups of wild-eyes kids, who grew up with no other source of personal power and simply kept on fighting and killing each other. The kids had become adults, but they knew no other world. What with the drug input these days, they needed no other world; they were a world unto themselves. They fought over large amounts of money. Drugs gave them money, lots of it. But in the end, it seemed to bring them down to the player's level. In the end, the user won, because everybody became a user. Then the killing went on as enforcement. Nothing left to do.

"No," Hey Hank said, clearly nervous about continuing this conversation in the hallway.

"That's why it's different here. Charlie makes sure there are no bosses on this street. Or the streets around here. He keeps them clean."

"Charlie does that?"

"Uh-huh. He and his friends."

"You mean Bubba?"

"Bubba and LeRoy and Big Mac. Plus a few white guys. That guy, Denys Fowler, he's one of them."

"But he doesn't live here."

"None of the white guys do. But they know Charlie."

I tried to fathom what Hey Hank was saying. Apparently, my street, and a few neighboring streets, came under Charlie Eusted's protection in some way. But what way? What Hey Hank had described didn't sound like the expected pattern. Tough guys make demands upon the people they govern. What did Hey Hank mean by "keeps them clean." The words were clearly an allusion. There was enough dirt and garbage in the street to qualify for renewal. Or was there? I had to think on that. Was I seeing things in one place and projecting them onto someplace else? In fact, these streets — these very few streets — were surprisingly clean. But that couldn't be what Hey Hank had meant. Could it?

"Yo' don' know nuthin'," Hey Hank said, suddenly. I caught a glimpse of a man on the stairs. He had just come in the whooshing door and paused on seeing the boy and me.

Hey Hank headed out the door the man had come in. The man went the rest of the way up the stairs, and I could hear his keys jingling as he worked his locks.

"Wait," I said, catching up to Hey Hank. "You're right. I don't know nothing. So teach me."

Hey Hank turned to look at me from off the stoop as I held the door open. He stared me in the eye. I felt as if he were the old, wise man and I was the recalcitrant boy. A stupid, stubborn, ignorant brat.

"Yo' gotta learn yo'self," he said, turning away.

"Okay, I hear you. So what do I do?"

"Get yo' coat. Let's go!"

"But I haven't..."

"Do it quick. Ma's fixin' breakfast. She won't like it if things be cold."

"She...? For me?"

Hey Hank nodded once. Then he folded his arms in his great, blue coat and waited.

I rushed back into the empty apartment and into the bathroom to do the things men do there. I got myself into my clothes as quickly as I could move. My drill sergeant was waiting, but the hell with him. She was waiting! Woman, in lovely, radiant form. Fixing me breakfast, yet! How to top that? I took one last sip of my coffee before heading out the door, one hand still locking locks, one hand still finding its way into the sleeve of my jacket. I was back out by Hey Hank within minutes, but I still had to run to stay with him as he strode down the middle of the street where there was more slush than snow.

Rebecca Coltrane greeted me with a cup of hot coffee in her hand. She appeared to be in no rush. I could have taken longer to get here. It wouldn't have mattered. I accepted the coffee and sent a wicked look at Hey Hank. He gave me that wondrously transformative smile in return. Then I was invited to sit at table where things were all prepared. I was treated like an honored guest, like a king. No, I was treated with respect; that's all. It was more than enough. I learned that this woman treated all people that way.

Except for a few.

"Have you read Gwendolyn Brooks?" Rebecca Coltrane asked me as I sat content, having filled up on ham and eggs, sweet rolls and homemade jelly. The sweet rolls were marvelous. They fell apart at my touch. The ham was honey-baked and the eggs scrambled to perfection.

"Gwendolyn Brooks?"

"Yes. Her *Aloneness*, say. That little book always reminds me of someone I know."

She was looking at her son, and he was responding to her with obvious affection.

"No, I haven't," I said, embarrassed.

"Have you read Albert French? His *Billy*, say?" Rebecca looked at me as if she knew I hadn't. And this first part of the test was the easy part.

I shook my head.

"How about *Moma Day*, by Gloria Naylor?"

My head kept shaking. As it did, I got to wondering. I wouldn't have expected this woman to quiz me, embarrass me in any serious way. Perhaps, I was wrong.

Then Rebecca smiled again. And laughed a laugh that was more like a giggle.

"I was told to ask," Rebecca said, with only a glance toward the source. "I was informed that, seeing as you were an educated man, you would have read about us. Us meaning Black folk, you know? We read those books around here."

"My education was an institutional one," I said, relaxing now that the quizzing was over. "You shouldn't expect too much from educational institutions. They have their own agenda. Afterwards, you can study on your own."

"You're hinting at something."

"I was remembering," I said. "After seminary, I made a discovery. Egypt, Babylon, Persia and Greece form the background to all that is Biblical. But I knew none of their histories, not from college or seminary. In spite of all I had learned, I was minimally educated."

"After seminary?" Rebecca said. Her eyebrows arched, revealing a pale blue eye-lining deep in the crevices behind her lids. It was like discovering heaven buried in the earth. A thunder-egg opened, revealing crystal; that's what it was like. A wondrous surprise. "I thought preachers never opened anything but the Good Book after seminary. It's all they need, isn't it?"

"You joke," I said. "But there I was a Doctor of Religion with a feeling of near-total ignorance. No Akhenaten; no Darius; no Alexander; no Caesar. Not even Homer; that discovery threw me. I didn't even know how to pronounce the name of the dramatist Aeschylus, never mind read his works. Amazing how much I didn't know."

"And now-a-days, what do you read?"

"I guess I'm going to read Brooks and French and...who was it... Naylor? Oh, I have read Ralph Ellison and the poet, Robert Hayden."

"Well, good for you."

"Sorry. How about *The Color Purple*?"

"The movie or the book?"

"Both. The one led to the other."

She nodded, approvingly, and then reached across the table and touched my arm. I watched her arm reach out and her long fingers unfold and the tip of one of the fingers tap lightly on the back of my hand. I shivered. The touch was familiar and frightening. Then Rebecca's finger began to trace circles on my skin, and I felt my hand tighten and freeze. Rebecca was staring at me across the table, as if she were examining my soul. She lifted her fingers from my hand and let them wave lightly in air. Then she picked up my hand and turned it over. She ran that same finger down the lines on my palm, sending a light, tickling sensation up my arm. Her eyes stayed on mine.

"You are afraid," she said.

I looked at her, saying nothing. A pale, blue glow had shifted the light of the room. It fell over us, blocking out any means of knowing where we were. Hey Hank was not visible; he sat behind the wall of light. I was frightened and calmed at the same time.

"You needn't be afraid," she said.

I jerked my head from one side to the other, like a wild animal trying to escape from a net. I tried to pull my hand back, but it would not come. It lay curled in her hand as if it belonged there. My hand was not mine.

"What are you afraid of?" she said.

I couldn't answer, my throat had constricted too much for talk. I was swallowing, and thick phlegm was sliding down, blocking my breathing tubes, taking breath and speech away.

"Two women," she said. "I see two women."

My hand lay quivering in hers. I was calling to it, and it was quivering. My hand knew who it belonged to; it needed only a single reminder.

"Who are they, Marc? Who are these women?"

"Their names...They are, uh, relatives of mine. I'm being led by two dead women, Rebecca. I don't know where they want me to go."

"Who are they, Marc? Who are these women?"

"My wife and daughter. They've brought me here. To Detroit, of all places. Why am I in Detroit, Rebecca? I don't know what I'm doing here."

I was crying, but there were no tears. I didn't have any tears. I had shed them all. My tears, unshed, broke the spell of the light. It glistened, momentarily, and faded, until the room was just a room. I was clearly a stranger in a foreign country, talking to two Black people who lived here and were being kind to me. I needed someone to be kind to me. The light became an ordinary bulb, hung decoratively from the ceiling in an ordinary house. But it wasn't blue. It was yellow, not quite white.

"They have names?" Rebecca said.

"Margie and Laura," I said. "My daughter was killed here. I don't know why. I don't even know what she was doing here. My wife sent me to find out."

My words sounded to me like the ravings of a madman.

"She sent you to me, Margie did. She sent you to me." Rebecca's hand left mine. Her fingers came up and slowly caressed my face. I felt my cheeks burning from her touch. There would be scars, tomorrow, from her touch. I could see them in the mirror of my mind, long and slender and raging like fire. "She sent you, Marc. She sent you."

"Why?" I said. "Why?"

"Because, I know," Rebecca Coltrane said. "I know who killed your daughter. You know, too."

"I do?"

"Yes. It was for money, Marc. Lots of money. Millions of dollars in money."

"But, how?"

"You know, Marc. You know."

I stared at her, baffled. What did I know? What could I know? Rebecca's eyes never left mine. Her hand left my cheek, and she leaned over and kissed the back of my hand where it tingled. Then she stood me up, brought me around to her side of the table and held me.

I looked over her shoulder, thinking to object to what was happening, because Hey Hank was there. But Hey Hank was not there. The chair he sat in was empty.

CHAPTER 21

On the short walk from Rebecca's place to mine, snow began to fall, light stuff, flaky. It blew gently this way and that in a cold wind. It fell on me as I walked, and soon my shoulders were covered, and my hair. Seeing as I had not bothered to wear a hat, my head was haloed in white, a sort of Christmas gift. A bit early or late, who cared? At my apartment steps, I paused and looked around me. A small boy was walking away from me, white on his black head. I felt, in that moment, at peace with the world. Serene, you might say. People seek serenity as if it could be the permanent thing it never is. Serenity, like spirituality, is a momentary affair. The spirit comes and goes, like the wind. It does not stay. So it is with serenity. But in one singular moment, it was as rich and full as it could get.

I shook the snow from my hair and wiped at the remaining wetness with my hand. Then I turned and went inside. The door whooshed its celebration of movement, its momentary freedom from the static life. I headed down the hall toward my apartment, leaving a trail of damp footprints behind me. I didn't make it all the way.

Mrs. Hedley had her face out her door as if she had been waiting for me. It couldn't be. I was not some grandson stopping by for a visit. I doubted she had a grandson. But she was smiling a toothless grin.

"You looked like you'd been crowned," she said. "That's what you looked like out there."

I flipped a bit more wet stuff from my hair, grinning myself.

She held out a small package, a box about six inches square with writing on it. "This came for you," she said. "It wouldn't fit in the narrow letter slots, and the mailman knows better than to leave it out. All we have around here are thieves."

With that pronouncement, her look changed. The smile vanished so quickly, I wondered if it had actually been on her face. Then she and her face were gone, squashed and then vanished behind the heavy wood of her apartment door. I held the box and turned it over. There was no name, except mine, and no return address.

I took the box into my rooms and dropped it onto the table until I had a chance to remove my boots and my coat. Then I picked it up and started to unwrap it. The brown paper came first. Then a small box lid, marked with the emblem of a nearby store. I lifted out a bundle taped all around, with tiny bubble stuff inside stuck to the tape. It took me a while to free it, not wanting to be rough, not wanting to damage whatever it was that had been given such care. Inside the bubble stuff was a plastic Baggie, and inside that was a paper napkin. I opened the napkin and took out what was inside it. Immediately, I dropped the thing onto the table top and took two steps backwards at the same time.

Holy shit!

It lay there, fleshy and thick. I swallowed big breaths to calm myself and came back to the table. My finger was poised above it and slowly came down to touch. I had never touched a human tongue before. Not one entirely out of someone else's mouth. It wasn't the whole tongue, of course. Just a good part of the tip. Enough to make it a little hard to talk.

I pulled up a chair and sat down. I stared at the piece of tongue, telling myself that it had to be fake, though I knew that it wasn't. I did not want to touch it again. And I did not want it here.

I got up, went over and placed a call.

"Sergeant Berra is out on a call," the voice said, pleasantly. "I can get him a message."

"Tell him, I need to see him."I tried to laugh, but it wouldn't come. I swallowed and refused to look again at the thing on my tabletop. It was there; it would be there whenever Sergeant Berra arrived.

"May I tell him what it's about?"

"Uh, no. Just say, it's important. At least, I think it is. I know it is."

"I'll tell him."

Within fifteen minutes, Sergeant Berra was banging on my door. I let him in, saying nothing, just waving him over toward the kitchen table that I had been staring at in disbelief all the while. Outside the snow was coming down more heavily, but I couldn't see that it was crowning anyone.

"How did you get this?" Sergeant Berra said.

I told him.

"When?"

I told him.

"You don't read the papers?"

I told him, no. I picked one up, occasionally. But I hadn't as yet started delivery. I still wasn't sure I was going to stay here long enough for that necessity. Why?

"A story," he said. "I clipped it out."

Sergeant Berra dug into his inner jacket pocket and brought out a thick notepad. He flipped open the notepad, lifted a piece of paper from it, handed the scrap to me.

"Right off the police blotter," he said. "Just about everything we know, at the moment."

I read the scrap of paper, read it again, handed it back to him. He folded it once and stuck it back where it had been. He closed the notepad and returned it to the inner pocket. Only then did he speak to me.

"Well?"

"Well, what?"

"The tongue belongs to the boy who enticed you close enough to get beaten up in the parking lot that day. But he will tell us nothing about it" Sergeant Berra smirked. "I mean, he will *write* us nothing about it. I've never seen a kid that scared, and a lot of kids get scared of things around here."

"It was done because of me?"

"Because of what happened to you. What else am I supposed to think? This tongue has to be his."

Sergeant Berra walked over and did what I could not do. He put everything, box, paper wrapping, bubble-stuff, napkin and tongue into a plastic bag.

He lifted the bag up for me to see. "There won't be nothing on it," he said. "But we'll look, anyway."

He waited for me to say something, but I didn't have anything to say.

"If you think of anything...," he said, as he went out my door. I went to the window and watched the man cross the sidewalk and enter a waiting police car. Another man was sitting at the wheel, and I saw Sergeant Berra raise the plastic bag as he gesticulated, giving emphasis to something I could not fathom. I could see the other man's head nodding. Then he started the car and drove away.

I stayed at the window a long time, trying very hard to think of nothing.

I was surprised to find Denys and Alicia at my door the next morning. They saw my bafflement and laughed at me. They reminded me that it was Saturday. "Saturday?" I said. "What's that?" "It's what you work the rest of the week for, those of us who work," they said. "Oh," I replied, grabbing at my coat as they dragged me out the door and into Denys's BMW. Denys whisked us off to a new shopping center out in Troy, Michigan, a city just north of Detroit. We ambled in and out of one store after another, Denys pointing happily to things he liked but would not buy. "I'll get them later, when I come back," Alicia whispered. "I make Denys do this once in a while, Marc. It's the only way I can get Denys's opinion about anything. What he might want, you know?"

Then Alicia let out a whoop, her arms wagging joy. She had spotted a friend.

"Marilyn! We didn't expect to see you!"

"You didn't?" the woman replied. "You know I live in the mall. It's my home away from home. I'm a shopaholic; I admit it. Why should I be anything else?"

The line was obviously a well-used one, though it was new to me. Shopaholics? Are there such people? Of course, there are such people. I could probably name quite a few, given time to think about it.

Denys got greeted by a kiss on the cheek. He grunted and waved a finger or two, but had eyes fixed on a window where sound systems by Bose were prominently displayed.

"And this is Marc McDaniel," Alicia said. "We're showing him around."

"Well, Mr. McDaniel, welcome to the Somerset Collection and the joy of spending all your money on frivolous things."

The woman was tall and very pretty, with dark hair and sparkling dark eyes. I couldn't be certain of their color. She wore pale blue clothing and silver jewelry. There were black accents, stones in the jewelry, and she wore black, low-heeled shoes. Everything about her said business woman, but there was a flare of playfulness in her dancing eyes.

"Marc, this is Marilyn Lanlaw," Alicia said, giving me an odd look of amusement.

"Marilyn," I said, taking the offered hand.

"Marc's living in Greg's apartment," Alicia added.

The life went out of Marilyn Lanlaw's face as if someone had blown out a candle and it had become cloudy and very dark.

"In Greg's...?

"Oh, sorry. I didn't think," Alicia said.

"It's all right, Alicia. I thought I was over it."

Alicia took Marilyn's arm and led her away a few steps. They talked for a while, and I tried hard not to pay attention to what they were saying. I could guess what was being said, but it was none of my business. I had been a catalyst for conversation and that was all. The rest did not concern me. I walked back with Denys, and we looked in store windows together. We had reached a store selling model railroad trains when the women caught up to us. Behind us, glassed-in elevators took people from one level to another in the mall. Down on the first level, there was the outline of pond the elevators looked down on. The pond had coins in it, as if it were a wishing well. Maybe, it was. I could see children staring down at the receding water, or at its advance. The children seemed mesmerized by the existence of water on the other side of the glass. Soon, perhaps, they, too, would get to toss a coin and make a wish.

Before I knew what had happened, I was sitting in a restaurant in the middle of that part of the mall called Somerset South. It lay on the far side of Big Beaver Road and was reached by a crosswalk over the street in which you could ride a people-mover, the kind they often have in airports. I sat there, having lunch with Marilyn Lanlaw. Alicia took Denys with her to Saks Fifth Avenue. She wanted him to see a few outfits she wished to buy for herself. They were on sale, she explained. Reason enough to buy them, if Denys liked them. Otherwise, the dresses were among the more expensive items Saks carried in stock. Saks stood at the far end of Somerset South, not far away.

Marilyn Lanlaw took charge of the conversation. It was natural for her to do so. That's what I concluded after being with her for a few minutes, seated in a restaurant in the open in the middle of the Somerset South. The teal blue of her blouse went well with the darker blue of skirt and vest. The silver ornament around her neck seemed to be an abstract of a pair of birds mating in the air. She fluttered long eyelashes, but there was no come-on in the act. Her eyes, in spite of the fact that I could not determine their color, were the most intriguing aspect of her. Here was a woman, I thought, who knew who she was and what she wanted, and knew how to go about getting it. I had to wonder what it might be she wanted.

The thought struck me, forcefully, when it came to me. This woman's eyes were exactly like Rebecca Coltrane's eyes, in spite of being a different color. They looked boldly at you, without being brazen. There was no fear in them, none that I could see. They were the eyes of someone confident and in charge, at least of her own life. I felt that — if the eyes could talk — they would say: "Trust me. What I am telling you is the truth!" There were a multitude of other eyes that never had that look. You'd better not trust them. Not if you wished to survive in this world.

"Yes, Gregory Barton, whose place you are living in, was once my husband. He moved there after we divorced. Greg was a good man, but he and I should never have married. It was a mistake, you understand?"

"Sure," I said, suggesting that it happened all the time. Many of us made the same mistake. Divorce was part of our cultural makeup, part of what happened, part of what we understood reality to be composed of, part of the inter-relational game we played. It may not be necessary, but it was about a fifty-fifty expectation.

Marilyn Lanlaw only glanced at me, but she had not missed the implicit judgment. The remaining question was whether the judgment was mine or, simply, society's. I saw her decide the latter. I was glad.

CHAPTER 22

Marilyn Lanlaw talked. She talked about Detroit and she talked about the automobile industry and she talked about the new Opera House and Symphony Hall and she talked about the particulars of all these things. We ate up a half hour talking about things educated people everywhere talk about. Nothing about the Tigers or the Red Wings. Nothing about the dirt of politics related to new stadiums. Nothing about the streets in the poorer parts of town. Nothing about crime. By the time she slowed down, I had learned about all the decent things I did not care about. But I was polite and educated and was doing the civilized thing, pretending interest and pretending concern. Take me to the museum, show me the stuff Diego Rivera immortalized. It would have been a better place to start.

When conversation began to drift, I said, "Would you mind talking about him?"

A cloud slid across Marilyn Lanlaw's eyes and, as quickly, disappeared. She sat up straighter in the chair she sat in. She took one slow look around her. There were few people sitting where we were sitting, more people walking beyond the restaurant dividers looking into the windows of the stores. One of the stores was a small bakery, offering doughnuts and cookies and bagels. There was a line at that store, none at the others. We were pretty much alone. As alone as you can be where other people are.

"I guess not," she said.

"I've kind of fallen into something," I told her as explanation for the request. "I'm not sure what it is, but it revolves, I think, around cultural difference. Can one group of people ever come to know another? Something like that. Your ex-husband, this Gregory Barton, he lived on the city side of Eight-Mile. It's like living on the other side of the tracks, I guess. People are different over there. At least, that's the supposition."

"Black, you mean."

"In this case, Black. I came from the other side of the tracks, Marilyn. That's what you'd say if you saw where I came from. In my case, the description is literal. It was the other side of the tracks."

"Lower class. Working class."

"Right. My childhood was the boom years after the war. It was up and down, you know. Families recovering from the depression, feeling prosperity's glow, then having to deal with the strikes that followed.

The manufacturers wanted to keep this spreading wealth all to themselves. There were, suddenly, things to want, and the battle was over who would get them and how big a slice of the pie each one would get. It took years, but I shed my class, Marilyn. I became what I wasn't in order to do that. Now I find that I never did really get away. It's all still in here. It's part of me."

"So what are you asking?"

"Was Greg like that? Was living in Detroit like going home for him?"

Marilyn perked up as I spoke. She realized I was not demanding anything of her. I had no judgment to make. I was merely asking for her opinion about someone she had known and about his situation. A guess as to why, perhaps. A peek into a man's mind. She leaned her long face on her cupped hands, elbows on the glass top of the table. She was thinking as she was studying me. What answer to give? What does this man wish to know? Why should he care? Why should I? Her eyelids fell away. She had made up her mind. She stared at my face, boldness returning. Marilyn Lanlaw was a strong and capable woman. I was impressed.

"Greg was a good man," Marilyn said. "I mean that, literally. He didn't know how good he was. He thought little of himself. I mean that both ways. He had no great expectations. Yes, Marc. He felt that he fit in, and he probably did. He was comfortable enough to stay.

"But he killed himself, I hear. That doesn't sound like someone comfortable with himself."

"I don't know why." Marilyn said. Her dark eyes lowered for a moment, and I noticed one hand curl its fingers over the edge of the table and play with the crack formed by glass and metal. One nail began to tap on the glass. She reached for her coffee cup and lifted it to her lips, then let it fall. The coffee was cold. She glanced around for the waiter; found him. She signaled, and he rushed over to fill her cup. She knew I was watching her, but it did not seem to matter. She was one confident woman, willing to let her body's language say whatever it said.

I tried to picture her with a man who looked something like me; a man named Gregory Barton, whom I did not know at all. It did not compute. Of course, she would have been a little younger back then. Was he a mentor for her? Perhaps, so. Perhaps, not. But a lover, of course. She was a hard woman not to love. I concluded that he wouldn't belong with her now. She had grown, and my image of him had uncertainty at the core. They could be friends.

"And yet, I guess I do," Marilyn said. "Greg talked about Detroit as a failed city. It wasn't any longer what a city should be. Which is probably why he felt like he fit in here. He was a failed man. By that, I mean, he didn't fit in with society in general. He was not what was expected of a man out there, anywhere else. You know: ambitious and competitive, wanting to get ahead, wanting to win. In Detroit, as it is, Greg did not feel so out of place. The difference was, I think, that he was far ahead of himself as a man, and Detroit had been left behind. So he fit in, but he didn't fit in. I'm not making any sense."

"Yes, you are," I said. "The Second Wave and all that. Men need to change. The only thing wrong with that argument is that some men are already what some women think all of them should be. Kind, gentle, less-ambitious, less competitive. The sort that don't fit into the business world, that is the world as men know it, today. This society stresses more and faster, lots of drive and efficient management. It had no acceptable place for those who stop and think, or those who find inefficiency attractive, sometimes. We are not all Puritans, Marilyn. Not all men fit the image. So we struggle to find a place."

"There aren't many places."

"No, there aren't."

"Is that why you're a minister?"

"Caught me, did you?" I laughed. "Yes, I guess it is. In part, anyway. I was interested in the general nature of the profession. And you do have some control of your time."

"You sound like him, like Greg," Marilyn said. "Not the same subjects, but the same bluntness and the same honesty. You don't spare yourself, do you? Greg didn't. It got to him in the end. That's what I think, anyway. The weight of the world; all that. He did what he could, but the loneliness and isolation. He had this need..."

"Don't, Marilyn," I said. "He was a man, not a saint. Of course, he had needs. One friend, anyway. My wife was that for me."

"I was his friend," Marilyn said, through tears. She did not dab at her face, just let the water run. I admired her for that. She'd make a great friend.

"He wrote a book," I said.

That made her laugh.

"He wrote a lot of books. Only one got published, the last one. Probably the only one he truly had within him. It died in the marketplace."

"I'd like to read it."

"It didn't kill him, Marc."

"I didn't think so," I said.

"How can you know him so well?"

"I don't," I said. "We just echo each other."

"Yes, you do."

Marilyn and I were holding hands across the table when Alicia and Denys showed up. Denys had a large package under one arm and a large bag hanging from his other fist. Alicia was holding onto Denys, a wide smile glimmering, her eyes bright and her cheeks aflame. They were a lovely, lively couple. I listened to Denys whistling a tuneless tune as they approached us, skipping by an attendant waiter. They ignored everyone else around.

"You guys look like you are old friends," Denys said. "I take it you hit it off."

"Don't mind him," Alicia said. "He's a matchmaker at heart."

Marilyn and I launched into "Matchmaker, matchmaker, make me a match. Find me a find, catch me a catch..." at the same time. It just came out. We ended up laughing at each other across the table. The power of a word not used that often.

"Broadway," Denys shouted. "Next stop, Broadway!"

We sang out, again, feeling as silly as kids.

Together, we stood up and bowed. There was applause from a nearby table. We bowed all around, smiling.

"C'mon, you nuts," Denys said. "Let's get out of this marketplace. I know a bar."

I was set on going but felt a tug on my arm.

"Can I borrow him?" Marilyn said.

Denys and Alicia looked at each other.

"I promise to return him unharmed." she added. "I know where he lives."

"He's a big boy. It's up to him," Denys said.

"Well... ?" Marilyn said, looking at me.

"We were talking," I said. to everyone. "I guess we're not finished. I'm not, anyway. So if you two don't mind too much?"

"Of course, not," Alicia said. "Denys will take just little ol' me to this bar he knows."

She nuzzled her nose into Denys's jacket, then pecked him on the cheek.

Denys shrugged, lifting his shoulders and almost dropping the package under his arm.

"Sounds like fun to me," he said. "See you guys."

He tried to wave goodbye but could not. Alicia did it for him.

"This way," Marilyn said.

The Jaguar we clambered into was a lovely car. Marilyn proved quickly that she used to be a race car driver. She scooted out of the parking lot and skimmed down Big Beaver Road then roared onto the freeway, heading south. A light snow had begun again. The car's wipers had no difficulty pushing it aside. After a short while, Marilyn pulled the car off to the side of the road, out of traffic. It was not a parking area, just the emergency parking pavement, a strip left barren in case of trouble. Ahead of us, the traffic diverged, some of it heading west. Marilyn had emergency lights blinking, though nothing was wrong. We rocked a bit as traffic continued by us.

"Over there," Marilyn said. "At the top of that banking, above the freeway, below those railroad tracks, Greg had a spot he liked to go to, to think. It was quiet, he said, though I don't see how. The traffic noise is constant here. Maybe, that's what he meant. A kind of 'white noise,' blocking out other sounds."

"Up there?" I said. I could see a break in the concrete where Marilyn was pointing, a huge crevice-like space that lay between banking and bridge.

"Yes. I've never told anyone this, but Greg had a dream one day. It was night, actually, though he seldom went there at night. He pictured himself walking down that cinderblock banking right into traffic. Not just any traffic. He stepped in front of a big, Mack truck."

I looked out and saw a number of trucks go by. There were all kinds of trucks, including an occasional Mack. I liked the looks of none of them.

"Symbolism?" I said.

"Yes, the bulldog."

"Oh, of course," I said. The Mack truck's symbol was a bulldog. It sat up front, above the radiator, leading the way. "He thought of himself as a bulldog?"

"No," Marilyn said. "Somebody else did. But the image fit him well enough. Not in shape; in attitude. He hung on, Greg did. It was one of his best and worst attributes. He sometimes chose poorly the things he hung onto, but you could count on him to stay."

I saw the single tear ease its way out of the corner of Marilyn's eye. I looked away, staring at the freeway, the banking, the bridges.

We sat for a long time, quiet together, at the side of the road. I was surprised a cop didn't stop to check on us; a few drove on by without a glance. I was tempted to reach over and take Marilyn's hand, to ease her grief, perhaps. But holding a person's hand had other meanings. Being quiet together had to be enough. Then Marilyn eased the car back into traffic, taking me home just a few blocks away. She offered to talk some more, but I said, no. I didn't think she needed any more questions of Gregory Barton and his reasons for living here in Detroit. I was, also, not certain I could stand being with this lovely woman, alone, for any length of time.

So I walked into my house to hide.

CHAPTER 23

I sat up in bed on yet another Detroit morning, aware that the philosopher and the believer in me were still battling. I needed a middle road, and I knew what that middle road was: wisdom. I sat up in bed and thought about the fact that wisdom was both religious and secular. If so, it was neither religious nor secular. It belonged to the world before such divisions were known, an ancient forgotten world. We moderns prefer distinctions, letting words lead us to them. Always deceivers, words urge us on. Hopefully, to wisdom. But the search for wisdom is a lifetime job, and nobody wants to work that long for anything. Not in this country. I got out of bed and drank my coffee and gazed out the window.

I watched a car force its way into a narrow parking spot at the curb out in front of me. The vehicle bumped the cars front and back, edging in. I watched a man climb out of the car and not bother to check for damage. He headed my way, and I saw him come up the steps and heard him stomp snow off his boots. I listened to him tramp down the long corridor and then heard his knock on my door. I thought to ignore it the knocking but slipped on my pants and opened the door, letting Sergeant Berra into my room. I offered coffee with a gesture, and he accepted a cup and went over and sat at my desk, leaving me the bed to sit on. I considered falling back on it, returning to sleep. I dared not. The man was not in a good humor, and I couldn't picture him waiting for me to awaken.

"You know a Ronald Weams?" he said.

Steam from his cup was rising up over his nose as he talked. He was watching my reactions through the fog.

I shook my head no.

"You know a Ronald Worthington?"

He was still watching.

"Sure. He's married to my daughter. Was married to her, I should say, before... Well, you know."

"Same guy," the Sergeant said.

The eyes were locked onto me, gauging.

"I don't..."

"Your son-in-law, Ronald Worthington, is Ronald Weams. He has connections in Detroit. The kind you'd need if you wanted to kill somebody in Detroit."

"You're joking."
"No, I'm not."
"I don't want to..."
"You'd better."

Steel gray, that was the color of his eyes. How come I hadn't noticed before? The color suited him. It went with his pale face. I pictured the man as a mercenary in the Roman army. One of those men from Gaul who would eventually take over and run things. Centurions, be damned! This man was a barbarian. But a clever one. And tough. You'd have to kill him before he was on to you, before he went berserk and took care of you. I would not want this man on my tail. At this moment, I would not want to be Ronald Weams, whoever he was. Could he be my son-in-law? I was having a hard time accepting that as actual fact.

"You have to be joking."

"I don't joke."

That I could believe, so I got to thinking it may be true. If it were true, that meant what? The handsome young man was a killer? Or a man who hired killers? My connection with police departments had taught me that anything was possible. But this was close to home. Too close.

"Think about it, Mr. McDaniel. Why would he want her dead?"

"Ron didn't want her dead. Her death threw him for a loop. He didn't anticipate her death, never mind have anything to do with it."

I was speaking from rote. But while I was speaking, a nagging bundle of suspicions were rising up to haunt me. I hadn't known my son-in-law that well. My daughter liked him and loved him; that was enough for me. Apparently, it should not have been enough. I should have done some checking. But why should I have, if I felt nothing was wrong? My sons also liked the guy, and they were not easy to fool. Obviously, I should have examined his past. I couldn't remember any mention of Detroit, anywhere, any time.

"Why would Ronald want his wife dead?"

Like a good cop, Sergeant Berra was being persistent. I knew, from experience, he would be going over the same ground again and again until he was satisfied that he had it all. Whatever it all was.

"He didn't," I said.

"All right. Let's say he did. Why would he want her dead?"

"I can't play this kind of game," I said, trying to picture Laura as *her*. Ron couldn't kill Laura. Could he?

Think!

"They owned the company together," I said.

"Yes, they did." The sergeant already knew.

"They started it together, ran it together. They did just about everything together."

"Maybe Ron got tired of it. Maybe he got tired of her. Maybe a lot of things. You tell me."

"I don't know."

"Sure, you do."

"Why should I tell you?"

"You want her killer, don't you?"

"Yes, but...?

"Does it matter, then, who that killer is?"

"It's always a relative, right?"

"A relative, an associate; someone close. Not all the time, but a lot of the time. This time."

"How can you be sure?"

Suddenly, the sergeant was playing coy. He sucked in his chest and made a face, his teeth tucked over his lower lip. He ducked his eyes and glimpsed me from under his dark eyebrows. He smiled the smile of the Cheshire Cat. He almost laughed, but not quite.

"Let's say, Mr. McDaniel, that I know how it was done. What I don't know is why it was done. That's what I need to get from you."

"He loved her."

"Sure, he did. Once upon a time."

"Okay, so they divorced. Don't we all?"

"We all don't kill over it."

There was that word again, the word that ends things. A life taken before its time. That's what the word says; that's what the word means if there is any sense to the concept: "its time." A life ended before it should end. It referred to a cutting of the cord, a breaking of a pot at the well. Dead before you should be dead. Being dead takes forever. Margie was dead; taken from me by disease. Before her time. Then Laura taken, too. But someone killed her. A person who could be named. Somebody killed her or had her killed. Both, it seemed.

"You're sure?"

"I'm convinced, Mr. McDaniel. But I don't know how to prove it. People here don't talk; not the people I need to hear from. And I don't have a motive, unless you can provide one. Which I think you can."

"You want me to accuse my daughter's ex-husband while she's still warm in the grave?"

"It's been months, Mr. McDaniel."

"I know that."

"He's beginning to feel safe. He made it."

"Ron?"

"Your daughter's, loving ex-husband, Ronald Weams."

"You're sure?"

Sergeant Berra sighed. He dug into his pocket and came out with a small, warn notebook. He flipped pages.

"A year ago," he said, "months before your daughter was killed, Ronald Weams...alias Ronald Worthington...made a single phone call to a number here in Detroit. It's a number we monitor here in Detroit. Have for years. They know we're listening in, so most calls are coded. They make no sense to us. But, once in a while, we get lucky. The guy calling is both angry and disturbed. He says the unintended. Usually he just says enough to set up another call we can't trace. Anyway, your son-in-law was upset. He asked, after a while, for a call back. I assume he got himself bawled out for calling at all."

"You assume?" I was floored by all this and was trying to find a way out.

"It gave away who he was."

"The mob is into the computer industry?"

"Sure. What aren't they into? Do you know how much Bill Gates makes?"

"A single call?"

"Yes."

"A wrong number?"

"Possible. Not likely."

"That's all you've got?"

Sergeant Berra flipped pages in his notebook again. The notebook had a maroon cover, and its edges were lined. The cover flashed its color each time his hand flipped a page. He let the notebook fall to his side.

"I traced the name...computers are wonderful that way...and came up with the connection. Not bad, huh?" It was a comment that needed no response.

"A single call?" I queried, again.

"The name *Weams* made it easy. We know who works for that family."

"You know who did the killing?"

"So do you."

My mind was racing. I felt thunder in my chest. I was trying to get enough moisture into my mouth to say a few words. Nothing came out. I lifted my hands part-way to my head and let the fingers spread open. I felt funny in my fingers. They were tugging at each other, working themselves into a frenzy. I closed the fingers into fists and beat with the fists on my temples. I stopped and stared at Sergeant Berra, who waited as if he had seen this kind of tantrum before. More than likely, he had.

"The man on the street," I said.

"His name's Jackson. Edward Custiss Jackson. He's got a rap sheet a mile long. A bad one that one. I'd love to put him away for a long, long time."

"Jackson?"

"He killed your daughter, Mr. McDaniel. Unfortunately, I can't prove it. I can't prove much of anything. But it explains how the car used in the killing vanished. The mob's into that, too. They've been making cars vanish for years, most of them a lot fancier than that one."

"What do we do?"

"Get me motive. I'll do the rest."

"Motive? The company, what else?"

"He got it all; that's what I would guess."

I nodded. Why shouldn't he? Ronald was the surviving partner. It was to be expected that Ron would get it all. But was it all more than any of us imagined? I'd have to check on that. Who would know? My sons might. They were his friends, still. They would know more than me.

"But what brought her to Detroit?" I asked. "How did he get her here? And why, Detroit?"

Sergeant Berra was laughing now.

"Why not, Detroit? All kinds of bad things happen here. That's what the world thinks of us. So why not, Detroit?"

I nodded, halfheartedly.

Later, I tried, but I could not reach either of my sons.

CHAPTER 24

I went out looking for Charlie Eusted. He was where he always was, regardless of the weather. Charlie had company. Hey Hank was sitting alongside him, with his teeth set and his hands jammed into his jacket pockets. If Hey Hank had not been snuggled so closely up to Charlie at the edge of the bench, he would have been shivering more than he was. He gave me what amounted to a grin, if you are able to do that with your mouth frozen shut.

"Hey, guy," Charlie said. "Take a load off."

I hesitated to say what was driving me. I did not want to upset a young boy. Then I remembered that this boy — and all others down here — had seen far more than any white boy from the suburbs. I hurled myself onto the bench and raged at Charlie over the top of Hey Hank's hooded head.

"His name's Jackson," I said. "Edward Jackson."

Charlie didn't blink an eye. His gaze went out to the street and the small amount of traffic passing by. He seemed smaller, crushed into his wheelchair, a tiny figure buried in a depth of cloth.

"I don't know the name," he said.

"Sure, you do," I said. "You know everybody.

"Who told you that?"

"Which? The fact that you know everybody? Or the fact that Edward Jackson killed my daughter?"

A car was thumping its way up Woodward, being driven by an old woman with a red bandana over her hair. The car rode the edge of the lane near the curb.

"You don't understand things down here," Charlie said.

"Of course, I don't. Why should I?"

"You need to."

"I do?"

"Yes, you do." Charlie seemed smaller.

"All right, convince me. Murder's not murder. And the witness to a murder has no responsibility, because he lives in the New Center area. Like right here."

"Down here, things is different."

"You sound like a broken record, Charlie. Mind explaining how things are different? Different in what specific way? Different, by whose say-so?"

"That's not all of it."

"It's not?"

"No, it's not."

I felt like someone trying to peel an onion with gloves on. I was getting nowhere. I felt like I was going to get nowhere, no matter what I did. No matter how hard I tried. I looked at Hey Hank, who hadn't said a word. He had not even moved, but he was listening. I wondered if he knew what was going on, more than I did. He probably did. Everybody knew what was going on better than I did. I didn't know what was going on.

"We run a clean neighborhood," Charlie said.

"That's what I've heard. And the Weams family runs the rest."

Charlie looked at me. His mouth came open and a fog of breath floated out of it to fall silently into his dark beard.

"Weams?" he said.

"You know, the other guys? The bad guys with the bad breath and the little machine guns that go around lining people against walls to give them what-for. It's a bit messy, what they do. But they do it so damn well, who cares? Somebody's got to do what they do, right? Yes, Weams. Like the Mafia family but in your neighborhood, Charlie. They own a lot of cars, I hear. And drivers, too."

Charlie was silent for a long time.

"They leave us alone here," he said, finally.

I looked at him and felt hate bubble up out of the deep caverns where I had banished it. He was the wrong man to hate, but he was here, present and available like the wife who was there when the guy came home from the argument he lost at the bar.

"Sure, they do," I said. "You think I haven't noticed. If they didn't leave you alone, you'd be like the rest of the city, wallowing in drugs and violence and stuff. What do you do, bribe them?"

"That's exactly what we do."

"Bullshit," I said. "You don't have enough money. You cause them trouble, I think, if they don't leave you alone. The kind of trouble they don't need. Trouble creates attention, Charlie. You don't want it; they don't want it. So it's a kind of stand-off. That's what I think."

"You could say that."

"For the sake of the children," I said, placing a hand on Hey Hanks' small head.

"You don't live here," Charlie said.

"I do, now."

"No, you don't. You're merely visiting."

"I'm here," I said.

Charlie shook his head. "Not yet." he said.

"Ah, shit, " I said. "What do I do, Charlie? What do I do?"

"Nothin'," he said. "Don't do nothin'."

"It's not in my bones to do nothing, Charlie. I live by that old adage that says, 'When in doubt, do something!'"

"Not this time, Marc."

"Why?"

"Think about it."

"I don't want to think about it. Tell me."

"I can't."

"Damn you! Just damn you!"

I hurled myself off the bench, forcing a cry from Hey Hank. My hand had slipped from his head to his shoulder. I grasped it in a grip that tightened hard. I hurt Hey Hank even through the thickness of blue cloth. I rushed back the way I had come, kicking hard at the snow all the way. I did not feel the cold.

In my room, fully clothed, I threw myself onto my bed. I felt the thick pulsation of blood in my chest and in my neck and throat and head. A man had killed my daughter. I was encouraged to do nothing about it because of a family named Weams, who caused her death. My ex-son-in-law was a member of the Weams family. And the initiator, it appeared, of the sequence of events that led to Laura's death. What was I to do about that? All of a sudden, I wanted a man dead. I had never had that feeling before, in spite of all the nasty things that had happened to me on this occasion or that. But nobody had killed — or arranged to kill — one of mine before. Why shouldn't I want to kill him? Or see to his killing? And what of the actual killer? What should I do about him? What could I do about him? Nothing, probably. About both of them, nothing. I was not a killer. I might consider killing them, toy with the idea as a pleasure of the mind. But to do it —?

I have been told that anyone, given the motivation, can do anything. It's a basic policeman's presupposition. You don It have to look like you could do it to do it.

I leaped from the bed.

I ran outdoors and down the empty street. I was in such heat, I did not feel anything. My breath was steam pouring out of my mouth. I heated the world. When I stopped to think where I was, I found I had ice on my mustache. My lips mere thick with it. I rolled my tongue over the sheet, and the ice came away. I had snow on my head and on my shoulders. I was beginning to shake with cold. My hands were quivering. I had not found Edward Jackson anywhere, not on any corner and not on any street. I had no idea of what I would have done if I had found him. I would have done something.

Bubba stood beside me.

The big man said nothing, did nothing. He was simply there. I stared at him, my breath pouring out of me in white gulps. My chest heaved up and down, up and down, like an old and beaten drum. I stared at him trying to penetrate his impenetrable facade. I could not. He stood there silent, calm as Buddha, chin lifted, arms folded above his chest. He did not say anything. He did not do anything. His arms were as quiet as his lips. Nothing moved on him, except for the slow rise and fall of his chest. His face was in repose. Bubba gazed at me with eyes that did not blink. I thought: What's he doing here? How could he have found me known I where I would be at this moment? I didn't even know where I would be. How could he? I had questions, again, but no answers. This was not the man to ask.

I turned, an immense anger swelling every pore of my aching body. I stumbled my way home.

When I got to my apartment, Hey Hank was sitting like a tiny statue in front of my door.

"You might as well come in," I said, reaching over Hey Hank to unlock the locks and open the door. I stepped over him and dropped my boots onto the carpet. I dropped my jacket alongside them. I dropped my hat and gloves. I dropped the bright scarf I had wrapped around my neck. I went into my bathroom and set the tub to running. I was cold all the way to my bones. A hot bath would take care of that. A little alcohol, as well. I poured a glass of wine and took it with me as I shed things. I climbed into the water as the tub filled itself. I felt the heat crawl into me, and I ignored the prickly pain as it did. I sighed deeply, hurting. Hey Hank sat outside my bathroom door.

"Who taught you patience," I finally yelled. "You get that from your Mom?"

There was silence.

"A lesson learned from dear old Dad?"

There was silence.

"How about Charlie Eusted? Did he teach you?"

Silence. The quiet had a eerie sound

"Patience is a virtue, you know?" I said. "It is something you are blessed with when you get old."

Nothing. Not a word from Hey Hank.

"Believe that, and I'll tell you another," I said. "And I'll sell you the Brooklyn Bridge."

Not a sound.

"Damn!" I said. I kept my eyes closed and let the hot water take me away. As revealed in *Shogun*, a hot bath was a Japanese tradition we might all enjoy. Take me away, heat! Take me far away from here. Close your eyes, and you can be anyplace, Marc, I reminded myself. Close your eyes, and you can fly across the world. You don't have to come back. I don't want to come back, not anytime soon. And then I felt the fingertips on the back of my hand.

Margie's voice: "It's all right, Marc. Things aren't as bad as they seem. What you need to do is take a few deep breaths and let it all out, slowly. Stay in touch with your essential self while the world does as it pleases around you. Stay calm. That's all you need to do, Marc."

I opened my eyes, but there was no one there.

I pulled the plug on the tub by reaching over and tugging on a long chain. I listen to the gurgling sound; water revolving down the drain. Water whirled in slow circles. I listened carefully to the sound. Let go, Marc. Let it go. My troubles were running down this drain. I let them ride the tinted water, saw them spin around and vanish. I lifted from the tub and looked around, as if all things were new and fresh. They weren't. Where are you, Margie? Where have you gone from me? Why did you leave? I took a thick towel and wrapped myself in it and sat back down on the edge of the tub. I sat there for a long time as water ran out of the tub. As water ran down my face.

When I came out of the bathroom, Hey Hank was sitting on the floor with his back against the wall. His face was set, like a mask. It looked like an old man's face. He did not watch as I got dressed.

Then suddenly he started talking.

"My brother was killed," he said in words thundering like a belch. My little girl cousin was killed...shot from a car. She didn't do nuthin'.

Pa was killed in da prison. Somebody put a knife in him. I got a uncle killed as he walk along a street. White man did it...some think. We can't be sure. Uncle was drunk and staggering along. White kids, Black kids, all kill drunks, sometimes. It's something to do. Makes 'em see yo' tough."

I was listening, but I wasn't listening. Hey Hank was sliding from street talk to white talk, all mixed up. Somebody once said, "If you do not listen, you will not hear. And if you do not look, you will not see." I tried to see what Hey Hank was saying, but I couldn't hear or see. I was looking at Hey Hank, but I wasn't listening to him. He was an old man, wiser than me. I wasn't sure I would ever hear. Hey Hank was walking a line, a golden mean, but I could not follow.

"You're too young to know that," I said.

He looked at me with his big eyes.

"Nobody's young here," he said. "Not for long."

"Nobody is..." I laughed then. "In Detroit?"

"In this city," he said, not rising to the bait. "In the inner city, anywhere. What you white folk call it...the only city they is."

"How did you get to be so smart?" I said.

"I live here."

"Yes, you do." I held myself back from saying: Sorry about that. "But he killed her, Hey Hank. He did."

"Whatcha gonna do?"

"I don't know."

"You will."

I almost damned him. For impertinence, if nothing else. Hey Hank was too small to be a guru. He was too young to be so old. "A child shall lead you," someone once said. But I never believed it. If a child led us, we wouldn't get any where. Have you ever followed a child going anywhere? They are so easily distracted. A child's wisdom is built on the distractions.

"My mother wants you," Hey Hank said.

"Your mother..." I swallowed a dose of laughter and found myself thinking: Mother and son, saviors of the world. Ancient images were banging around inside my head.

But I reached for my clothes, grabbed Hey Hank by the hand, and headed out the door.

CHAPTER 25

Rebecca Coltrane sat in an easy chair in her living room and let her concern wash over me. "My mother was a witch," she told me. "There are powers we can use.

"A witch?"

"You might think to call her that."

"I don't know her."

"She's dead."

"But she gave you these powers?"

"She gave me nothing. She gave me everything."

"That makes no sense."

I sat across from her on a small sofa. A maple table sat between us. On the table was a small bouquet of flowers. In the midst of the flowers was a gold crucifix. There was nobody hanging on the cross.

"Do you always talk in riddles, Rebecca?"

"I use plain talk. I say what I mean." She gave me her glorious smile, the echo of her son's.

"Sure you do," I said.

I was enamored of Rebecca Coltrane and pleased to be in her presence again. She represented both beauty and mystery to me. Her hair, I saw, had a tint of red to it. I thought of the henna washed into the hair of a Pharaoh's daughter. There was a dancing in her eyes, and the color of her cheeks reflected the darkness of her irises. She was wearing a long gown, bright red in color, too rich for me, that made her glow and the chair she sat in shine as if it were formed of forged copper. There was a rug lying on her chair. It was African in design. There were a pair of black lions embroidered on it, roaming against a rusttinted hillside. One lion looked directly at me over Rebecca's left shoulder. It seemed alive.

"Shall I finish it for you?" she said.

"What?"

"The criticism," she said. "The one about male prerogatives. The one that says a woman should know her place and not disturb a man, ever. As in not bringing into view the possibility of witches and their power. Men tend to kill witches, after all."

"I wasn't thinking that."

"What were you thinking?"

What was I thinking? What a city! That's what I was thinking. Killing a man! That's what I was thinking. A lovely woman! That was part of my thought. I had a collage of disparate images in my head, none of which went together. What should I be thinking?

I raised my hands and shook my head.

"I could put a hex on them."

Rebecca laughed at me. It was a lovely laughter.

Hey Hank sat on the other side of the room, staring out a window, saying nothing. It was his job, apparently, to say nothing unless asked. He was good at his job.

"You loved your daughter," Rebecca said, quietly.

It was not put as a question, but I reacted to it as if it were.

"Yes, I loved her."

"And he did not?" The smile was gone, but the compassion remained. Rebecca's head was cocked to one side, a posture for listening carefully.

"I don't know. She married him. So she thought he loved her. What else do you have to go on?"

"Of course," Rebecca said.

"Of course," I said. "People lie. They lie as often with what they do as with what they say. He said he loved her; he made love to her. What more is there?"

"There's more," Rebecca said.

"Our world is based on lies, Rebecca," I said. "The truth is not in them."

"That's a quote, is it not?" Rebecca said.

"Close enough," I said. "Honesty is what the country needs. But we won't get it. No commercial gets built around the truth. Only one was, and it was a lie at heart. Most lies are harmless. That's the story."

"No lie is harmless," Rebecca said, echoing a sermon of mine preached long ago to people who could not hear. I sometimes cannot hear, myself.

"The power of words," I said.

"You understand that, too?"

"It's Biblical," I said. "'My word shall not return to me void.' A thing spoken has a way of fulfilling itself."

"I could love you," Rebecca teased, "if you weren't a white man." She was still smiling.

"Why should that make a difference?"

"It doesn't. I was joking. A way of getting at the truth, you see...slant."

"Dickinson," I said. "I like her poetry, too."

"A white woman," Rebecca smiled. "A sister of mine."

"I have an unending argument with God," I said. "God made a mass of people with a mess of languages. Any respectable creator could do better."

Rebecca quoted: "Tell the Truth, but tell it slant — /Success in Circuit lies/too bright for our infirm Delight/The Truth's superb surprise."

And I responded: "My Maker — let me be/Enamored most of thee — /But nearer this/I more should miss —."

Then we rested in our separate thoughts, feeling as close together as we could get, given who we were.

There were people in my apartment, a lot of them, more than the two rooms could hold. I knew Denys and Alicia and Charlie Eusted. The others were friends from the party I attended at the Fowler's house. The party-goers were here that were there. I was not certain of that. Maybe all of the party-goers, plus a few. The people were talking and eating, and drinking refreshments they brought with them. I eased my way through my door, leaving behind the complaining chatter of Mrs. Hedley out in the hall. Alicia greeted me and, tugging at my arm, pulled me toward the window where Charlie and Denys were located. The crowd, jammed together as they were, made way for me slowly. A number of people patted me on the back as I slid by. There were supportive comments made to me, words of encouragement. There were a number of sincere smiles on various faces.

I raised my hands to Denys and Charlie, while mouthing the words, "What's going on?"

I wasn't sure they could hear me over the noise. A big boom-box was making what sounded like music in a corner. I thought, maybe, it was rap I was hearing.

Denys came close and cupped a hand over my ear, his mouth inside the cup. "Thought we'd have a party, Marc. It was your turn to play host. We didn't have a chance to tell you."

"Thanks," I yelled.

I made out "...welcome," before his hand pulled away. Charlie Eusted pulled Denys down to tell him something. Four feet away, I could make out nothing but noise.

A drink was placed in my hand and I made use of it. It was nearly dark outside, but inside it was very bright. I had the feeling that some of the parties these people held were in places worse than mine. Maybe even smaller than mine. Nobody was paying much attention to my apartment. They were intent on each other. Soon, we were all roaring. All it took to have a good party was to gather together a number of people who liked being together. Very obviously, these people did. I expected cops to show up at my door before the evening was over. But maybe all the tenants knew that Charlie Eusted, the owner, was inside. Maybe they allowed for an occasional beer blast. Maybe a lot of things.

By the time everybody left, I was exhausted. Charlie was the last person to leave, just after Denys and Alicia said their goodbyes, Alicia making a fuss over leaving me. Bubba came in to get Charlie. He rolled the bulky wheelchair through my doorway, then picked up Charlie and the chair. He carried both man and chair down the front stairs, passing through the whooshing door I held open. Bubba did not pause to thank me. He was doing his job and me mine.

When everyone had gone, I turned off the lights and lay down on the bed. I got to wondering what had been said by the party that had just taken place. The fuzziness in my mind locked onto the issue. I couldn't let it go. There had to be a reason, more than the fun involved. That's what my suspicious nature said to me. I made a guess as to what the purpose of the gathering had been. The thought annoyed me and pleased me at the same time.

I had not called for help — or cried for it — but it had come to me, anyway. I was an accepted one, the party had declared to the neighborhood. Best to leave me alone.

Then I got to thinking of my visit to Rebecca Coltrane. I got to thinking about what I had been thinking then, about killing a man. I didn't know how to go about it, I concluded. And I shouldn't go about it. Years in the ministry had not prepared me to be a killer. I might pray for marines going off to war, as I did during the Vietnam years, but I had no dealings with war. But what of my daughter's killer? Couldn't vengeance be mine?

I tried to sleep, but it would not come. I stared at the frame of yellow light surrounding the blinds on the window. I could even see the light when my eyes were closed. It poured into my brain, like a picture frame surrounding an image that moved, refusing to stay still. My mind went back over my thoughts, reiterating them again and again like a film stuck in a machine, recycling over and over. What was I to do? What was I to do? What was I to do? Then it was morning, and I could not figure out where the night had gone. I only knew I did not want it back.

I woke up, because the phone was ringing. My son, Rick, was on the line. He had gotten my message. It wasn't the message that made him anxious, but my tone of voice. "What's troubling you, Dad? It's we who trouble you all the time. Seems strange to have you sounding so anxious. What is it that's troubling you, Dad?"

Before I thought about it, I told him.

Silence, when I was through.

Then Rick said, "Geez, Dad! Don't tell Jim."

I asked him why not.

"Jim'll kill the guy."

I said I didn't have proof. Jim wouldn't do anything, when all I had were suspicions.

"Jim won't need proof," Rick said.

"Do you need proof?" I said.

Silence, for a long minute.

"I dunno, Dad. I can't picture Ron doing it. Why would I think Ron did it? Nobody suggested Ron. Laura was killed in Detroit, not here. Geez, I dunno, Dad. Ron loved her, didn't he? Once upon a time?"

"Laura never said otherwise," I said. "But Laura wouldn't say, would she? She kept a lot of things to herself. Maybe we didn't listen good enough to what she told us. Maybe I didn't. People don't fall out of love in a minute. It takes years, normally. Ron loved her for time, but it ended."

"I remember us talking about it, Dad. Ron was older than Laura; thirteen years, wasn't it? She was very young back then when they started the business. Ron let her be president of the firm to protect the investment from his ex-wife, remember? He was a technical engineer, anyway. He didn't deal well with people. So Laura ran the business and got good at it. She grew into the job and became quite a woman in the process. She got strong, Dad. Ron didn't like that, but it left him free to do as he pleased."

"Yes," I said. "I'm with you. I don't think Ron appreciated a strong woman as partner. Emotionally, he took himself away from her. Laura lamented it that the magic was gone, but that happens in relationships."

"Do you think he killed her, Dad?"

"It looks that way to me now. But it can't be for that reason, Rick. Under her leadership, the business was doing well. They had a firm niche in Silicon Valley. He wouldn't kill the goose that made that happen."

"But something to do with the business?"

"I think so. It would be the most likely motivation. But how would he benefit from Laura being gone?"

"He's selling it, Dad. I thought you knew."

I felt like I had been kicked in the gut.

"It's in the papers, Dad. A Japanese firm, I think. A Pacific Rim country, anyway. I'll look it up for you. He's going to get rich off of this."

"Damn!" I said. "Laura would never sell it. The business was her baby. The employees were her children. She was always seeing to their welfare. No other company would do things as Laura did them. He's going to sell it?"

"Yes, Dad. The article said something about his grief over the loss of his ex-wife. It mentioned how he missed her expertise in running things. He said he didn't have the desire to continue the business without her."

"Truth is, he couldn't run it without her," I said.

"What are you thinking, Dad?"

"If he had decided they should sell the business before she died, and she didn't want to..."

"He might kill her. Or arrange for her death, if he's connected back there, as you say"

Jim and I were thinking along the same track. But I still felt uncertain.

"Especially if Ron felt nothing at all for her. She'd merely be somebody in the way."

Just somebody-in-the-way? Was that how it was viewed when you were a gangster? If somebody's in the way, you get them out of the way. As simple as that. Too damned simple, it seemed to me.

"We need to know why she came to Detroit," I said. "Without that, we have nothing, Rick."

"I'll ask him," Rick said. "I like the guy, Dad. I can't believe this. But I'll ask him as if it's bothering me. Which it is. Maybe Ron will say something incriminating. He must know why. I'll let you know what he says."

"I know you like him," I said. "Ron's a nice guy, easy to get along with. We just didn't know him as well as we should have, apparently."

"We didn't try to find out."

"No, we didn't."

CHAPTER 26

I went looking for St. Edward's Catholic Church and found it. Its tall steeples were an easy mark. I entered the nave and passed through into the sanctuary. I was out of my element to anyone intent on noticing. I did not light a smoking candle, I did not cross myself, I did not kneel. I sat in a pew halfway down the long aisle to the sacristy and composed myself to wait. I did not expect Father Rene would be there. But I was mistaken. In moments, he was by my side. Someone intent on noticing had passed the word to the tiny priest. Rene sat quietly by my side, waiting. I let the waiting go on. Father Rene did not mind. He was at home in this place. As with every good priest, the sanctuary gave him comfort. The statuary, the stained glass, the smell of incense held him as a baby is held in a warm blanket.

"The word is on the street," Father Rene said after a time. "I'm glad you came."

"Do you hear everything?" I asked. "Do you know everything that goes on around here?"

"I wish. There are many secrets. I hear some."

"They killed her, Rene. He killed her."

"That is what I hear. You are in pain."

"Pain? I am raging, Rene. I feel no pain."

"It is the conflict," he said.

"What conflict?"

"The usual one, between belief and grief. How am I to believe when this has happened to me?"

"If that's what you think, you are mistaken."

"In moments of grief, belief gets tested. It is then, in that place between, that a human being finds out who he or she is."

"You getting philosophical on me?"

"No. Simply practical."

"The stages on the way," I said, flatly. "Anger comes first."

Rene turned to look at me, his eyes brimming with compassion, his thin hand reaching over to touch my knee. I was surprised at how cold the touch was.

"Will you recover?" he asked, quietly.

"You're asking me?"

"Who am I to ask?"

"Your God, of course. God knows everything, doesn't he? The holy, omniscient One can envision the future, right?"

"Do not mock God."

"I can't mock someone I no longer believe in."

"On the contrary, it is then that you can."

"Then, I do," I said.

There was the sound of a sharp, indrawn breath. I thought that Father Rene was going to flee from me, as from the devil. His hands were shaking, but he did not leave me.

"You stand on the edge of a precipice, Marc," Father Rene said, being what he was to his core, a priest. "Heed this warning, my friend. Do not endanger your soul."

"You would warn me!" I said.

My gut stirred, and I could feel a hardening of muscle tone. I had a hand on the back of the pew in front of me. It was either hit Rene, hard, or leave. When I dared look at him, I could find no trace of fear in his eyes. I was the one who fell away, jamming my stiff back against the pew. I slammed hard enough against the wood to cause me to gasp. I lifted my shoulders, but could not reach where it hurt.

"I am not the one you should be talking to," Rene said, finally. "I am not the one."

"I thought I could talk to you, and you would understand," I yelled at his receding back. "Obviously, I was wrong."

Father Rene did not answer me, but walked to the front of the sanctuary and crossed himself. His hands folded in prayer. Kneeling, he seemed such a small figure that I felt sorry for him. Who would hear such a little man's prayer? I knew who he expected would hear.

Above him hung a figure on a cross. It was a rustic carving, a figure the likes of which I had never seen. No crucifix looked like it. The hanging figure was small and the agony on his face immensely large. That agony, I felt, could swallow the world.

Outside of the church, the wind was cold on my face. I wiped at my face so that it wouldn't freeze. I did not want frozen streaks on my soft skin. I willed myself to go slowly down the hard concrete steps of St. Edward's. I walked carefully for there was ice on them. It was slippery ice. Except by the railing on the side of the stairs, where somebody had sprinkled salt. The salt was green until it melted. Green ran up the length of the stairs like a carpet.

A man stood across the street, fingering his ever-present cigarette. Mr. Edward Jackson smiled at me. The man had killed my daughter, and now he was trailing me, smiling at me, mocking me, threatening me. The man had killed my daughter by running her over with a car. Now he was covering his ass, perhaps. Or looking to cover it.

I crossed the street and stood in front of Mr. Jackson. I stared deeply into his battered face. He looked back like a cat amused by the odd antics of a strange mouse. Did I actually think I could hurt him? Didn't I know that any physical harm I might do had been done before. I was merely old news. Could the man know fear, I asked myself. I didn't know how to answer the question. I didn't know how to answer any question — or even ask it — so I gave up. I wasn't certain what point I had made, except to confront my own fear. Perhaps, that. After long minutes, while he blew smoke constantly into my face, I turned away from him and walked off. Squaring my back to Edward Jackson, killer, I strolled down the street toward home. There was a peculiar tingling sensation in the middle of my back. Head high, I was offering myself as target.

Nothing happened.

At my apartment, I found a car by the curb with a door coming open on the passenger side. In the driver's seat sat Sergeant Berra. He did not look at me. I sighed heavily and slid onto the seat alongside him. I wondered if I should buckle up, but did not.

Sergeant Berra was whistling, but no sound was coming from between his lips except f or the bleat of air, itself. Finally, he turned to me. There was muted anger in his eyes. I expected a lecture and received it.

"That was stupid," he said.

I said nothing.

"He's out to get you at this stage. One way or the other, he's out to get you."

I said nothing.

"The way you reacted, facing up to him like you did, now he'll have to kill you. He'll figure you don't scare. So he'll have to."

"He knows I can't prove anything," I said.

"He knows shit. All he knows is that you are a threat to him. More all the time. So he'll have to kill you."

"That won't get you off his back."

"You don't see it, do you?"

"See what?"

"Death is a way of life around here."

I opened my mouth, but nothing came out. I was hearing an echo in my head — *Death is a way of life* — and I was trying to adjust to the fact that Sergeant Berra meant sudden death, death that was violent and cruel and quick. It was the kind of death you talk about in war; nobody easing into a peaceful sleep at the natural end of a long life.

"Read the papers," Sergeant Berra added. "Almost any day. The gang killings you hear about. Old ladies robbed, raped and killed. Kids shot on the playgrounds or on the sidewalks in front of their parent's houses. Any day, you can read about it. Sometimes, for days in a row. Find out if I'm kidding you. Read about it."

"It can't be that bad."

"Of course, it ain't," he said.

I was silent, because he was not kidding. I remembered some things in the papers but had not paid them much attention. It was what I expected to see about Detroit. So death had not struck me. People were dying all around, and I had not noticed, not enough to care.

"What do you want me to do?"

"Leave this fuckin' stuff to me."

"I'm not sure I can."

"Look! As long as you're around here, stirring things up, but staying alive, I can stay focused on this. But when you're gone, nobody's going to care. You got me? If you leave here...or get yourself killed...there's nobody to care. The whole business dies."

"The police give it up? I would think..."

"Forget it! We have hundreds of unsolved cases. Thousands. More every day. Another one just about every day; we can count on it. You figure it."

I stared at him while my mind turned over in a turmoil, trying to grasp at realities, trying to know what was the thing to do.

"It don't mean nothing to me," Sergeant Berra said, as if it were his final word on the subject.

"You'll stay on it?" I said. "As long as I'm around?"

"What do you think?"

"But how...?

"It helps, believe me, your being around," he said. "You got me interested. I have my bosses thinking I might actually solve this thing.

And get them some other answers, too. You've got clout, Mr. McDaniel. Even if you don't know it, you've got clout. Being an outsider; being an educated man; being Somebody from Somewhere. I use that, don't you see? Image. Mr. McDaniel. Detroit has this image a lot of people are trying to change. All right, there have been riots and killings here. Downtown is dangerous. But they're going to build stadiums and casinos here. Lots of money, you know? Image. Detroit's got to be seen as a safe place. It is a safe place. That's what they want everyone to believe."

"Image is everything," I said, disconsolately.

"You got it."

"I don't want it. Detroit's not my problem."

"Yes, it is. Your daughter was killed here. Okay, so it was initiated in California...Silicon Valley, no less. But the deed was done here. So you got to deal with Detroit, like it or not."

"Meaning you?"

"Meaning me. And this city."

"So what do I do now?" I said.

"Hang tough. That's all I can tell you. But don't be confrontational. Not with that guy, anyway."

Sergeant Berra rubbed at the steering wheel as if it were a comforting friend. His hands rolled down the black circle from top to bottom, from top to bottom. I pictured a large-bosomed woman, and found a different expression on Sergeant Berra's face when I looked again. He had gotten what he wanted from me. I wondered if he had any women friends, at all.

"And what do you do?" I said.

"First, I'll hassle Mr Jackson. See if I can get him to think of me enough to leave you alone. I'll inform him that if anything happens to you, I'm going to assume he did it. He won't want that. He knows me."

I already knew that I wouldn't want that.

My answering machine was full of a single repeated message. My son, Jim, had been told what was going on. Rick told him. Jim was — as we thought he would be — raging. But his anger was directed at me.

He couldn't have done it," were Jim's first words. "Not Ron. He's a competitor, sure. But he plays fair. He sure wouldn't kill to get what he wants."

"He didn't kill," I said. "He just arranged it."

"He didn't do it, Dad. He wouldn't."

"Look, son. I know how you liked the guy. You and Jim both liked the guy. It burned your sister up because you kept liking him even after."

"He is honorable, Dad."

"Is he? How do you know that, Jim? How can you be so sure?"

"I know, that's all."

"Okay, now we're dealing with your ego, your feelings about the man. But tell me how you know."

"I don't. I just..."

"Jim, ask any cop. Anybody is capable of doing anything, whether we think so or not. What we're talking about, now, is plenty of motivation. Millions of dollars worth. It breaks through the barriers of self-limitation. Money has caused a lot of problems in this world. A single death, it seems, is among the least of them."

"He wouldn't..."

"Wouldn't he? That's the kicker, Jim, isn't it? For a few million dollars, what would you do? What would your brother do? What would I do?"

I could see Jim's mind clicking. What would he do with a million dollars. Fulfill his obligations and still have a bundle of money to enjoy his freedom. That's what you could buy: things; a soothed conscience, perhaps; time. It is how Americans judge themselves, by the amount of money each one had. Why not count from the top?

"Ron doesn't come from Detroit," Jim said, forcing the argument. "He's from San Bernadino."

"If what I'm hearing is correct, Ron has family roots in Detroit."

"That's bull."

"How would you know, son? We didn't meet the guy until he married your sister. What did he tell you about himself? What has he told anybody? We know nothing, Jim, beyond what Ron told us. We accepted that. Why shouldn't we? He lived in San Bernadino, he said. Why go back further?"

"But Weams?"

"I know. No, I don't know. I'm finding out. It's what the police here tell me. That's all I know. Ron's real name is Weams. And he has close connections here among gangsters and killers. Why would he tell us that?"

Jim hemmed and hawed, but at least the anger had dissipated and was not so forcefully directed at me. Anger was still there, but it was without specific focus. It lay in him like an unbearable pain.

"Anything else you want to talk about, son?" I said into developing ilence. Jim told me, no. He was simply stewing, and this problem nerely added to all the rest. He didn't know what to do about any of hem. The most minor of his difficulties was the hotel he was in, as his lane had been forced to sit on a runway and go nowhere. He felt lucky o have a room at all. Passengers come first, it says here. Jim laughed t his own comment. The airline took care of him better than he leserved. Most of the time.

"Thanks for being so blunt, Dad," he said, as closure. "I used to hate ou for it, but now I find I do it myself. We all become our parents, I uess."

I laughed at him, for neither of my sons would ever be me. I would ot let that happen.

CHAPTER 27

I stood above the roar of traffic, out of the snow by the protection o the railroad bridge overhead. The freeway below me was coated in a white curtain, cars running out of a clear zone and back into thicker whiteness. There was no wind to speak of, so the large flakes o snow fell peaceably down.Wipers on the vehicles cleared them away but an accumulation was gathering on the roofs of cars and trucks. The heat of an engine melted snow away, revealing shape and color. If I had been an artist, I would probably have painted the colors as living and vibrant. They were the careful brush strokes of a Cezanne, the accu mulation of which gave you value of depth and line. Here, the brush strokes would not sit still. There was, therefore, no painting to gaze a or meditate upon.

Gregory Barton dreamed here, I told myself. In one of his dreams he slid down this long, cinder-block slope, then walked out into traffic He was crushed going onto the first lane by a big Mack truck. Greg did a lot of thinking here, Marilyn Lanlaw had told me. The traffic noise had the effect of white-noise, under cover of which a mind might work its wondrous magic. Thinking required an aloneness, which Greg found here. In so many ways, the man was like me. If I lived here, I would need a place like this, though I would rather be out in the woods by a rolling stream. Obviously, when in the city, you made do.

I turned my back to the traffic below me and looked around. It wa late afternoon, and all the place looked like was cold. Its gray wall and floor were streaked and stained. The train tracks above led to Hamtramck, once a truck-building center called Poletown, because o all the Polish people living there. And, of course, Grand Boulevard ran above me. It was a roadway surrounded by industry, if you went east Grand Boulevard circled the city of Detroit from the New Center area to the Detroit River. Industry was gone now. Gutted buildings remained, rusted-out and broken-windowed and crumbled brick, the result of years of unuse. I looked along the dull slot as it ran along the slope leading to the freeway. I walked along the edge looking down. It would be easy to slide downhill, step into traffic and die.

Back at the apartment, my rooms looked gloomier than before. What to do? I dug in my pockets. Marilyn Lanlaw had given me her phone number. Now was the time to call it. It wasn't too late in the evening to call, I hoped. Perhaps she wouldn't mind talking to me some more. About him, of course. About death, naturally. About him.

She answered on the second ring.

"Sorry, if I'm disturbing you."

"Who is this?"

I told her, including an apology if my timing was bad.

"Oh. That's all right. I'm just settling in for an evening of easy listening. That's Mahler, you're listening to. I hope you won't mind if I leave it on."

"Sounds good to me."

"How are you doing?"

"Okay, I guess. Maybe, not. I need to talk about, you know."

"That's fine. I'm past grieving, so it's okay. If it proves not to be, I'll let you know, and we'll stop. Okay?"

"Fine. Yes, that's fine."

"What do you want to know?"

I said, "I still don't know how he died, Marilyn. No one seems to be able to tell me. I hear he was murdered. I hear he was a suicide. I don't know what to believe."

"I don't know, either she said. "Not for certain. The police report said it was an accident but that there were indications it might have been suicide. There are some who think the police have evidence they are not releasing, just in case, you know?"

"In case of what, Marilyn?"

"In case Greg turned out to be the last victim of the war."

"What war?" I said.

"Oh, you don't know? You really don't know? I...?" She let it hang, her words mixing smoothly with Mahler's Ninth Symphony. Then I was listening only to music, as if the mouthpiece of the phone was now directed away from Marilyn's mouth and toward the CD player. Perhaps the phone lay in her lap, and she fiddled with it. I could hear a clicking, like fingernails on plastic.

"Marilyn? Marilyn?"

"I'm sorry. I thought you knew. You were with Denys and Alicia Fowler. I thought you were one of them."

"One of whom, Marilyn? What are you talking about?"

"I'm sorry. It's a little war, that's what I've called it. Just over those few streets. You didn't know? What am I saying? I shouldn't be telling you. It's over now, anyway. At least, I hope it is. Greg would want it to be."

"Marilyn?"

I had the feeling she wanted to hang up on me but felt it impolite to do so. She became quiet, letting me bear the weight of conversation.

"Let me guess, okay?" I said. "It was a only a little war, except it was a different kind of war. It was over cleaning a few streets, the streets where I'm living. How am I doing?" I was praying she didn't hang up on me. But who against whom? Oh, God! "Charlie Eusted and company. Am I right?" Come on, Marilyn, I urged, tell me something. Tell me, yes; tell me, no; tell me something. "Alicia and Denys and the rest are claiming the streets around here as a safe zone, sort of, where I am living." Still, no affirmation from Marilyn. A new thought struck me. "Against the Weams family, right? That's who runs drugs and stuff around here. The Weams family. Like the Mafia. So they went to the mattresses," I laughed, speaking right out of dozens of old gangster movies. "until they worked out a compromise. Just these few streets. That's what Charlie Eusted watches over when he sits out there in the cold. He's holding the line for the residents, against hoodlums."

Marilyn said nothing. I waited, holding my breath. The whole idea seemed preposterous, something out of a fiction story. How could anybody hold off a gang, when the entire United States government had trouble doing that? This city was replete with gangs. What resources would Charlie Eusted have to use against a mob? A few veterans of various wars, some foreign, some domestic? How could any of them hold off an entrenched system of violence?

"Marilyn," I said. "Assume I know. Tell me what I don't know. I have a right to know"

"He died," she said, simply. "He was not anywhere near the war, not in his heart or in his mind. He was a peaceable man, a gentle man. He would never hurt anyone, deliberately. Not ever."

"You mean, Greg?"

"But just because he lived there, they assumed..." Marilyn's voice faded away into silence. I pictured tears slipping down. She was dabbing at her eyes, using a tissue from a box at her elbow. She was working hard to compose herself. Mustn't reveal any weakness. Must be always strong. Must be what you can't always be, when you're talking to a man.

"Marilyn, it was an accident, right?"

"Yes, I think so. Both sides assumed things that were not true, not about Greg. He didn't choose sides. He wanted a better life for everybody, but he was concerned with the means, too. He would not condone violence, not even against other violence. Violence shattered any chance for harmony, Greg often said. And it killed the voice of the moderates. Then nobody would listen to anybody, anymore."

"So the compromise gave Charlie a few streets to watch over, and it gave the Weams family less violence to deal with in their territory they controlled? It must have been hell to arrange. You don't bargain with killers."

I was still saying things I was guessing at, but it seemed true enough. It has often been said that America was a violent country and, earlier in our history, anyway, some balance of forces kept violence in check. We don't get rid of criminals, but we limit their impact. We don't get rid of prostitution, but we keep it under control. We don't get rid of thieves in high place, either, but we jail the worst abusers of privilege. People honest with themselves see it as a kind of balancing act. We can't change who we basically are, but we can work together to control life, to keep it safe if not sane.

"Did Greg try to intervene?"

"Exactly," Marilyn mumbled. I listened to a few sobs, accenting some of the world's finest music. Then she added, "Each thought he worked for the other side. I don't know which side killed him."

"He was killed, then?"

"There was no proof, and it looked like he took his own life, which Greg would never do."

"You loved him," I said. "You still do."

There was silence.

"How do you stay in love with a memory?" she said.

I knew the answer to that question, but I could not put it into words. Better to stick to the subject.

"So it looked as if Greg killed himself," I said. "But the police may have some evidence suggesting otherwise. Of course, they're not saying anything. But with Greg's death, a series of killings stopped?"

"Yes, Marc. Other things, too. In the block you live in, there are no drugs being sold. Or violence, except on occasion, for which there is immediate retribution. Then it quiets until the next time. That block of streets is safe, comparatively."

"But across the street?" I said, thinking of a rape a priest told me about and a beating I received, my self. "Outside a few blocks, it all goes on as before. Nobody can stop it. Sounds like you've made a study."

"No. I just kind of keep track, Marc. I think you'd be like that, too. So I'm glad you know now. It helps to know somebody else can see what you see."

"So what can be done about it?" I asked.

I could visualize a slow smile forming, and it made me wish I knew this woman better. Maybe that could happen. But not in this moment. I was facing relational hazards enough. Connection had to wait; other things were more important to me right now.

"Nothing," she said. "At least, nothing I can think of. Perhaps it's better if nothing is done right now."

"Maybe," I said.

CHAPTER 28

I couldn't sleep. I tossed and turned and had snatches of dreams that seemed to surround me like a pack of wolves intent on feasting. I could not remember any of them, when I climbed out of my restlessness in the morning. Sleep was a thing desired, but it had eluded me and left me with slips of rest that made me more tired than I was before I went to bed. I staggered into the bathroom and showered long enough to drain the tension from my shoulders. The effort left me without any energy. I spread a thick layer of peanut butter on a piece of toast, thinking to replace what I had lost. It was expecting a bit much.

I threw on my clothes and went looking for Charlie Eusted and I found him in the usual place. I sat down heavily on the bus stop bench, alongside his wheelchair.

"I'll tell you what I know," I said.

He did not respond. He was writing in his little book, and his eyes were on a pair of men holding each other up on the far side of the street. I assumed he knew them, but I was not sure of that. He scribbled in his book and closed it with a flourish. He stuck it into his pocket and rubbed his heavy hands together. He did not look at me. It was as if I was not there.

"I'll tell you what I know," I said, again, louder this time. He could not help but hear. He would have heard me if he were deaf.

"You don't know nothing," he said.

"I know what I know, Charlie."

"I don't care what you think you know. Study your German, Marc. There are two kinds of knowing. You don't know nothing."

"I took German in college," I said. "It was required, more or less. So I understand you. The German language has two words for our one word. To know, as in knowing the details that make up something. And to know, as in being familiar with. I know some details, Charlie. Let's put that against your familiarity with Detroit."

Charlie turned to me, smiling slightly.

"I keep underestimating you, Marc McDaniel. You're more than you appear to be," he said.

"So indulge me, Charlie. Talk to me."

Charlie stuck his hands into the pockets of his coat. He leaned back and looked around. Nothing of consequence was happening on the street.

"They got back from the war," he said. "Some good kids came back. They took a lot of shit, but there was nothing to be done about it."

"You mean, Vietnam? That was a few years ago."

"Not so many. Their war. A different war. Different homecoming, too. You understand it was different?"

"I was at a church near Camp Pendleton in California, dealing with Marines that took that shit, too. The whole scene was unfair and screwy. The guys all got caught in the middle."

Charlie looked as if he were going to object to something I said. Then he let it go and got on with what he had determined to tell me.

"A few years ago, we had us had a meeting," Charlie said. "It wasn't planned, but it happened. We decided to make use of the skills our fine government taught us. Take back the streets of Detroit for the people."

"This block of streets," I said. "Your idea?"

Charlie nodded.

"We ended up with only a few, but that's something. On these streets, right here, a few people are relatively safe. More like normal city life, say."

"But there are drugs here," I said.

"Yes, there is," Charlie said. "But nobody sells drugs here. Across the street, maybe. Not here."

Charlie glanced up Woodward, and I followed his gaze. There was an old, decrepit house across the street with a front porch on which I had seen men congregate. It was an obvious spot for using and selling. Cars slowed by, going south. Some stopped. Often, the same cars had circled the block in some sort of ritual. I had noticed but had not given it much attention. I figured drugs went on here and were tolerated, being impossible to stop.

I turned to look behind us, up and down a few streets. How many, actually, I wondered. I had been here only a little while, but I could guess. Accurately, I thought.

"No peddlers? No crack house?" I said.

"No. We don't allow it."

I said, "How do you stop it?"

"Fear," Charlie said. "Like in Vietnam. We're merchants of fear." He smirked, his lips cracking.

"You're proud of that?" I said.

"We're proud of nothing," Charlie said. "We're doing what we think needs to be done. That's all."

"But your not against drugs? Or against the crime that comes with it? How can that be?"

Charlie sighed, sagging in his wheelchair.

"What we are is for the people who live here. We want them free to make choices. That's it. If they are after drugs, they can get it by crossing the street. It's like going to the store. But we don't let the hustlers intrude into their home space. As it is, they're free to choose. As you can tell, a lot of them choose to be free of drugs. At least, relatively. Crime, too. Capers are allowed, sort of. Not heavy stuff. You ever read about inner-city drug life? Nobody can stop it."

"Everybody tries," I said, thinking of all the effort of communities and of governments. "You don't think anything can work?"

"The effort comes from outsiders," Charlie says. "What do they know about such a life?"

"Can't you tell them?"

Charlie laughed that uproarious laugh of his. He laughed until he was crying, and he had to take a gloved hand from one pocket and wipe his face.

"Tell them?" Charlie said. "Nobody listens."

"If they did?"

He settled down, thinking, while his eyes roamed the streets, as watchful as a hawk's.

"Tell them to read a book called, *The Corner*," he said. "It's about inner-city Baltimore, written by a news reporter and a cop. But they got it pretty right."

"Baltimore is not Detroit," I said.

"No," laughed Charlie. "It's worse. Maybe."

"And the Weams family?" I said.

Charlie turned to look at me.

"I can't help you with that," he said. "There are certain agreements. We'll hold up our end. Which means that what happened to your daughter happened out of our territory. We have no jurisdiction."

It was my turn to laugh.

"You sound like a cop, Charlie," I said. "Out of your jurisdiction? It happened just across the street, over there on the corner."

"But it was across the street."

"So you won't help me?"

Charlie said nothing. I swallowed developing anger and asked, "Where does the fear come from? What do you merchants of fear do? You injure people? You kill? You cut out a boy's tongue, dammit!"

"That wasn't meant to happen. Not where it did."

"Out of your territory, right? You got yourself a loose cannon, Charlie? One of you doesn't approve of the limitations your agreements set, right? C'mon, Charlie. What's happening here?"

"We're meeting about that, tonight," Charlie said. "I will arrange for you to be there. Okay?"

The totally unexpected had suddenly happened, and I was at a loss to respond. Charlie seemed to shrink into himself, and I expected at any moment to find myself lifted to my feet by a big, burly man called Bubba. More than to my feet; lifted into the air and tossed out into the middle of traffic. If I survived that, I would find him tramping his big feet onto my head until it was pulp. I had offended the man Bubba worshiped, or trapped him in a corner, or something. Nobody gets by with offending Charlie Eusted. Nobody. Not while Bubba was around.

Nothing happened to me.

At my door was Hey Hank, looking like Bubba had just punished him.

"She don't understand," Hey Hank cried, as I took him by the arm and ushered him into my rooms. Hey Hank was crying unconsolably, as if his world had just ended.

"What happened?" I asked.

"We're moving," Hey Hank said. "We're going to California. I don't want to go there. I want to live here."

"California's a nice place," I said. "I lived there for a while. Good weather all the time. Great beaches. You'll like it, Hey Hank. It's quite a place."

"I don't want to go."

"You want to stay here?"

"I live here. I've always lived here. My friends live here. I don't know any other place. And Grandma's house is here. I don't want to leave."

Every sentence was a gasp, a breathing between sobs. I have seen upset kids, but none more than this. Between the pile of sentences came the phrase, again and again. "She don't understand! She don't understand!" More than anyone I knew, I thought, Hey Hank's mother would understand.

I waited for a break in the jerking of the small boy and asked, "Why, Hey Hank? Why does she want to go to California? What's out there for her?"

"A guy," Hey Hank said, vehemently. "That's what it is. A damned guy!"

"Who?" I said.

"This dude she thinks she's in love with, that's who. Name of Rafael McHallius. He's gonna be an actor. Got him a part in a movie comin' out. Makin' a lot of money."

"Well, it's nice she knows someone," I said.

Inside, I was feeling turmoil. I had this sudden desire to make love with Rebecca Coltrane. I could see her lithe body moving on a bed, my arms around her as we did what a few special couples did, both of us enjoying it immensely. I dismissed the image, forcibly, and focused on a small boy's pain. It was a common one, but no less a pain for all that. Moving was the American lifestyle. Who stayed where they were born, anymore? Who stayed long anywhere, anymore?

"Sure," Hey Hank said, bitterly. A gentle knock came from my door. I opened it to Rebecca Coltrane and all the lovely feelings rose up to swamp me.

"I thought he might be here," she said. She walked easily past me and sat down alongside Hey Hank on my bed. She put a long arm around him and he fell into her breasts and wrapped his arms as far as he could around her. She kissed him on the top of his curly, dark hair. They wept together, as friends do even when they disagree.

"When do you go?" I said.

"Tomorrow. We're flying out. I'll come back after a while to have our things sent out there. But Rafael wants us, now. He wants to show Hey Hank all there is to see out there. If Hey Hank still doesn't like it, well..."

She shrugged her slender shoulders and gave me a sad smile. Her eyes raised all the questions.

"Life," I said, nonsensically.

Rebecca nodded and let her son go. He dragged himself to his feet and plodded his way out of the room, down the long hallway and into the street.

"He likes you," she said, not following him.

"I'm glad for that," I said. I almost added: I'll miss you. I'll miss you both.

"I am, too," Rebecca said. "Hey Hank could use an older man-friend. I'm not sure Rafael can be that."

"Have him write me," I said. "I'd like that."

She nodded, slowly, tears in the corners of both eyes. She was staring at the doorway as if she expected Hey Hank to return.

"Funny, I said. "This is home for Hey Hank. Yet he has to leave, while I'm trying to learn how to live here. When will I know I can live here, Rebecca?"

"When will you know you can live here, Marc?" Then she smiled an odd smile. "On the day you discover you're not white, that's when. There is no such thing as white, Marc. Whiteness is an invention, much like childhood. Or America, for that matter. It's an imposition on reality, a recent one at that. Whiteness came when Black slavery came to America. Meaning, it's almost always been here. To learn to live as an American in America, you have to learn to be white. It's not a native state, Marc. And it's a false image. It controls both Blacks and whites. That was its purpose, of course."

"Where did you get that?" I asked.

Rebecca sighed, as if she knew I could not understand and never would. She knew I would not understand before she told me.

"Blacks are born knowing this, Marc. Whites don't wish to learn it. They might have to change."

"But I am white," I said. "White, Anglo-Saxon, Protestant; all that damned stuff."

"Not in my eyes, you're not. You're just confused."

"I am now," I said.

If it was sympathy I was looking for, I didn't get it. "You are sumpin' " she said, patting me lovingly on her way out to find and be with her bewildered son. She left a bewildered lover behind. I would never be her lover, of course, except from a safe distance. There would never be a safe distance. Safe distances are not part of any active life.

CHAPTER 29

In the days when I was heading for seminary, the big religious question had to do with mystery religions. In its beginnings, was Christianity simply one more of those secret societies that sometimes had at center a dying and rising god? The cult of Mithra seemed closest, with the handsome youth pictured slaying a bull. Mithra was honored among Roman soldiers, who saw him as the unconquerable sun. More popular was the worship of Isis, goddess of Egypt, and her re-animated husband-brother Osiris. The power of resurrection offered hope for Isis' followers and a rejuvenation of nature as well. But the most mysterious cult met at Eleusis in Greece and practiced rites we still do not understand. There Demeter was worshiped, an earth-mother powerful enough to save her daughter, Persephone, from Hades.

Nobody talks about mystery religions anymore. There is little talk about the mystery of the Kingdom of God. Or of the Messianic secret in the Gospel of Mark. All secrets are passe. We know it all; it's on the Internet. Gone is the phrase that suggests, "The more you know, the more you know you don't know." We know too much. The truth is that we all have tons of information, but little knowledge. What we know does not get incorporated into our lives. It's "out there." Nothing's "in here." At least, not much. The Internet is a resource access tool, but it has little relation to human wisdom.

Secrets. The world is full of secrets, and one of them had to do with what was happening on a few streets in the historically humiliated city of Detroit. For some reason, I was being let in on the secret. That's what I felt as I waited for the day to go by. Sometime, before it was over, I would be taken by Charlie Eusted to wherever his companions met to determine what response would be appropriate to the events that occurred on these few streets. Waiting made it the longest day of my life. Or it seemed that way, as I twiddled my thumbs and filled my gut with coffee and wine. I sat in my window waiting and, looking out, saw nothing that happened. My eyes, as they say, were turned inside my head. All was turmoil within my head.

At seven o'clock, Bubba showed up at my door. He didn't say one word. He simply waited patiently as I slid into my boots, and dragged out and put on my jacket, hat and gloves. I nodded when I was ready, and he went out. I followed him and thanked him as he opened the rear door of an old LTD. The car had seen a lot of years and a lot of wear. But the engine turned over at a touch, and Bubba eased the car smoothly out into the street. There was another man in the passenger seat, but I was not introduced to him. I imagined him a hit man, and I was about to be eliminated as an unnecessary problem Charlie and company had already decided to get rid of. But we drove around for an hour, and I was certain when we stopped that we had not gone more than a few miles, if not blocks.

Bubba let me out in front of a store. I looked both ways and saw burned out buildings and broken down residences and a few empty spaces where other structures had once been. Bubba nodded toward the store, and I saw, then, that the place had been converted to a Church, more or less. *The Wonderful Peace of a Wonderful Savior* was sprawled across the doorway in letters a foot high. I didn't know if that was simply a way to welcome those who entered or it was actually the name of the church. I never did find out. Bubba let me look for only a moment before urging me into the darkness inside. Then the door closed and lights came on.

There were six men and two women seated at a table in the center of the hall. All were Blacks. Two of the people, I recognized: Charlie Eusted and Rebecca Coltrane. I felt disappointed that Denys and Alicia Fowler weren't there. I expected them to be, though I could not imagine quite why. I took the chair that sat empty at the end of the table and fitted myself into it. Charlie nodded once to me but did not provide any introductions. All of the faces looked familiar from the two parties I had been to, at Fowler's and at my own place. They had all talked to me then. Now — except for a glance my way — they all ignored me. The meeting began, with Charlie Eusted presiding. There was business to be taken care of and I, apparently, was to see and hear. Nothing more.

What I heard, I could hardly believe. This had never happened in any neighborhood I had ever lived in. They went down every street in the few blocks this group controlled and discussed every incident that had taken place there. It was an easy night, obviously, with no big decisions to be discussed. This person was drinking, as usual. There were people on dope and coke that needed to be watched over. There had been two robberies — call them capers, not real crimes — but nothing serious. A bit of damage involving copper tubing or aluminum siding, a screen door that the group was to replace. There had been a knife fight in one backyard between a man and a woman with blood spotting the snow by the time it was over. No great harm had been done as both parties had been so spaced out they couldn't do it right. It turned out the man and woman were husband and wife. The group laughed, as at a story they had clearly heard before.

Then came the more serious stuff, about outsiders who tried to penetrate these streets. There had been attempts, but no successes. Each attempt had been nipped in the bud. I heard that but had no desire to learn how the attempts had been nipped in the bud. I was beginning to figure it out for myself. This was the executive committee, making the essential decisions. The work was carried out by others who were skilled in that activity. I considered Bubba, but the man was too obvious a choice. Better as defense, any way I looked at it. Who then? The man out in the car, acting as lookout? Probably others, people I couldn't know and was better off not knowing. People of the caliber of an Edward Jackson, who worked for the other side.

I was listening to the details of a war being fought, a war that ran sometimes hot and sometimes cold. For the most part, it seemed, the present time was more cold than hot. Except for the cutting off of some kid's tongue. That act had probably been dealt with at an earlier meeting, I thought. And it was across the street. This was a territorial war, as with Vietnam for the Vietnamese. What was being fought over was home. At least, symbolically. Not all of these people lived on these few streets. Maybe, that was intended as a start. Maybe, that's what the mob really feared. If these folk succeeded here, wouldn't they naturally want to extend their success into Detroit's larger neighborhoods. And, eventually, into the whole city.

Three hours later and the people had gone, except for Rebecca Coltrane and Charlie Eusted. They chatted quietly at the far end of the table, before turning to me.

"Well?" Charlie said.

"What did you expect me to think of that?" I said. "I will have to think about it for a while."

"No," said Charlie. "We need your first impression."

"It's illegal," I said. "The approach is that of the vigilante."

"Yes," Charlie said. "As happened, necessarily, on the frontier."

"It's not the same, Charlie. There is law here."

"Your limited law," he said. "Your white law is a poor approach. We simply do what's necessary."

"The law doesn't work in this case, therefore, you take things into your own hands? Aw, Charlie, that's shit."

"You people don't even see the problem," Charlie said. "It's too late for law to solve anything."

"So the inner-city's another country," I said, laughing at him.

"It lives its own life," Charlie said. "I thought you might notice that, if you lived here."

I flicked a glance toward Rebecca Coltrane. She was leaning with her elbows on the arms of the chair, listening carefully to every word.

"I need to forget I'm white," I said, not knowing whether I meant that symbolically or factually. It might have even been a question, directed at Rebecca.

Charlie glanced at Rebecca, quizzically.

"I tried to explain," Rebecca said.

"That's another issue," Charlie said, after a minute. "Blacks in the city live lives you whites can't comprehend, even when you try. And drugs...? Well, drugs have created a lifestyle and an economic system you folks can't even see. So you panic. Making stricter laws and building more jails ain't going to make the drug scene go away. A lot of people within it...Black folk, Marc... fight the drug scene, too. Every day. We win some and lose some. Where you are living, we have tried to create a safe zone. Call it another American experiment if you want. This country is known for its experiments. So here's another. But this one is being made by Blacks for Blacks. With a little help from our friends."

Suddenly, I knew who their enforcer was.

"You use them," I said.

Charlie stared at me. Rebecca caught her breath and held it. Then Charlie smiled a disarming smile. I liked him and disliked him, all in one second of time.

"Tell me who," Charlie said.

"White folk," I said. "Those who sympathize with you, with the plight of Blacks in this country. Especially with those who live in the decimated areas that white folk have left behind. Like the inner city."

"You naming names?" Charlie said.

"Sure. Denys and Alicia. Especially Denys, for his skills. But Alicia, too, if only to hold Denys together. It is a holdover from Vietnam, isn't it? And Denys was among the best at killing. A good man to have working for you."

Charlie's head was shaking, slightly, but he didn't answer me. Nor did Rebecca.

"Probably Father Rene, too," I said. "The man is an innocent. He might live down here for a hundred years and remain an innocent. Nice man. But, if he really knew what he was being used for, I'm not sure he would like it. He might even grow cynical."

"We don't force him," Charlie said. "Anybody else?"

I could only think of one other person.

"Sergeant Berra," I said. "It would be helpful to know what the police were doing. Or going to do."

Charlie's smile became permanent.

"Damn," he said. "Remind me not to play poker with you. What gave it away? Something specific?"

"No," I said. "Pieces. They just suddenly fit together in this way. I couldn't think of any other way. Admittedly, I'm still guessing."

"You guess damn good." He was chuckling.

"Should I believe that?" I said.

Rebecca Coltrane nodded at me. "Pretty much," she mouthed. Rebecca seemed to have relaxed. I had not disappointed her and ruined her expectations. I had not failed at this guessing game.

"What about my daughter?" I said. "How about telling me what you know about what happened? I think I've got that figured; I'm not sure. Do I have it right, Charlie?"

Charlie let air run out of his mouth in a soft whistle. He flicked a look at Rebecca and I thought, for a moment, he was not going to say anything more. That had been his practice on this subject, thus far.

"I didn't know you then," Charlie said, finally. "And it happened out of our territory. I still won't show you anything, but what you think happened is what happened. I can't see you liking that idea."

"He's my son-in-law," I said. "Or was. And he did love my daughter, once upon a time."

"What are you going to do?" That was Rebecca Coltrane, injecting her concern.

"I don't know," I said. "Leave it to Sergeant Berra, I suppose. He made the connection to Detroit in the first place. I never would have. I don't even know why my daughter came here. I don't know what would have gotten her to come. She might have come for business reasons. Only dear Ronald would know that. All I know is, she came and she died."

The feelings welled up, and I shoved them down. I was in no mood for tears.

"What about the kid with the tongue?" I said.

"That was a mistake," Charlie said. "The man who did it did it for you, personally. You understand?"

"For friendship?" I said.

Charlie nodded.

"Like you were one of us," he said.

"He was good, then," I said. "At killing and such."

"Denys was the best," Charlie said. "That's what I was told by his buddies, some of whom came from here. He was just another greenhorn for awhile, over there. Then he changed. Nobody knows how, for sure."

"He became somebody else," I said.

"Huh?" Charlie said. "Yeah, like that."

He was looking at me like I was some kind of divine spirit sent down to earth to haunt him.

"Scary," I said.

"Yeah."

"And the kid with the missing tongue?"

"He doesn't remember doing it, Marc. Denys doesn't remember a lot of things."

I remembered the room Alicia Fowler had shown me. I could almost hear her descriptions of Denys's nightmares. When he remembers, I thought, he remembers too much. Sometimes, it's good to forget.

CHAPTER 30

The next morning, I walked circles on the corner of Grand and Woodward where my daughter died. I walked quite briskly, banging my arms to my sides to keep warm. The weather had cleared but gotten colder. Ice coated the old telephone pole on the outside edge of my circular pathway. Ice coated the red brick of the building on the inner side. I slid on ice as I walked my circles. I skidded and slipped and righted myself, and skidded and slipped again. I glared at cars going by on the street. A few of the drivers, making a slow turn on the corner, looked surprised to see my face. They tended to speed up, in spite of the hazards of going faster. They thought I was about to leap out at them and do damage to their fine vehicles.

Then I broke stride and headed for the GM Building, where I walked corridors and climbed stairs until I found someone who looked important enough to tell me what I needed to know. That person, a woman in a sharp uniform, got on a telephone and grunted and nodded at the sounds she heard. I thought she was talking to a spaceship circling the planet. Or to Mars.

"He's not here," she said to me, finally, her hand over the mouthpiece of the phone she used.

"Where is he?" I asked.

"Out of town," she said. "He won't be back until sometime next week."

"Where out of town?" I asked.

"I'm not at liberty to say."

"You're not at liberty?" I almost laughed at her. She looked as if she stood on the other side of power to me. Perhaps, the master, as well as the slave, is without liberty.

"Is there anything else?" she said, most politely.

"Not a damn thing," I said, walking away.

I went back to my room and dialed the Fowler's residence. An answering machine said it would take my message if I would wait for the beep. I did not wait.

I threw the phone down and immediately regretted the action. I picked the phone up and lay it carefully in its cradle. Then lay down on the bed and fell asleep, trying to make up for being up all night, thinking. It was an old motto of mine: Don't think serious thoughts before going to bed, or you won't sleep.

Obviously, I had forgotten it.

Morning was a riot of loud noises. I staggered out of bed and opened the window blind to glaring light. The sun reflecting off snow made me wince. Outside, a snowplow and car were in touch with each other. The driver of the car was reaching up to the window of the snowplow and banging on it with his fists. The driver of the snowplow was yelling obscenities of his own, though I could not hear them. But he was leaning on his horn. The din had drawn other people out onto the street, and they were cheering for one side or the other. Or just cheering the diversion from winter boredom. They all had winter's cabin fever, and any diversion was appreciated.

The truck driver shoved his vehicle into gear and pushed the car another few feet out of his way. Then he shifted and roared his noisy engine down the street. The driver of the car clung to the side of the truck, almost to the corner. But he lost his balance and fell into the white stuff piled high where the gutter used to be. He seemed unable to get to his feet, but his voice was as loud as before. I thought I knew every swear word in the book, what with the mills and the military. But these words hadn't made it into the book yet. You live and you learn.

The noise outside had covered over the light rapping inside. I scuttled over to the door and opened it. Alicia Fowler stood there, looking sad and bedraggled, which was unlike her, in my view. I reached out and grabbed her arm and dragged her inside before she could vanish away from me, as dreams often do.

"Where'd he go?" I said.

"He flies out of state a lot," she said..

"Timing," I said. "Not image, but timing is everything."

She stared at me, cocking her head.

"You sound like a commercial," she said. "Denys had to fly to San Francisco on business, Marc. He heads out that way a lot. He goes wherever they need him to save them a bundle of money. He visits manufacturing plants and dealerships and whatever else he needs to see. He examines their books, then he comes home and thinks about things and faxes them suggestions on how to save money. Why are you so interested, Marc?"

"Who decides where he goes?" I said, ignoring her question. "Who decides when and where?"

"Why, he does. Why do you ask?"

"And you don't go with him?"

"Sometimes I do. If he's going to a fun place."

"San Francisco's not a fun place?"

"Sure, it is. I've been there a lot of times. But this time, I didn't go. I had things to do."

"What things?" I said.

"No," she said. "No more, Marc. First, you tell me what's going on. Why all the questions?"

I thought: What does she know, and what do I tell her? Could I really be sure of anything? Was everything I thought merely part of some weird dream. I had to do some thinking of my own before I brought anyone else into this new understanding of reality.

"Do you know anything about what it means to be white," I said, shifting tack.

Alicia shook her head, trying to catch up with me. That would be pretty hard to do, seeing as I didn't know where I was, myself.

"I heard a couple of days ago that whiteness was a new thing. It was also an American thing, Alicia. Being 'white' arose because of Blacks. Because of negro slavery, Alicia. I'm trying to get a handle on that idea."

"But why Denys?" Alicia said.

"He's here. Denys knows a lot of Blacks. I thought he might be able to help me."

"Oh," she said, not sounding like she really believed me.

"What are you doing down here?" I asked.

"I came down to get Deny's check and deposit it," she said. "Besides, I wanted to see how you were doing. We haven't really had a chance to talk since early on, Marc. What are you wound up about this morning?"

"Nothing," I said. "Not really. The noise out there startled me awake. Usually, I wake early. I shouldn't sleep in. Or go back to sleep, once awake. I end up dull-headed all day. Or a crank. Sorry about that."

"It's all right. How about breakfast?"

"You mean, in a restaurant? Somebody else's cooking? That's sounds wonderful. I'll get some clothes on."

"But I'm buying," Alicia said.

"Fine with me."

I washed quickly and threw on some clothes and let Alicia lead me to a restaurant a few miles away that I had not been to before. The place specialized in breakfast, and it was a joy to savor every mouthful. I learned that the restaurant had once been a Presbyterian church and was now named *Ashley's*, after some girl the owner had once loved. Ashley had died of pneumonia at twelve years of age. The man had a crush on her as a boy that would not quit. An idealized sketch of Ashley was on every napkin. A painting of the girl was hung prominently above the spot where I assumed the baptistry had once been. Another pose would bid farewell to you as you left the place. Good food and good romance; what could be better in starting a day?

"Now what's this about being white?" Alicia said. "And why is it bothering you so much?"

"James Baldwin, I guess, primarily," I said. "He's the one I know about that says you have to forget color if we are ever going to solve the race issue. We are all colored. Being 'white' is a fiction, picked up, now, in its own way by those who wish to see themselves as 'Black.' Which amounts to a lot of people, if you ask me."

"Just about everybody," Alicia said.

But our view was corrected immediately by a glimpse of our waitress, who was decidedly Japanese. At least, as far as ancestry was concerned.

"We're all colored," I said, surrendering.

Alicia laughed and touched my hand across the table with her own warm fingers.

Too many things to think about. Too much, too soon, as the old saying goes. I left Alicia at the curbing in front of my home after she let me out of her sporty little car. I thanked her, profusely, for the fine breakfast. Especially for her company. I asked her to let me know when Denys returned, as I would like some conversation with him. She told me she would be talking to him by phone that evening and would have him call me. Perhaps, I could have the conversation I required long distance. Don't worry about cost. The company paid for Denys's calls when they sent him on jaunts. But they hadn't sent him, I reminded myself. He had chosen to go. That was both policy and practice.

Then, as I watched Alicia swing the corner onto Woodward, I saw Edward Jackson. He was watching me, smoking, hands in his pockets. Clutching what? I had no way of knowing. Probably nothing. Not this early. Not in public. Not on this street.

I stood still and stared at him, putting on the blank face Hey Hank had told me about, the one you needed to wear to survive down here. I stood still and stared at him until he smiled and nodded his head and sauntered off, walking slowly, with that limpy, foot-dragging swagger

Hey Hank had also described. Edward Jackson was the epitome of life in the inner-city, and I was immediately angry for allowing myself to be turned into a carbon copy. In the way I looked and acted, at least. Yet, how else does one survive, except by knowing the enemy and copying him? Old King David had done that with the Philistines until he learned their strengths and weaknesses. Until he figured out how to defeat them.

The danger was, of course, that I would become him or someone like him. Then what would happened to me? There is a conundrum nobody talks about.

I turned and slowly climbed the steps of the building I lived in. I let myself through the whooshing door. Out of one corner of my eye, I saw Mrs. Hedley with her door open a crack, watching me. She didn't miss much, I figured. She was simply another sad person with no life of her own. I went into my apartment and picked up the Potok book I was nearly finished with. I couldn't read it. To read a man like Potok, you had to pay attention as you read. There was always much think about. I had nothing else on hand, no James Bond stories, no true adventures, no Westerns. So I dropped the book and picked up a pen and began to write notes to myself.

I listed the people involved, the men and women I had met since coming to Detroit. The names multiplied quickly, beginning with Denys and running through Charlie Eusted and company. Then I listed events as they had occurred, beginning with the first phone call from Sergeant Berra. All the things that came after filled five pages. Thinking about it, I could have added other details, small things said, a few things hinted at, clever conversations. When I had nearly a dozen pages, I spread them out on the bed and began to make charts and graphs and scribblings of all sorts. Some of them made no sense at all, had no connection, I could see, with the rest. Others fit together like pieces of a puzzle. I concentrated on those that appeared to go together and felt, again, that my guessing had been good, too good. Yet, I also felt like a student taking a final exam who was putting together the best argument he could, but remained ignorant of the intent of the big question at the heart of the exam, the one worth the most points.

How could any of this go on, anywhere?

I didn't know and couldn't figure it out right now. So I got out some tape and stuck all my pages to an empty wall. Then I sat with my back at the head of my bed and stared at the collage the pages made.

Something should click. I was a smart guy, wasn't I? I was one of the intelligent ones, so this should be a cinch for me. But it wasn't. I was no detective in a roomful of detectives, putting together the details of a crime. Nor was I a prosecutor making a case out of materials handed to me. I was just a guy, a thinking man living where he did not belong, dealing with things he knew far too little of. Who could say that any conclusion I came to was valid? Only those intimately involved. Little chance of any of them confirming my educated guesses. Even Charlie could lie, naturally. How could I tell?

I gave it up as the phone rang. I looked toward the window and discovered the day had ended. It was Denys on the telephone. For the life of me, I couldn't remember what it was I wanted to talk to him about. What I actually wanted to talk to him about, I could not talk to him about. Denys made it easy, by reiterating what Alicia had told him of her conversation with me. We spoke generally of Black and white association, coming to no conclusions. He guessed at what James Baldwin might mean by arguing that we should all forget color, as it was merely an American convenience, a bit of our private history and heritage. No validity anywhere else in the world.

I said goodbye and put the phone in its cradle. My hand was shaking, and I felt a tingling on the back of it. I felt as if somebody was writing me a letter. Or, perhaps, filling out a page of material I had not noted in the papers that filled my wall. But I couldn't read the writing; I only felt the touch. It elated and it frightened me.

I put my face in my hands and cried.

CHAPTER 31

Days went by without a phone call. Days went by without a knocking at my door. I went out only to get groceries from the store. I talked to no one, except clerks who were only interested in taking my money. I bought food and cold drinks and wine and beer. I settled in, like Admiral Byrd at the north pole. But I had no dials to read, no sounding to make, no concern for the weather around me. I scarcely glanced out the window, until one day when the sun shone brightly, and I thought it might be April. The snow melted, and the icicles dripped off the roof, falling in liquid drops to the hard ground far below.

Then Denys Fowler appeared at my door.

"Where's the priest?" I said as he came through my door, unbuttoning his camel-hair coat.

"He's sick," Denys said. "Father Rene was helping some people in the cold weather. He took a bad case of the flu. He was in the hospital for awhile. Now, I guess, he's in the rectory, recuperating."

"I hadn't seen him," I repeated. "I guess I had gotten used to him knocking at my door."

"He knocks on everybody's door," Denys said.

"Not yours," I said.

"Too far out," Denys replied. "Not in his parish."

"Lucky you."

"What's with you?" Denys said. He completed the slow removal of his coat and lay it with hat and gloves on my unmade bed. Then he caught sight of the wall and studied the writings. I kept quiet until he had finished.

"A pattern of connections," I said.

He looked again, and I saw his face change. In that moment, I grew afraid of my friend Denys Fowler. It was a long while before he looked at me again.

"Looks confusing to me," he said.

"Does it? You're good with figures, Denys. You should have no trouble at all with this."

"Why this?" he said. He looked once more, carefully. His eyes, coming away, went blank.

"Think of the novelty of it," I said. "I'm considering writing a report about it. You know, something for journalists. Titled, maybe, *These Few Streets*. What do you think?"

He was the wrong man to ask. I should be asking this of Charlie Eusted. Denys' face darkened, and the fear of him I felt intensified. But I couldn't help myself. I was like the canary caught in the bird's claw, singing anyway.

"You shouldn't," Denys said. He stepped the couple of steps to his coat and hat and gloves. He put them on, one at a time, slowly. He took time to adjust his hat on his head and smooth the lines of his coat and the depths of his gloves on his fingers. Then he walked to my door. At it, he stopped. "You don't understand," he said, glancing again at the wall covered with papers. It was as if he saw the devil's sign. "You shouldn't be doing this."

He went out.

I listened to his footsteps going down the hall. I made sure to hear the whoosh of the outer door. I got up and went over and locked the door. I made certain every bolt was in its slot. Then I went to the window, reaching it just in time to see Denys turn the corner down the street. His back was the back of a soldier, stiff and solid. His walk was a march of troops on parade. I relaxed. He would be dangerous, I told myself, when that facade vanished. Then he could become the commando, the guy who coated himself to look like nature and slid along the ground like a shadow until he found an enemy to kill. Denys would only be that if allowed. And the orders had to come from someone else, the man in charge. In this case, my sponsor, Charlie Eusted. I thought I was safe for a time.

It was only an hour until Charlie Eusted appeared at my door. He came in saying nothing but leaving Bubba out in the hall. He rolled to my wall and examined it, carefully. "You have a choice," he said, when he was finished. "You can stay or you can leave. If you stay, we're going to assume you are one of us. If you leave, we'll let you go knowing you're not. So if we hear anything..."

"You threatening me?" I said.

"Call it what you want."

"What did you expect, Charlie? A white guy ignorant as some of those you obviously dictate to?"

"They're not ignorant," Charlie said. "They understand far better than you ever will, apparently. They know enough to take a good thing when they see it."

"A good thing? You're joking."

"You didn't live here before. You don't know."

"I know the law," I said. "I know this is a country based on law. What law applies here, Charlie?"

"You don't know nothing. None of that works here. It's too big for the law to handle. You're never going to have enough cops or jails to handle it. Drugs is big business, Marc. You can't squelch the desire for drugs, and it has created an industry larger than anyone imagines. So forget the law! And all your do-gooder social programs, too. It's gotten too big and too powerful. Drugs has created an economic engine that runs by itself, Marc. You can't stop it. Nobody can."

"But you do, here."

"We're not fools," Charlie said. "We hold a small strip of territory. That's what we fight for. We keep them out, and we deal with what gets brought in."

"You just drive...what are they called?...the touts, the runners, the fiends, to some other part of Detroit, Charlie. You've made an island, that's all. And the price you pay to keep it clean is pretty high."

"Right, right! You've got it! But that's something, isn't it? Isn't it?"

I looked at Charlie and saw that his huge eyes were wet with unshed tears. I realized I could not comprehend — and probably never would — the pain and the frustration of those who lived here and bore witness to the degradation of their lives. I have never witnessed an entire community rolled under until a drug culture, alone, had meaning. For these streets, life had been redefined. A neglected community had found meaning for itself, again. The price was staggering. Over against this stood Charlie and company, offering a middle ground. The whole situation seemed horrendous to me. But who was I to judge?

"Charlie," I said, falling on my knees in front of his wheelchair, so as to look him right in the eye. "Why me, Charlie? Why let me know what's going on? Why let me guess as to purpose, as to cause?" I had my hands on his arms and felt the muscles in them quivering. "I'm just a guy like you, Charlie. You don't need my permission to do what you do. You don't need my judgment, either."

"Don't I?" Charlie said. "I've been in charge of this for years now. It's too much for me, Marc. I didn't know what I was getting into; how it would go, you know? Tell me it's all right. Tell me I didn't go too wrong?"

"Why me, Charlie? Why tell me all this?"

"I don't know," he said.

There were tears sliding down in bright, slim rivers on the man's dark face, washing it.

"Sure, you know, Charlie. So tell me."

I felt like a priest with a penitent. Or like an itinerant evangelist with a man on the edge of conversion. I had given up that traditional practice early in my ministry. I could not bear seeing grown people cowering. I felt that it degraded our common humanness. We all make mistakes, so why grovel? Because Christ is king? No! He's our companion, an understanding fellow sufferer. In this country, we had little use for kings. Why do we seek for one in religion?

Charlie was staring at me, calm all of a sudden.

"Because you're a preacher, Marc. That's why, because you're a preacher. We all have to respect something, and I respect preachers. It's in my blood."

"In your blood?"

"My mother was a preacher. In Harlem. I was a little boy in the back row, but I can still see her. She used to bang out the beat of the songs the people sang. The songs came, spontaneously, one after another. Everybody looked to my preacher-mother for the beat. She kept them together by banging away on the arm of the throne-like chair they made for her. She sat up there keeping the beat. She was some great lady-preacher, my mother."

Charlie was smiling, a wide-eyed smile. He was seeing himself in another day, in a day long before such caring, such anguish, such pain as today.

But while he talked on about his mother, telling me of the overwhelming impact of her character on him — a force so strong that not even being in war could take it away — I thought of something I had read about the value of the stranger to Judaism. If a stranger accepted Judaism as his or her religion, it confirmed the value of being Jewish as nothing else could. He or she had no ancestral motivation for belief; it was purely present-day. A stranger who accepted Judaism's practices as his or her own affirmed the value of all Jews; of Judaism, itself. In times of doubt, there was no one to be honored more than the believing stranger. There was no one more righteous.

I was a stranger in Charlie's world. But I found that, as much as I admired him, I could not condone violence as a way of bettering human life, anywhere.

Charlie Eusted lived as I could not, if what I knew, now, was truth. I could not condone his actions. He saw it in my face, and his broad smile slowly vanished.

"I thought..." he began.

"It's all right, Charlie. It's me, not you. I'm not a part of this world you live in. So I won't judge it. But I do feel for you. And for the others. I'm an outsider who can't make the required leap of faith."

Charlie's sad eyes stayed on my face.

"You're all right," he said. "For a white boy, you're all right."

I laughed lightly with him, but felt as if I had let him down. He had been let down before, obviously. He was used to bearing burdens all by himself.

Charlie sighed and rolled himself toward the door. At it, he stopped and spun around.

"I keep hoping, " he said. "And, maybe, one day I'll find somebody. In the meantime, you take care of yourself, you hear? I'd hate for something to happen to you."

"Thanks," I said, both of us knowing, in that moment, I was going to head home. "I'm glad I met you Charlie Eusted. You're quite a guy. By the way, don't I owe you rent? I've been here awhile."

"No, you don't," he said. "My treat. I hope you'll come back one day, Marc, when things are better."

"I will," I said.

We both expected things would get worse.

Charlie nodded and called for Bubba. The big man took up Charlie, chair and all. I did not watch them go out. I sat at my desk, instead.

CHAPTER 32

I was doodling and the phone was ringing. I picked it up and listened to my son's voice. It had an edge to it, so I was slow in listening to words. By the time I caught up, Rick was saying, "Dad? Dad? You there?"

I said I was and apologized to him for not being truly attentive. I asked him to repeat what he had just told me. Rick told me Ron Worthington was dead. I asked what, where and how. Rick told me.

"An accident," he said. "On his way to Vegas. He went off the side of the road, Dad. It was a long fall. The car, you know, that new, red Viper, it burned up. They had a hard time getting him out of there, what was left of him. So he's dead, Dad. We don't have to think about him anymore."

After they had been in business for a few years, and things were finally going successfully, my daughter and son-in-law were advised that they should buy some property, as a tax-offset as much as anything. They looked for a long time and finally settled for a large house not far from the casinos and Lake Mead at Las Vegas, Nevada. The house had been lived in by the man who built it. It had the most marvelous living room fireplace. The fireplace ran two stories up the wall and had the look of a running waterfall. Laura decorated the falls with birds and fish, figures that fit into the niches and crannies of the falls-looking concrete. Ron got that property in the divorce settlement. He may not have, if Laura had wanted it anywhere near as much as she wanted the divorce. It pained her enormously to let the house go.

It was toward that house Ron was heading, as he often did on weekends, either by plane — he got their airplane, too — or car, when he went off the road. Parts of the road were treacherous Being late in a long day, maybe Ron was tired and dozed off at exactly the wrong time.

Fate or divine judgment, take your pick.

"That will take some getting used to," I said, only half facetiously. "He's really dead?"

"It's confirmed, Dad. Besides, you know Ron. He would never loan that car to anyone."

"If I remember right," I said. "Jim drove the Viper once. He raved about it for days. Wanted one of his own, I believe. Loved the damned thing."

"Yes, Ron let him drive it," Rick said. "On the way to Vegas for the weekend, with Don in the car. No way to take it alone. Jim tried. He tried to borrow the car, to show it off to whatever woman he was seeing at the time. No way, Dad. Ron wouldn't."

"Ron's dead, then."

"Yes."

"It's over."

"Yes.

"Okay. Thanks for telling me, Rick. I guess I'll be heading home in a day or two. Why don't you come up to Oregon and see me. We'll go camping or something."

"It's winter, still, Dad. Where are you?"

"Oh, yeah, right. I'm a little rattled, I guess."

"Then it's time you went home." Rick laughed, and it was good to hear him laugh. It felt good to hear anybody laugh.

"Yes, it is, son," I said.

But I didn't feel like laughing.

Rick's call was followed by one from Sergeant Berra of the Detroit Police Department.

"You heard?" he said, without preliminaries.

"Just now," I said. "My son called."

"What do you want me to do?"

"What can you do?" I said. "The man's dead. If we got evidence together to take him to trial, what would it get us? A verdict of capital punishment, if we were very lucky? But that's already happened. Somebody else arranged that. I guess, we quit, Sergeant. You've got other things to do, I'm sure."

"Yeah, yeah. Always. You're sure. We could get the truth out. Wouldn't that help?"

"We already know the truth, Sergeant. I thank you for that. The only mystery remaining is the question of how he got her to come to Detroit. I guess it'll remain a mystery."

The Sergeant was quiet for a moment.

"I already know that," he said.

"You do?"

"Yeah."

"Well, tell me."

"You sure you want to know?"

"Sergeant!"

"While she was in Boston, he sent her a cable, telling her to come to

Detroit, sign in at the St. Regis, meet him on the corner where she was killed. He signed it with your name, Mr. McDaniel."

"Laura thought she was meeting me? Oh, my God!"

If I asked her to, Laura would come. She'd come without question. Ron knew how close Laura and I were.

"Sorry, I only learned this last night. It took some tracing, as you can imagine."

"That bastard!"

"Yeah, yeah," the Sergeant said. Then he let the line hang silent. "You still want to stop the investigation? I could do it on my own, of course. But you're my motivation. I'll continue, if you want."

"I'm leaving, Sergeant. I'm going home."

"I see. Well, we suspect the Weams family of a lot of killings. Your daughter was only one more in the files. I guess, I hoped. Aw, hell! Look, I'm glad to have met you. If I do get more, I'll let you know. Wherever you are in the Wild West."

"Oregon," I said and gave him my address.

As I hung up, I found myself repeating, Ah, shit!, Ah shit!, and thinking of Hey Hank. The language of the street for the life of the street. One thing appropriate to the other. Smart little boy. Very smart. If I had been as smart, I would never have come to this city. Detroit had been a liminal experience for me, a slight crossing of a cultural thresh-hold. I did not wish to fully cross. To cross all the way meant I would have to stay.

It was a day for phones to ring and knocks to come on the door. Mrs. Hedley stood outside, holding a small package identical to one she had handed me before. She giggled like a schoolgirl handing a boy a present at recess. Then she scooted down the hall and vanished behind her door. But not before glancing back at me and laughing.

I held the package, but I couldn't open it.

I shoved an arm into my coat, made sure my boots were laced and went out, leaving the package on the table. I went first to the corner of Woodward, looking for him. He wasn't there, not by a pole, not on the street, not near the store on the other side. I turned around and walked faster, back past the purple house where Hey Hank had hung on the fence. By the end of the street, I had not found him. I started to run, clomping along in my heavy boots, exploring each and every street in the neighborhood. He was nowhere to be seen. I passed behind Charlie

Eusted without saying a word to him and threaded my way through a line of people waiting for the bus. He was not there, not on Grand, not on Woodward, not down the roads leading toward New Center. Nowhere. I couldn't locate him, and I was beginning to panic.

Then there he was in front of my house. He must have been sitting in somebody's window, waiting for me to come out. Or he had a spy, nearby, letting him know.

I walked right up to Edward Jackson and looked him in the eye. The usual smile was stuck to his face and a lit cigarette to his front teeth. I was smiling as I went up to him. I couldn't help myself.

"I'm glad to see you still have a nose," I said.

The cigarette popped out of his mouth, riding the tip of a red tongue. It quickly vanished into his mouth, entirely, only to reappear in its usual place.

"And you have your tongue," I added.

I breathed a deep sigh of relief and headed back up my stairs just a few steps away. I paused at the whooshing door, looking back. Jackson's smile had vanished, and one of his hands was scratching his head up under his cap. I waved at him and let the door close.

Breathing more easily, I let myself into my room and hung my coat on the rack. I sat down at the table and fingered the package. It was just a package, after all. All kinds of things come in similar packages. Not all of them scary. Not all of them frightening. Not all of them human body parts.

But, as I unwrapped the box, I got a bad feeling. It was wrapped exactly as before, with packing inside a plastic bag and another smaller bag inside the packing. When I tipped up the smallest bag, a piece of flesh fell out onto the table. It took a moment for me to figure out what it was. I didn't touch it, didn't want to touch it. I took a knife and let the blade move the piece of flesh back into its bag. I took the bag and wrapped it in the smaller piece of paper. I placed the paper in the jacket of my coat. The rest I threw away, without examining it further. Whatever it could tell me, I really didn't want to know.

Alicia answered on the first ring. I told her that I had decided to leave Detroit and that I was planning to go tomorrow. I had gotten a flight out early in the day and was simply anxious to go home.

I told her I would like to take her and Denys out to dinner and thought that, maybe, the St. Regis Room would be a good place. That was where this all started. I suggested she call Denys at work, if he were at the G M Building today, and we could all meet at the St. Regis Hotel. It would be more convenient for everyone that way. She said she was sorry I was going but could understand why. Homesickness is a difficult thing, she said. So she would call Denys and then call me right back, which she did. We were on for six-thirty. We could talk more, then.

I packed, slowly. As when I came, there wasn't much to pack, a few books and the clothes I wore and the new boots on my feet. I took my time, avoiding the wall with its collage of scribbled-on papers.

Then I called my son, Jim, and left a message saying I was heading home and would be reachable there by tomorrow evening. Hanging up the phone brought me close to the wall. I looked it over once more, and it made no sense to me. I could not find myself in it. Taking the papers one at a time, I stacked them on my desk until the wall was bare. I remembered, then, that there was a barrel in the backyard of the building that was used occasionally to burn trash. I didn't know if it was legal of not, but I put on my coat and went outside, making sure there were matches in my pocket.

It was very cold, though there wasn't a breeze. I held the papers in my hands, like bread and wine. I lifted them to my lips and kissed them. I lay them on top of the snow that lay on top of the ashes a few inches down inside the barrel. I put a match to one corner of one page and watched it sputter and catch. The flame ran along the page while, underneath, the snow melted, taking the pile of papers slowly down with it. Soon the mass of papers were burning. Before long, the last page was ash, and the fire was out. A thin trail of smoke continued rising into the cold air. I stayed where I was and watched it until it was gone, too, fading into nothing.

CHAPTER 33

I shoved my plate aside with a motion that was noticed by our hovering waiter, so that it was immediately removed from the table. I nursed the wine, as Alicia picked at the last of her meal and Denys waited for us both to finish. He was chewing, abstractedly, on nothing but his teeth. We had eaten and talked. It appeared we had run out of ordinary things to say. The rest was serious. The table was empty, except for cups and saucers. Napkins, out of our laps, lay folded on the table cloth. Denys took his cue from Alicia's slow, deep sigh.

"There's no other way to say it," Denys said. "We're going to miss you, Marc. You sure you don't want to stay in or around Detroit. It's an interesting city."

"What about what's going on here?" I said.

"Here?" Denys said, his hand waving around so as to include the neighborhood. "Well, I put it this way, Marc. We lost both wars, the one Alicia and I were in, and this one for the inner city. What you see going on here is just a holding action, nothing more. Alicia tells me that Western Civilization led us to this, but I don't know about that. I only know that we're trying to hold on until somebody works something out. But nothing seems to be working."

"You're rationalizing brutality." I said, remembering that this man had maimed a young boy. He was probably guilty of murdering my ex-son-in-law, though there seemed to be no way of proving that. What else had he done?

"Sure we are," he said. "It's necessary. And it gives meaning and purpose to our lives: Charlie, Alicia and me, all the others. What else should we do?"

"I don't know," I said.

Alicia had it right, of course. Western Civilization had been heading in this direction for a long, long time. There had been no awareness for consequences. Civilization had plunged ahead, no apology asked for or given. We had exploited the earth's resources and its people. Ourselves included. Even God remained silent. But, then again, maybe God was in the silence. Maybe God was the silence. A heavy silence that lay beyond our words, beyond any words, even beyond the scriptural words.

A *holding action*, yet? What could I say about that? Nothing I could think of, being no fan of warfare or its rampant terminology. Better to be silent.

“Well, I need to go,” I said. “I’ll walk you to your car.”

And I did just that, walking with Alicia and Denys, walking on the other side of Alicia; talking with Denys, while holding her hand. A peck on the cheek and a shake of a hand and it was done. Their car slid out of the parking structure, then turned north on Woodward, heading home. I stood, waving, until it was out of sight.

I walked back to my place. Surprisingly, I got no glimpse of either Edward Jackson or Charlie Eusted. Maybe, I thought, the present standoff was adequate. With me leaving, a source of friction was taking itself away. They could all relax for awhile. Until the next catalytic situation arrived. Until then, the present frame would hold. Both sides would see to it. But, unfortunately, no set boundary lasted forever. Human beings, sensing advantage, would see to that, too.

The next day, a black City Cab took me to Metro Airport in plenty of time for my flight. But, when they called it, I felt a tug on my sleeve, dragging me out of line.

“Sergeant Berra,” I said. “Nice of you to see me off.”

“Just doing my job,” he said.

“Sure,” I said. “What’s up?”

“Finally got a full report on that accident out in California. Point of curiosity for me.”

“Oh?” I said.

The sergeant shifted from one foot to another and I felt myself bumped by somebody, running toward my plane. I needed to board soon, before they gave my seat to a stranger.

“Yeah,” he said. “Coroner’s report, you know. Had this peculiarity. The man was missing a piece of an ear. It’s a bit odd, but, you know, odd things happen. It’s accidents I’m speaking of, you understand?”

“I think so,” I said.

“What they figure is this. His body was thrown against a partly opened window. The glass cut a bit of ear off, and the wind tossed it away. Out there in the hills someplace. Maybe, an animal grabbed it. Coyote, whatever. I don’t know what animals they have out there. Wild dog, maybe.”

“I’ve got the idea, Sergeant.”

“Well, I figure this. It was kind of hot that day. Not winter like here. Muggy, dirty, dusty, windy; you know. Bad day. They didn’t say, but I figure a guy with a Viper, he likes all the comfort that thing can give you. And it has this wonderful stereo system for music that sounds better when the windows are closed. So why is the window open, if it is open? It's hard to tell from the wreckage. The thing was totaled, you know. Nice car; too bad."

"It was a marvelous car," I said. "I see one on the highway, now and then. Never saw Ron's. Heard it was a sweet thing, though. That's my son's description. He got to drive the car, once."

"Oh, that right?"

"You figure you know what happened to the ear? Or the piece of an ear that's missing from Ron's very-battered body?"

"I think I do," he said.

"I think you do, too," I said.

I put a hand into the inside pocket of my jacket and came out with a small plastic-wrapped package and gave it to Sergeant Berra.

"Thank you," he said.

"You're welcome," I said.

And we shook hands.